Praise for *Finding Mr. Write*

The idea of two writers falling in love with each other has always intrigued me. (Hey, a novelist can dream, can't she?) Perhaps that's why I adored Carol Moncado's delightful new book, Finding Mr. Write. Jeremiah and Dorrie's individual stories hooked me right away and the merging of their lives offered twists and turns that kept me flipping the pages, wondering what would happen next. Highly recommended! ~ **Janice Thompson, author of the Weddings by Bella series**

Oh my goodness—if you've never been to a writer's conference before, this is the book for you! Light-hearted and fun, *Finding Mr. Write* captures the essence of a writer's journey on the road to publication and love, offering a fresh and frisky glimpse into a truly novel romance. ~ **Julie Lessman, award-winning author of The Daughters of Boston, Winds of Change, and Heart of San Francisco series.**

Finding Mr. Write is a mega-romantic story with amazing chemistry between the two characters, and Jeremiah is one of the most memorable and loveable heroes I've read in a long time. Carol Moncado's writing reeled me in and hooked me, and I was eager to see how Dorrie and Jeremiah would overcome their secrets and unusual circumstances to find true love. I loved this story! ~ **Melanie Dickerson, award winning author of *The Healer's Apprentice***

General Praise

Sharp-witted dialogue, clever plots and engaging characters - Carol Moncado is an author to watch and, more importantly, READ! - **Jennifer A. Davids, author of *Buckeye Dreams***

Author Carol Moncado's stories are truly irresistible! With endearing characters and make-your-heart-smile romance, you'll keep turning pages, never wanting to reach 'The End'... Go ahead and make room on your favorites' shelf, because this fresh voice in contemporary Christian fiction is here to stay. ~**Kristy Cambron, author of *The Butterfly and the Violin* and *A Sparrow in Terezin***

CANDID Romance

Finding Mr. Write
Finally Mr. Write
Falling for Mr. Write

Montevaro Monarchy

Good Enough for a Princess
Along Came a Prince
More Than a Princess

For Andrea
Thank you for raising a good man
And for always loving and supporting
all of us.

And Rich.
For all you have done
And for all you do.

Chapter One

*W*hat do you think they're arguing over?"

Richard Antonio David Nicklaus, spare to the heir of Montevaro, didn't take his eyes off the two trail guides while he answered Dennis. "Probably us." Rick hitched his backpack a bit higher. "Writing me off as another pretty boy and you two as my best-friend-tagalongs living off trust funds. Same as always." It wasn't the first time. It wouldn't be the last.

Dennis, Rick's bodyguard-turned-friend, moved to stand next to his backpack outside the headquarters of Ozark Outdoors as they watched the two leaders in a heated discussion.

Rick had spent the last four years seeing the world on his own terms, doing things just like this around the globe. If only he could convince his parents - and his sister, once she took the throne in a few months - something like this would thrive in their corner of the Alps. With Italy to the south and Switzerland to the northeast, they had a prime tourist area to work with. Directly north lay Montevaro's sister country, Mevendia. Between them they could create something spectacular.

"Maybe next time you should go buy the same clothes everyone else wears." Steve, his other bodyguard, brought Rick's attention back to the trail head in Missouri. "Try to blend in."

"Off the rack? I don't think so."

"And you wonder why people think you're a pretty boy," Dennis muttered.

"Don't start." For all his outdoor-loving, Rick didn't like wearing off the rack. His height made it hard to find clothes his size in the first place, but his proportions were off for a guy as tall as he was. Tailor-made was the only way to go.

"Okay, everyone!" The guy leader walked toward the two groups of three. Richard and his two bodyguards/best friends stood together. A woman stood to one side and another woman and a man seemed to be a couple. "I'm Trent and the cranky gal back there is Ellie. You've all been told the basics of what's going to happen. We'll be together most of the time, but you'll also be in groups of three that stick together no matter what." He nodded toward Richard and his friends. "Since you booked together, you'll be one group." That was good. Dennis and Steve wouldn't have let it happen any other way. Trent looked at the other three. "You're with me."

"That means you guys are with me." The girl introduced as Ellie pointed at Richard and his two friends. "Who's Richard?"

Rick stepped forward. "I am."

He heard her muttered, "Of course." Then louder, "Then who's Dennis?" His friend to his right raised a hand. She nodded to Richard's left. "Then you're Steve." He nodded. "We've got a long way to go today so let's move out." She pointed to the path. "Get started. Wait at the first tree you come to."

Rick raised a brow at Dennis, who shrugged. They started off, his friends trailing behind him. He turned to walk backwards, eyeing Ellie in the distance. She'd snapped at him, made judgments about him based on the quality of his clothes, and wanted nothing to do with him, but all he could notice was how the sun gave her brown hair gold highlights from this angle.

"So, Ellie," Rick called as he walked backward toward the

trail. "I take it there's no orientation meeting about how far we plan to go today or how many different camps we'll set up over the next few days."

"No." The one word answer told him everything he needed to know - for the moment at least - about how this week was going to go. She'd be bitter and snappy until he could prove he really did know what he was doing when it came to camping out and surviving in the wilderness.

A wicked grin crossed his face. Or maybe he'd feign ignorance and let her help him with everything. It wouldn't get him on her good side, but it sure would be fun.

All six of them set off down the brown dirt trail through the field next to the Outdoor Ozarks building. It was narrow enough the thigh-high weeds on either side brushed his legs as he caught up to and passed Dennis and Steve. He reached the tree she'd indicated, walked a few feet further into the woods of the Mark Twain National Forest, and stopped to wait.

Another pretty boy. Just what I need. Ellie Brewer stuck another protein bar in her pack before surveying the group of six as they walked away for the next several days of survival training in the Missouri Ozarks. Three of them looked ready for the trek. Two women and one man with appropriate gear who wore it well.

The other three...She stifled a sigh, knowing Trent would catch on immediately and, as the senior guide, he'd assigned them to her. The tall one - Richard? - was the pretty boy. The other two looked comfortable enough but none looked like they were ready for this.

Unless she was really honest with herself. But then she'd have to admit the pretty boy actually wore his gear well, too. His boots were sturdy but worn. There were scratches and scrapes on his pack showing it had been well-used, but still in good enough condition it wouldn't fall apart the first time he tossed it on the ground. The camouflage pants had pockets on top of pockets stuffed with additional supplies to be kept on his person at all times.

But even though the clothes were worn, when new, they had to have cost more than her monthly salary. Not that she made much.

"You about ready, Ellie?" Trent slung his pack on one shoulder before sliding his other arm in and buckling it around his middle.

"As ready as I'll ever be." She yanked the zipper shut and winced when it stuck. She'd need a new one soon but that wouldn't happen until her parents realized this wasn't just a whim or until one of her survivalists decided to give her a big tip for helping him survive in the wilderness because he wasn't smart enough to realize he wasn't the ourdoorsy type. A face flashed through her mind, but she shoved it out of the way as she situated her pack. If only Trent would help that memory stay gone. "You get the pretty boys."

Her efforts to walk off before Trent could protest didn't matter, because his laugh followed right after her. "Not on your life. Assignments are already made, and I didn't make them. Not this time."

Ellie swiveled on one heel and her eyes met Trent's in a stare down for the ages. "You would do that to me? After everything I went through, you won't trade me?"

Trent shrugged. "You know what they say to do when you get bucked off a horse."

"This isn't like falling off a horse or a bike or anything else. This is getting your heart broken, and you like me too much to watch me go through that again."

His trademark grin in place, he walked past her, whispering in her ear as he did. "Then don't fall in love with this one."

They started down the trail watching to see if those in front of them could follow the very basic instruction of "stop at the tree." Ellie stifled a sigh. Five of them had. The pretty boy was six feet further in and grinning like the Cheshire cat. Of course.

After Trent lectured all six of them about listening to your guide and doing what you're told, they took off again. Only four more days and she could ditch this guy. As much as she loved the outdoors, this was one time she'd rather be home sick.

An hour later, the pretty boy behind her didn't bother to lower his voice. "I can't believe Maddie talked me into this."

"Your sister hates it when you call her that," one of the other guys told him.

"My sister's not here."

"Don't let her hear about it," the other guy said.

"Then don't tell her."

"And she didn't have to try hard to talk you into it."

"I'm just a glutton for punishment."

Right. Of course he was. He was too good looking not only for his own good but to be traipsing around the woods. Sure, the clothes looked worn in, but maybe he'd borrowed them from a friend who hiked a lot. Never mind that her traitorous brain had taken note of not only his height, but the broad shoulders, lean waist, and long legs. He wouldn't be able to borrow clothes from just anyone. Her rebellious mind had also noted his easy smile and thick, dark hair.

Ellie wasn't going to fall for another pretty boy. Even as she thought it, she knew it didn't really apply. Yes, he was good-looking, but not in a sissy-pretty-boy way. Yet she knew, no matter how ruggedly handsome other women might find him, she needed to keep her distance. Instead, she focused on the trail in front of her as they neared a clearing. Four days with these three yahoos and she'd be asking for a raise. She wouldn't get it, but she'd ask.

The next three hours passed both too quickly and too slowly. Too quickly because the sooner they reached their camp site, the sooner she'd have to help them set up shelters. Too slowly because of the incessant stream of chatter from Pretty Boy and the somewhat amused replies of his friends. At least they'd kept up. Trent and his group had fallen a fair bit behind, but she wasn't worried about them. Every half hour, he checked in over their radios. There was no cell phone service in the middle of nowhere, but if they needed help they could get a hold of the home base.

They stopped for a quick lunch. Protein bars and trail mix along with the allotment of water were downed by all of the men as they sat on a group of rocks. Ellie sat off to the side, against her favorite tree at this particular rest spot. She let them sit for about twenty minutes before she stood.

"Time to move out." She hoisted her pack up and moved to the trail out of the small clearing, waiting there for them to pick up the trash. As soon as they had their backpacks on, she started down the trail.

"Hey!" Rick stopped a couple feet away, forcing her to stare up at him. "I know we're doing the whole minimalist thing, but there'll be a cabin nearby right? Just in case."

Deep breath in. And out. In. And out. She counted to ten. Then twenty. Then in Latin. "No, Ricky. There won't be any cabin. Just what we can carry or find or kill." Spinning on one heel, she started up the trail. She sent up a prayer - or two - and tried to tune out the chuckle she was sure she heard coming from behind her.

"You're not being very nice." Dennis walked next to Richard for a few feet where the trail widened. "You know all this stuff. We lived in the Amazon for three months with less than we have now. What're you doing?"

Richard shrugged and made sure Ellie was far enough ahead

she wouldn't hear. "She made snap judgments about us. I didn't want to disappoint her."

"Don't do it. I get why. I know how sick you are of being written off as a pretty face or a spare - and not in the fun sense of the word - but playing up to that role isn't going endear you to her. Once she finds out you're not as helpless as a newborn kitten out here, she's going to be madder than the rhino on that safari."

"I know." But he wouldn't be able to help himself. He knew that. Dennis knew that. Or maybe he'd just tell - or show - her the truth.

Steve called from behind him. "How much farther? I'm not complaining, just curious."

Ellie turned around and Rick caught a glimpse of a scowl that disappeared almost before it began. She walked backwards as she called out. "About two more hours to the campsite, where there are no cabins and no facilities of any kind - except a nearby stream."

Rick hid his smirk until she turned around then let it break loose. Dennis just shook his head.

The next two hours went quickly and before they knew it, the forest opened up into a clearing. He dropped his pack and took a deep breath of clean air. The clearing wasn't too big, but also not too far from a drop. The incline wasn't nearly steep enough to be called a cliff, but it did allow them a decent look over the Ozark Mountains. The view wasn't as awe-inspiring as some he'd seen in other places around the world - including his home country - but...

He started softly and grew louder with each word, not caring who was around to hear it. "'The heavens declare the glory of God; and the skies proclaim the work of his hands!'" Rick's arms spread wide over his head as he yelled the last.

"Are you done?"

Rick turned to see Ellie standing there, arms folded across her chest and eyes snapping. A slow grin crossed his face. "For now. But look..." One arm swept across the expanse toward the hills. "How can you look at this and *not* shout about God's glory? If we're silent, 'the stones would immediately cry out!'"

Ellie rolled her eyes. "Luke 19:40? Really? That's not exactly what Christ was talking about, and I'm sure you know it."

"You're right," he conceded, "but..." With his eyes closed, he drew in another deep breath. "I can't help it."

With another glance heavenward, she turned and went to start unpacking. Dennis moved to his side and mimicked the deep breathing.

"You know you don't have to yell everywhere." His friend put his hands on his hips and inhaled again. "I know it's your thing but..."

Rick let out a chuckle. "When you see the world from the top of Kilimanjaro, what else are you supposed to yell?"

"Nothing?" Dennis shrugged. "Most of us are happy enough with a quiet moment of reflection."

With a slap to Dennis's back, Rick took a few more steps forward, coming close enough to the edge to make his bodyguards-slash-friends look at him twice, but it couldn't be helped. Whenever he had a moment to stop and reflect, he took it. Especially when confronted by the glorious tapestry spread out in front of him. Maybe it had something to do with growing up in the shadow of the Alps or in the middle of one of the clearest lakes in Europe. Surrounded by those during his formative years likely affected his perspective.

Chuckling to himself, he turned back to the campsite and started to set his things up.

He'd be on her last nerve before the day was out.

Ellie did her best to be patient, but some men just made it

impossible. The only consolation she had was to watch Trent and his crew - two of whom, despite how they'd appeared at headquarters, were less experienced than her Pretty Boy and hadn't kept up nearly as well on the hike.

Just a few days and they'd get back to the trail head, and she could ditch all of this for a long-overdue vacation. The tall, unfortunately handsome one she was trying to ignore had even brought his camera with him. Who did that on a minimalist trip? And a very nice camera at that. He'd get some great shots, she admitted, although grudgingly and only to herself. She sighed and looked around the camp. The bear bags were hung. Water bladders were filled and purified. Trent was helping his people finish their shelters. Her team had finished much more quickly than she would have expected. Ellie tried not to remember how Rick's fingers felt under hers as she helped him with the knots. Or the feeling of his breath on her cheek as he asked one astute question after another.

Ellie finally turned her back to the man filling way too many of her thoughts. She poked at the campfire with a stick. The stove was off to the side and had a pot on it. The water would boil soon and they'd use it to mix with their dehydrated meals for dinner. She'd bet her three boys had packed their own then been forced to take the ones Trent provided when he disapproved.

A nudge to her gut made her rescind her internal criticism. They had outperformed her expectations today. Even the pretty boy only had to be shown once how to tie the knots.

Normally, Trent enforced a fairly early bedtime, but Ellie saw the sly look he was giving her as the stars began to appear. He tilted his head toward Rick. She just rolled her eyes and went to sit on her favorite rock.

"Is this seat taken?"

Ellie looked up to see Rick standing there. "If I say it is?"

He gave her a cocky grin. "Then I'd guess you were saving it for me."

"Don't be so sure," she muttered when he sat down anyway.

A crunching sound caught her attention but she refused to give into her curiosity. "You do this all the time?" he asked around whatever it was he was eating.

"Sit and watch stars?"

"Lead groups of people who have no clue what they're doing into the middle of nowhere and hope you all survive."

The comment stung. "Glad to know you think we're incompetent."

"I don't think you're incompetent."

"Then why would we only *hope* to survive? If Trent and I are any good at our jobs, and we're very good at our jobs, then everyone will survive just fine, thank you very much."

"I didn't mean to insult you. You seem quite competent." This time she saw him take a rather large bite of an apple.

Ellie should have brought some fresh fruit along but she hadn't wanted the extra weight in her pack this trip.

He held it out to her. "Would you like a bite?"

"No, thank you." She didn't need anything from him.

Even if the next crunch of his apple made her mouth water. The crunch after that made it even worse.

"So, what is on the agenda for tomorrow?"

"Weren't you paying attention?" Did he expect her to repeat everything over and over just for him?

"Yes. I was hoping you could give me a bit more detail. Pack up camp, hike for a while, and set up camp again isn't much in the way of information."

She'd give him that. Trent was pretty sparse with details. "If you and your buddies keep up the way you did today, we'll hike for about three hours, break for lunch, hike for two more hours then set up camp. We'll stay there tomorrow night and the next night then pack up again. Another day hike to our last campsite. After a night there, we'll retrace our steps."

"Why two nights at the one spot?"

"We'll practice some more survival skills. You'll set out your own snares and dress the squirrel or rabbit then cook it yourself. No stove."

"Sounds easy enough."

He would think that.

"I'll even share my rabbit with you." That cocksure grin was back.

And made her traitorous stomach do slow flips as he took the last bite of his apple.

Rick knew he shouldn't try so hard to irritate her, but it was so easy.

And so fun.

His mother would tan his hide. Well, not really. Hide tanning wasn't in his mother's genteel nature, but he'd be grounded for a month.

A shrill whistle behind them caught his attention. "Lights out. We gotta pack up early." Trent's voice carried to where he and Ellie sat.

"That's our cue." She stood and brushed the back of her pants off with her hands. "Dawn comes early and we have a big day."

"Sleep well, Ellie." He watched her walk away, one corner of his mind wishing she wore shorts so he could appreciate the long legs hidden under her cargo pants. The rest of his mind felt guilty for his deception. Tomorrow, he'd have to come clean.

That had been his plan but Ellie woke up on the wrong side of the bedroll. When she started snapping at all three of them first thing after dawn, he fumbled his way through packing up his part of camp. He could have done it with his eyes closed, or in his sleep, but instead she had to help him get everything folded and packed right.

A hand on his shoulder as they started off stopped him. "This is going to backfire, sir."

Dennis's voice wouldn't carry far enough for anyone else to hear him, but Rick glared at him anyway. "Don't call me that."

"Then stop the charade. I've got a bad feeling about this."

Those words stopped Rick in his tracks. "What kind of bad feeling, Dennis?"

The bodyguard-turned-friend shook his head. "I don't know, but nothing good can come of it, and something is churning in my gut. It won't end well."

"I won't do anything stupid. You know me better than that."

"I know you won't do anything *you* think is stupid." Dennis stepped directly in front of him. "You *will* listen to me, to Steve, and to Ellie. Understand, Your Highness?"

The barb struck where it was supposed to. "Don't call me that."

"Then behave yourself. Do as you're told, and don't pretend you're incompetent." One more withering look and Dennis turned to follow Steve and Ellie.

Rick sighed and trudged after them. He knew Dennis was right. He just needed to remember that the next time the opportunity arose to annoy her.

"Rick! Get back here!" Ellie charged after him as fast as she could through the dense underbrush.

"We won't go far!" His long legs carried him further and further away from her faster than she could follow him.

This was what happened when you took arrogant, self-centered pretty boys on hikes. They didn't listen, did their best to get lost, and she had to save them. It wasn't the first time. It probably wouldn't be the last. This time she wouldn't rescue the guy from being hopelessly lost, lose her heart in the process then get it broken again. She'd shove him, hard, and watch him land on his backside.

"This is the coolest cave around, right?" Rick called back.

"Yeah, but this isn't the best way to get there." Like that would stop him.

"But we can't get to the best way to get there from here, right?"

"Rick, we can't go this way. Stop!" She hurried as fast as she could, but his long legs carried him further away from her.

His two buddies weren't being much help. They'd yelled after him when he'd first taken off, but once he'd insisted, they'd exchanged a look she couldn't interpret and followed in his wake.

She thought about grabbing the walkie-talkie and calling Trent, but what could Trent do? They were only checking in every ninety minutes during this hike and Rick had waited until just after the last call to make his move into the woods. Besides, if she stopped to get the walkie out of her backpack, Rick would be long gone. He had grabbed her map and compass, so he wouldn't need her. Instead of wasting time, she followed him, hollering at him to stop every few minutes.

But he just kept going.

After almost an hour, they broke through the rugged forest onto the trail that would lead directly to the cave. Ten minutes after that, they stood in front of the entrance.

"We won't be in here long," Rick promised looking up at the mountain above the opening.

Ellie crossed her arms in front of her. "That's because we're not going in at all. We don't have the equipment for wandering around in the cave."

"We won't wander around." Rick hiked his backpack a bit higher. "We'll just go in and look around for a few minutes then get back to where we're supposed to be." He headed for the entrance. "Come on."

She heard Dennis and Steve muttering behind her, but they

didn't try to stop him. If they didn't go far, they'd be fine, but she didn't trust Rick not to push the limits.

With a frustrated growl, Ellie ran after him until she could grab him by the arm and spin him around. "Okay. Fine. Look. It's my job to keep you safe. You won't listen to me and turn around, and I won't let you go on by yourself. So you're going to listen. You'll stop when I tell you to stop, and we'll leave when I say to leave, understand?"

Rick's smug grin was more than she could handle. She put both hands on his chest and shoved. Just like she'd planned.

He didn't move.

Annoying pretty boy.

She turned and stalked into the mouth of the cave, pulling her flashlight out of its spot on her backpack.

The sound of water trickling in the distance caught her attention first. Cool air greeted them as they moved further in. Stalactites and stalagmites reached for each other, glistening as their headlamps illuminated the space.

"This is amazing," Rick whispered. He tilted his head down toward the opening in front of them. "How far down does that go?"

"Not too far. I forget exactly but maybe fifteen feet or so." She turned and crossed her arms across her chest. "We are *not* going down there."

His eyes narrowed. "I wasn't suggesting it."

"You were thinking about it."

He sighed. "Okay. I was. But you're right. We don't have the equipment." In the dim lighting she could see a gleam in his eyes. "But we *can* explore this way a bit more." He turned toward the path that led along the side of the cavern.

Ellie smothered her frustration and started after him.

But her boot slipped on the loose gravel.

A scream ripped from her as she dropped her flashlight and plummeted into the darkness.

Chapter Two

Rick scrambled down the embankment, yelling at Ellie. A curse or two slipped out under his breath. He'd let his experience and desire to poke at her for being annoying override his common sense. You *always* listened to the guide. Unless you *knew* they were flat out wrong about something with regards to survival, you listened. And obeyed. The guide *always* knows the area better than you do.

Period.

So why had he charged off into the woods when she told him not to?

Because he was just *sure* he knew better than she did. Or at least that she was just being stubborn and obnoxious because she didn't like him.

He slid to a stop at Ellie's side near the bottom and right before the fifteen foot drop. That probably wouldn't have killed her either but she'd have been in worse shape.

"Where's it hurt?" he asked, getting down to business.

"My arm's broken," she ground out. One hand propped her up, the other rested against her stomach. "Radius, ulna, or both. And I wrenched my ankle pretty badly."

Dennis and Steve skidded to a stop next to them. Rick looked at Dennis for guidance. He'd dealt with injuries before, but wasn't a trained medic like his friend. "What now, Dennis?"

Dennis swung his backpack off and set it down. "We assess." He asked Ellie a series of questions, probed a number of places gently then sat back on his haunches. "I think the worst is the arm. She's going to be sore and bruised, but as best I can tell here, the bones are our main concern. We'll keep an eye on her and reassess as necessary, but for now, we'll work on the arm and ankle."

Ellie finally glared at them. "What makes you qualified to make that assessment?"

Pulling his canteen out, Dennis twisted the lid off and handed it to Ellie. "I'm a trained medic. Steve is too, but my training and experience are a bit more recent."

Taking a big swig of the water, Ellie nodded. "Okay. For the record, I agree with you." Tiny beads of sweat broke out on her brow. "For now the pain is manageable, but we need to call Trent and get rescue personnel headed our way." Rick helped her slip her backpack off, completely undoing the strap on the side with her broken arm. "It's in the front pocket."

Rick unzipped it and pulled out the walkie-talkie. "Um, I think we have a problem." He held up the cracked and broken plastic. "I don't think this is going to work."

Steve took it. "I'll see what I can do with it in a bit. First, we need to get Ellie stabilized and out of this cave. We can start back and when it's time to stop tonight, I'll try to fix it. Otherwise, we're burning daylight on a long-shot."

After discussing it for a few more minutes, they decided to splint both her arm and her lower leg, just in case. Steve went to get some stout branches to use for the splints. While he was gone, Rick and Dennis dug out several bandannas and worked them into place under her leg.

"Can you lean back? Get comfortable?" Dennis looked up

from where he was checking her foot for blood flow and feeling.

Ellie was propped up with her good hand behind her, but there wasn't anything nearby for her to lean against.

Rick moved to her side and slid behind her. "Here. Lean on me." He bent one knee and pressed his shin along the ground against her rear. Leaning forward a bit, he put his hands on her shoulders and guided her backward until her back rested against his chest. Without thinking about it, he wrapped his arms around her until his fingers laced together on her stomach.

He breathed a sigh of relief as she relaxed into him, her good hand coming to rest on top of his. The rightness, the feeling of protectiveness, caught Rick off-guard. It was his fault she'd been hurt. Why couldn't he have listened to her? And Dennis. And Steve. And his conscience.

How long had it been since he'd held a woman in his arms? Had he ever? He'd been on precious few dates. Rick made it home for the balls when he was required to - for the Christmas Eve Ball and the Anniversary Ball celebrating his father's coronation. He always escorted someone to those, but never anyone he had a romantic interest in. He'd gone on a few dates during his year in college but when your bodyguards had to go with you it was awkward at best.

Though it had been three days since any of them had taken a proper shower, he could still catch hints of Ellie's flower shampoo. Her fingers tightened around his as Dennis touched her arm. But then she sank back into Rick, expelling a lungful of air.

With Ellie a bit more relaxed, Dennis gently felt along the arm, determining it was likely a clean break. After about fifteen minutes, Steve reappeared at the top of the incline with two stout branches. Ten minutes after that, her arm and ankle were immobilized with the splint and bandannas.

While Steve was looking for the branches, the three left behind had strategized how to get Ellie up the embankment and then out of the cave. Rick unfastened the Paracord bracelet on his wrist and handed it to Dennis to unravel while he held Ellie steady. It wasn't the first time it had come in handy. By the time Steve returned, two of them were undone and they had plenty of it to do the job. As the tallest, Rick would stay with Ellie after she was situated in the homemade harness. Steve and Dennis would be at the top hoisting her by pulling on the Paracord ropes while Rick would help her balance most of the way. She'd use her good hand and leg to help when she could but otherwise the men would pull her out.

Getting up took significantly longer than it had taken them to get to the ledge, but they made it to the mouth of the cave before nightfall, though barely. They decided to make camp just outside the cave, under an overhang. Once Ellie was situated against the rock face, the three men set about gathering wood and making a shelter. They never left her completely alone, but the look on her face made Rick believe she'd never felt more useless.

Hot tears stung the back of Ellie's eyes, but she refused to allow them to fall. The three men went about the tasks of setting up camp without talking much about it. She'd known from nearly the beginning that Dennis and Steve weren't new to this kind of outdoor trek, but Rick had been a total newbie.

Or he'd pretended to be.

His movements were sure and competent as he used the fuel brought back by his friends to get a fire started. He knew all sorts of things they hadn't covered in their three days in the mountains. His friends were still out somewhere - getting more water from the nearby stream maybe - when he spoke.

"How far are we from cell phone service?"

Ellie screwed her face into a grimace. "A full day, maybe more, without a busted ankle. I don't think we want to send someone tonight, but first thing in the morning two of you can head for civilization and get help."

Rick shook his head but ignored her return glare. "No. We stick together. None of us know where we are. It would be too easy for the two who are going to get lost and not be able to tell rescuers where to go even if they did."

"We're not anywhere near where we're supposed to be, though. By now, Trent has called in that we're missing. Rescue operations may have started already, though they'll be called off for the night soon. They'll start again in the morning either way, but they'll be miles from here and have no reason to look this way. This cave isn't on one of the regular trails used by anyone really. The odds of us running into someone are slim, and they won't look here. They'd get here eventually, but we'll have to find a way out on our own. I don't think I can wait three or four days, or longer, for them to find us."

He stared into the flames beginning to flicker up the twigs and small branches then nodded. "Okay. First thing in the morning, all of us head out together. Down the trail, not through the woods, and toward civilization."

She nodded. "Okay." First, though, she'd have to make it through the night with a broken arm, an aching ankle, no pillow, no bed, no comforts of any kind. She often slept under the stars, but never like this. The ibuprofen took the edge off the pain and between it and the acetaminophen in their packs, hopefully she could keep it at bay until she could get to a hospital.

"If it was just the ankle, we could try to fashion crutches." Rick didn't seem to be talking to her as he pulled a protein bar out of his pack and held it out to her.

She took it, gratefully, and nodded her thanks as she thought. "If we had real crutches, maybe, but I can't put any weight on the leg at all so even if I didn't have a broken arm. With one under my good arm, I'll do the best I can but..." Ellie shrugged. "It'll take a long time, but I don't know what other options we have."

Rick didn't look at her when he told her what he thought they'd do. "We'll carry you. We've got a poncho blanket, I bet they're finding two long branches and we'll make a litter to carry you as much as we can."

As much as Ellie hated to hear it, she knew it was the best way to travel and she nodded. It would be humiliating but at least she'd get home.

It was one of the longest nights of Rick's life. Not the sleeping outdoors part. He did that all the time. No, the part where he relived how his arrogance and stupidity gave Ellie a broken arm and severely twisted ankle.

He stared at the night sky long after Dennis's snoring told Rick his friend was asleep. He knew Steve was. The man could sleep at the drop of a hat. A good thing, he supposed for a bodyguard for whom regular sleep wasn't always possible. His mind wandered a million places besides the edge of a cave in the Ozark Mountains, though all rabbit trails could be traced back, in one way or another, to the woman sleeping on the other side of the campfire.

After all, her cousin was marrying his sister.

Or would be once Charlie got around to asking.

It wasn't official, but he'd had a long video chat with Addie before booking this trip two months ago. She and Charlie were madly in love and his sister adored Charlie's eleven-year-old daughter. But they'd decided the official engagement would wait until life settled down a bit. Like after her coronation.

For the moment, Rick was second in line for the throne of Montevaro, and he liked it that way. Once his father abdicated due to recent injuries and overall failing health, he'd be first in line. He hoped Charlie proposed soon - and that Rick was an uncle at least twice sooner rather than later. He'd do his duty if called upon, but he'd much rather spend his time in the outdoors. Creating a tourist environment for outdoor enthusiasts. Making it the "go to" place in the southern Alps for camping and hiking trips like this one. It was the whole reason he'd decided to go on one last trip before taking some time off to help Addie prepare for the coronation and do all the other official Prince-slash-brother-of-the-practically-queen stuff required of him in coming months. He'd tried to get in touch with her en route from the Himalayas, but with the time differences, he hadn't been able to.

He'd have balls to attend. Fundraisers to plan for Addie's favorite charities on her behalf as a coronation gift to the people of Montevaro. Galas. Thinly-veiled attempts to find him a steady girlfriend before the coronation and definitely before the wedding. Rick knew his father would love to see him settled down in the next year. The king had been quite clear on that. With Parkinson's taking over his body, Father didn't want to be seen as a doddering fool with all the attention those kinds of events were sure to attract. If Addie, Rick, and Rick's slightly-younger-twin-sister, Ana, were all happily married in the next twelve to eighteen months, their father would be ecstatic.

The restless night stretched into eternity, but not long after Rick finally dozed off, dawn began to break. It still wasn't fully light out when they started stirring around camp. After a quick breakfast of granola bars and trail mix, Dennis and Steve assembled the litter while Rick covered up the fire.

Half an hour after the streaks lit the sky enough to wake them, Ellie was on the litter. Rick took the poles near her head while Steve took the ones at her feet. They started down the trail for what was sure to be one of the longest days of his life.

Chapter Three

*T*his was the longest day of her life.

Ellie closed her eyes and tried to will herself to sleep, but though she trusted the men not to drop her, there was no way she could doze off. She even tried her virtually fail proof trick of breathing in for a four-count, hold for eight, out for ten. Didn't work.

"Time for a rest." Steve's voice drifted back to her. He'd carried her feet for a while, then they'd traded around. They'd likely switch again after this break.

Rick was carrying her feet now. She'd spent too much time watching his back and, yes, even his rear end. Ellie didn't spend much time ogling men - had she ever ogled one? - but though Rick annoyed her to no end, even she had to admit he was more well-built than she'd originally given him credit for. She had precious little else to do but notice.

The feeling of his arms around her after the fall had gone farther than anything else in calming her fears and helping her relax. How long had it been since she'd had a man hold her in his arms? Too long. And even then she'd never felt safe and protected like she had with his arms around her.

"We're gonna set you down now, Ellie."

She looked up to see Dennis looking down at her and nodded. Though they did their best to be gentle, the jostling caused pain to spear up her leg and through her arm. Tears were involuntary and though she did her best to keep them from spilling over, she couldn't. Hot liquid leaked down the side of her face and into her ears. When she opened her eyes, Rick was standing between her and the sun. When their eyes met, he held out a hand and pulled her into a sitting position before handing her some water.

"How are you?" He sat next to her, propping his forearm on his knee.

Ellie tossed back some more ibuprofen. "As good as can be expected, I guess. It hurts, but the pain meds are helping. I know you're being as careful as you can."

He pulled the map out of her pack. "Can you tell me where we are?"

She studied it and looked carefully at their surroundings before pointing to a spot on the marked trail. "About here." She traced her finger south to the other trail. "They were expecting us to be right around here."

"Would they have found the trail we left into the woods when I took off?"

"Unlikely. You followed a game trail for the first bit. Not a big one but I doubt we disturbed the ground enough for them to notice."

Rick looked straight into her eyes, his face as somber as she'd ever seen it. "I am sorry, Ellie. I know better. I should have listened to you and then asked you to take us to the caves after our trip was over."

One thing he said stuck out. "You know better?"

A grimace crossed his face. "I'll just say this is not even close to the most difficult trek my friends and I have done."

"It's not?" She tried to figure out what he meant by that. They obviously had some experience, but just how much?

"No..."

Dennis called to Rick, interrupting whatever he planned to say. He squeezed her good leg, just below the knee, as he rose. They stood, several feet away from her, looking at the map and talking. She couldn't hear what they were saying and it annoyed her.

"You know," Ellie called. "I know this area better than any of you. You might include me in these discussions."

Rick stuck the map in his pocket. "There's nothing to talk about. I was just telling them what you told me."

"Five minutes and then we'll get moving again." Dennis took a swig from his canteen. "We need to make it as far as we can before nightfall. We won't make a full camp like we have been, just enough to get by so we can hike longer today and start earlier tomorrow."

Ellie nodded, like she had a choice in the matter. "At the pace we're going, we'll get back to the Outdoor Ozarks building late tomorrow afternoon. We should have cell phone service before then."

They didn't say anything but nodded. When they started again, Rick led the way while Steve and Dennis carried her litter. Once again, she closed her eyes. And once again, she couldn't sleep.

"Guys?"

Rick looked down at the pale face on the litter. "You okay?"

Tears streaked down Ellie's cheeks as she shook her head. "Can we take a break?"

How long had she been in pain without saying anything? Rick hollered to Dennis, fifteen yards ahead then turned back to Ellie. "We'll find a place to stop as soon as we can."

If he had to guess, it was about four in the afternoon and he knew Dennis wanted to go for a couple more hours, but if it was going to be too hard on her, they needed to stop. Rick was in the best shape of his life, and he knew Dennis and Steve were as well, but he needed a break. Ellie weighed next to nothing, but carrying next to nothing through a hiking trail all day would wear on anyone. His shoulders were feeling the burn. They walked for another fifteen minutes before they found a clearing big enough for them to set up camp.

They set Ellie down and Rick helped her unhook her arms from her pack. Holding it on her chest couldn't make it easy for her to breathe. He reached out a hand and helped her to her foot. Before she could protest, he lifted her into his arms and carried her over to a tree. When he set her back down, she looked up at him.

Her hazel eyes were filled with tears again.

He reached out and brushed some of the hair off her face. "I am so sorry, Ellie."

She nodded, and he wanted to pull her into his arms and tell her it was all right to cry. Instead, he helped her lower herself to the ground. "What do you want for dinner?"

Following her direction, he dug a meal out of her backpack and opened a granola bar to hold her over while they got a fire going and water boiling. He and the other two men set up the camp quickly and efficiently. By the time set up was complete, the water was boiling. He poured it into the bag and handed it to Ellie.

By about six, they were done eating and Rick found himself sitting next to Ellie. Dennis and Steve went to replenish their water supply from a creek she told them ran nearby.

"Are you ready for some more meds?" Rick asked her.

Ellie didn't nod, but just held out her hand. "Thank you for making them stop. I don't think I could have taken much more of the jostling today."

"It means we might not make it back tomorrow." He shook the acetaminophen into her palm. "We've got plenty of supplies, but it'll be that much longer before we get you to medical care."

"I know, but there's only so much I can take."

He wanted to make sure she knew he would take care of her medical expenses and any lost wages, but his friends chose that moment to come back. Dennis motioned to him and Rick nodded. "I'll be right back."

"How is she?" His friend handed over a canteen.

"Tired and sore, but otherwise, holding up, I think." Rick glanced over to see her eyes closed and her head resting against the tree. "She said her body just couldn't take anymore right now." She hadn't said much to any of them while they ate, only to refuse help while she fed herself with one hand.

Dennis nodded. "We'll have to push that much harder tomorrow, though. I don't want to be out here another night."

"Agreed."

"She hasn't gone into shock and seems to be all right physically, but she needs a hospital. They're probably going to have to do surgery on that arm."

Rick had already come to that conclusion, though he wouldn't say so to Ellie.

Dennis took hold of his upper arm and pulled him further away, his next words laced with sarcasm. "Pardon me for forgetting my place, sir, but what were you thinking? You know better."

Rick glared, knowing Dennis's place was to keep him safe, period. "You're right. I do. I'm going to apologize, take care of all the medical expenses, and any other financial repercussions for her and Outdoor Ozarks."

"You need to tell her who you are. She's headed to Montevaro for her aunt and uncle's investiture as the new Marquis and Marchioness of Montago and her cousin's knighting for service to the crown and protection of the royal family above and beyond the call of duty. She'll find out then, and she'll hate that you didn't tell her sooner."

"I know. I will." He would. Soon. But he hated how people changed around him when they found out his title and his family heritage. Maybe at dinner the next day, as late as he could tell her before they arrived at the base. Or maybe afterward. Stay until she was out of surgery and tell her as she came out from under the anesthesia. *Coward.*

He took a long pull from the canteen and walked back toward Ellie. She held out a hand, and he opened it before handing it over.

"Thanks." She took a long drink before resting it on her good leg. She stuck her chin toward Dennis and Steve. "What're they saying?"

Rick let out a breath and sat next to her. Before he spoke, he picked at a blade of grass, splitting it long ways into strand after strand. "Dennis got on my case for running off. I know better."

She seemed to absorb that for a moment before replying. "You know better than to run off?"

"I know to listen to your guide. Always." He tossed the grass down and picked up another blade. They'd started the conversation earlier. It was time to finish it. "I'm not nearly as incompetent as I tried to portray. The three of us have traipsed all over the world together."

Another pause. "All over the world?"

"Yep." He picked up the Paracord from where it lay beside him and maneuvered it around the plastic piece that held the bracelet together. Once it was situated, he began reforming the bracelet.

"Like where?" She didn't sound like she believed him.

"The Andes. African safari. Dog sledding. The biggest cave in the world in Viet Nam. The Himalayas. You name it, we've probably done it."

Her sarcasm deepened. "No Alps?"

"I grew up in the Alps, so I've been all over my part of them." Should he tell her the rest? Tell her his true identity and give up time spent with someone who knew *Rick* and not *His Royal Highness Prince Richard*? Before he could decide, she spoke.

"That's nice. I suppose Mommy and Daddy paid for all of it, too." Ellie didn't mean to be snarky, but she couldn't help it. "Or was it a trust fund?"

It took Rick a minute before he replied. "Something like that. My family has enough money that I can do this sort of thing without worrying about it, but I will be taking a substantial role in...the family business when I finish this trip." He continued to refashion his Paracord into a new bracelet.

There was something off about how he said "family business" but Ellie didn't take the time to analyze it. "Must be nice," she mused. "Not to *have* to work. To buy a new backpack whenever you want."

"It is," he answered slowly, as though he was measuring every word. "I can admit it makes life much easier. It comes with its own set of pressures and requirements though. I will likely always be under my father's thumb, no matter how much I wish to break away. Once he is no longer head of...the family business, my sister will take over, and I will answer to her. It is probable that I will never truly be my own man with my own life outside of the family. When I am home, my time is not my own. When I'm not in a remote wilderness, my every move is watched by more people than I care to admit."

A familiar face flashed in front of her eyes. One she wanted to forget. But she could empathize with not wanting anyone to control your life. "Your family is well-known?"

A wry grin crossed his face. "Very."

"So I could do a search and find you on Wikipedia?"

"I would imagine so. I've never looked. I'm sure my family has a page, but I don't know if I have one of my own."

How would she feel if her life was spelled out in an online encyclopedia? Every date analyzed. Every business decision second-guessed. Every clothing choice picked apart and ridiculed. Ellie shuddered, wincing at the pain as it shot through her arm. "I guess maybe there are parts of it that aren't all they're cracked up to be."

"Sometimes, I wonder if I couldn't find a happy medium somewhere in the middle. Enough money to do things like buy a backpack or take a vacation, but not so much that the paparazzi parks outside my home."

She turned her head to look at him. "Paparazzi? Really?" She hadn't thought he was that serious.

"Oh, yeah. News. Tabloids. You name it. Not much outside my country and our sister countries. At home, it depends on what's going on, but there's usually a few around."

"Okay. That part wouldn't be any fun." She grinned. "I bet you have a cool house, though."

Rick chuckled. "Yes. I do live in a very cool house. It belongs to my parents, though. And my grandfather before that. My great-grandfather before that. My great-great grandfather and great-great-great grandfather before that. And so on."

"No grandmothers in there?"

He shook his head. "Not in the line. My family followed the traditional rules of primogeniture until this generation. My sister will inherit most everything."

She blinked rapidly. "Primogeniture? Did I even say that right?"

"Yep." Rick's head rested to the side, allowing him to watch her. "It means the oldest son gets everything."

"Until now, you would have inherited everything?"

"Not everything, but close enough. But I'm good with it. I'll live beyond comfortably for the rest of my life, as will my children and grandchildren. My great-grandchildren possibly not quite as much, but it depends on a number of factors. I won't ever have to worry about where to live. My parents' home is plenty big enough for all of us to live without ever seeing each other if we don't want to, plus there are several other properties owned by my family in my country and in our sister countries."

"Must be nice," she muttered. "Sorry." How much was she willing to tell him? "My parents don't really approve of my job choice. I only finished one year of community college in Serenity Landing, my hometown near Springfield, Missouri. I make enough money to live on, but not enough to do things like buy a high quality backpack or boots that will last longer than a few months out here."

"I didn't finish university either." He looked up at the sky. "My parents aren't happy about it, and I will likely return to finish my degree after this trip."

She rolled her head to look up at the sky with him. "If you could do anything you wanted, what would it be?"

Rick reached over and lightly grasped her uninjured hand in one of his. "This."

Chapter Four

The next day was a carbon copy of the one before. By the time Ellie insisted they stop for the night, they were still at least a couple hours from Outdoor Ozarks headquarters.

"Do we want a couple of us to keep going?" Ellie posed the question as she ate her rehydrated meal. "If one of you stayed here with me, the other two could be back at headquarters before dark. We might even make it out of here tonight."

Dennis shook his head. "No. I still don't think splitting up is the way to go." He looked at his watch. "But it's only seven. We could make it by nine or so if you're willing to try?"

Rick watched her face closely. It would tax her endurance and her ability to take the pain, but she nodded her assent anyway. "I can take some more pain meds. Let's do this. We all have headlamps. By the time it gets too dark, the trail will be a lot easier. The roughest part is coming up in about half a mile or so but after that it's smooth sailing."

He exchanged a look with his friends. They would keep going.

Twilight had given way to dark when they finally reached the tree line along the path to the headquarters. Rick was leading the way while the other two carried her, and he stopped as he broke through the trees.

"Um. We may have a problem."

"What's that?" she asked from her spot on the litter.

"News crews." Ellie didn't understand the grim tone in his voice.

"We should have expected that." Dennis's voice reflected Rick's.

"Why? What's the big deal?" Not that she was thrilled she'd end up on local television or newspapers looking like something the cat dragged in, but the men seemed to be making it into a bigger deal than she would have guessed. Sure, they didn't look great either, but who cared? Or was it Rick's paparazzi?

"Nothing." Rick's tense voice told her he was hiding something. "They're mostly on the other side of the building. Maybe we'll come in unnoticed."

"I wouldn't hold out much hope for that." Dennis sounded weary. "I'm sure your parents already know."

"Maddie's gonna be thrilled," Rick snorted.

Steve let out a short bark of laughter. "Don't call her that to her face. She'll never forgive you."

Who was Maddie?

"Let's just get this over with. Trade me spots, Dennis." Rick took the branches at her head. "Are we going to make a statement?"

"We'll see how it goes." Steve broke through the tree line. It was about a quarter mile through waist high grasses to the building. About the time she figured they were nearing the headquarters, she heard a shout.

"Here they come," Rick muttered. She didn't think she was supposed to hear him.

Flashbulbs popped and questions were shouted their direction, but Ellie couldn't make out what they were saying. She pointed toward the door on the side of the building. "Through there."

"What happened?" one of the reporters yelled.

She heard a couple of them saying something to Rick - or "Richard" anyway. But then they were through the door and Rick and Steve set her down on a couch.

"I need to talk to you." Rick's mouth was set in a firm line. "Before it gets..."

Trent appeared at her side before Rick could go on. "Ellie, are you okay?"

She accepted his hand, and he pulled her to a sitting position. "Arm's broken, ankle's a mess, but otherwise, yeah. We're fine."

"What happened?"

Ellie glanced up at Rick. She didn't want to play the blame game. Sure, he shouldn't have defied her, but he'd come through when it counted, and she didn't want to set it solely on his shoulders like she would have a couple days earlier.

"I'll tell you everything," Rick told Trent, clapping him on the shoulder. "But first can we get Ellie some medical attention?"

As though they'd heard him, paramedics, and assorted others streamed in the room. She was separated from Rick, Dennis, Steve, and Trent. Questions came at her from the left and right. She answered them as best as she could and struggled not to feel abandoned and alone. The four men huddled in the corner with Ed, her boss - who looked both furious and relieved. The medics left the splint in place, started an IV with some morphine, and decided it was time get to the hospital as quickly as they could.

Without giving her the chance to say anything to anyone, she was transferred onto the gurney and into the ambulance that had pulled up outside the back door.

The last thing she saw before the doors shut was Rick, staring at her, a sad look on his face. His eyes closed briefly, and he turned back to the group.

She was alone.

"Are we going to make a statement?" Dennis looked to Rick.

Rick nodded. "I want to make sure the world knows that I take full responsibility for what happened. Outdoor Ozarks had nothing to do with it." He turned to Ed and the assorted authorities gathered. "I will pay all expenses for Ellie and the additional costs for the search and rescue. I'll reimburse funds to the rest of the group and something for their inconvenience."

Ed seemed to relax a bit. "Thank you."

"It is only right. I did not listen. Once she knew I would not do as she said, Ellie did her best to keep us safe, but it is my responsibility. I know better."

The man gave another nod. "You'll all need to go to the hospital and get checked out."

Rick started to protest, but stopped when Dennis glared at him. "I will make a statement to the media gathered outside, and then we will go to the hospital."

It was an hour before they were ready to go out and face the masses. He spoke briefly with his sister who was both relieved and mad - just as he'd known she would be. The local sheriff was the first in front of the microphones, and he introduced Rick just as he'd been instructed.

"Next, His Royal Highness, Prince Richard Jedidiah David Nicklaus of Montevaro. He will make a statement. He will not be taking any questions."

Rick moved in front of the microphones. "Ladies and gentlemen, thank you for coming and for following this story. I am taking full responsibility for the situation we found ourselves in. Outdoor Ozarks is in no way responsible for my recklessness. I would like to thank all of those who have spent the last few days searching for us. Ellie went above and beyond the call of duty in helping us and paid the price with a broken arm. I would ask that you leave Ms. Brewer in peace. I will do my best to make myself available to answer questions after my friends and I have been examined at the local hospital. Once again, thank you for your efforts on our behalf, and I apologize for the concern that we caused as a result of my actions."

The reporters yelled questions but he didn't answer any of them. He did turn to wave as he, Dennis, and Steve climbed into the waiting SUV and headed for the hospital. Once there, the doctors checked all three of them out and wanted to keep them overnight for observation. Rick protested but Dennis and Steve overrode his decision.

"Can I see Ellie?" he asked the nurse. The ground would be preferable to the hospital bed, but they wouldn't let him out of their sight. He felt so helpless, and there wasn't even anything wrong with him.

"She's in surgery, sir." The nurse gave a bit of a bow toward him. Great. Deference. It was nice sometimes, but it got old fast. "They had to reset her arm."

"Very well. Please see that I am informed of her status." It wasn't a question.

The nurse nodded. "I'll let you know when I hear anything."

The hours of the night dragged on and on, but Rick finally managed to get some fitful sleep. When he woke the nurse told him Ellie was resting comfortably but sleeping so he wouldn't be able to see her until later.

Except later wasn't going to come. He was being summoned back to Montevaro, and he didn't dare wait any longer. Not even to wait for Ellie to wake up so he could see her before he left.

Ellie used the remote attached to her hospital bed to turn the sound up. One of the local news stations was replaying the press conference from the night before.

The sheriff, the father of one of her early childhood friends, took the podium. *"Next, His Royal Highness, Prince Richard Jedidiah David Nicklaus of Montevaro. He will make a statement. He will not be taking any questions."*

Ellie blinked rapidly as she attempted to assimilate what the sheriff said. Before she could, a knock sounded at the door. "Come in."

Trent walked in holding a teddy bear and a giant Hershey's bar. "Hey, kiddo."

She nodded at the television. "What's all this about?"

"Pretty amazing, huh?"

"I'm not sure."

"You haven't figured it out?" Trent asked as Rick continued making his statement.

"Who is he?"

"A prince in some small country in Europe. His family was about ready to convince the president to send in the National Guard to look for him and his bodyguards."

"Bodyguards? Is that who Dennis and Steve are?" A lot of things suddenly made a lot more sense. The looks they exchanged. The attempts to get him to stop. The frustrated acquiescence when he refused.

The doctor walked in interrupting whatever else Trent had planned to say. A steady stream of people were in and out of her room until it was finally dark, and she was alone. Her parents were on a cruise and she didn't even know for sure if they knew about her little escapade. Her brother and cousin-who'd-grown-up-with-them were both overseas visiting her cousin's fiancé.

His princess fiancé.

What were the odds Rick was related to Charlie's girlfriend? There couldn't be that many royal families in Europe she'd never heard of, could there?

Her cell phone buzzed from its spot on the side table. "Out of area," she muttered, swiping her finger across the screen. "Hello?"

"Hello, Ellie." The voice on the other end of the phone warmed her insides.

"Rick?" He was already halfway home, wasn't he? "Where are you?"

"On the Montevarian jet on my way home."

"Montevarian?"

"I am sure you have been told who I am."

"The prince from a country in Europe."

"Montevaro. Your cousin is going to marry my older sister, Adeline." She could hear the smile in his voice.

"I wondered." She wished for an old fashioned phone so she could twirl the cord in her fingers. Instead, she twisted the blanket.

"I want to make sure you know I will be taking care of all expenses, including compensation for your time off work."

"I heard."

"I would also like for you to come visit Montevaro as soon as you are allowed to travel. I can either send the plane for you or provide for your airfare."

Her mouth hung open. He'd do that? "You'd send a plane? For me?"

"Absolutely. I am hoping to start an organization, similar to Outdoor Ozarks, in my country. I would like you to help me set it up."

Ellie's head spun. "Sure. I'd be happy to." Did he mean it? She knew enough about the company to help him get started. And what she didn't know she could find out.

"I will see you soon then?" A voice sounded in the background. "We are about to begin our descent and the pilot is telling me I must get off the phone."

"Yes, you'll see me soon."

They said their good-byes and Ellie clicked the button on the top of her phone. She clutched it to her chest with her good hand. She'd spent four days in the woods giving a prince a hard time. A *prince*! A prince who could probably hike circles around her.

Even if he was a pretty boy.

Chapter Five

*T*he dichotomy of his surroundings was not lost on Rick. Even on board a plane, he had access to luxuries he'd only dreamed about two nights before. Shower. Soft bed. Razor. The scruff did not bother him, but it did his mother. He often went days – sometimes weeks or even months – without shaving when he was on a trek. His mother would have passed out if she'd seen him when he first came out of the Andes after four months.

"We'll be landing in about fifteen minutes, sir." The pilot's voice came over the intercom.

"Your sister is going to kill you." Steve sat across from Rick and put his seat belt back on.

"Most likely." Rick held his nose and tried to pop his ears as the pressure increased. "I'll have to make sure she knows I'm not going anywhere until after the coronation and wedding. Maybe in the mountains near home. I'd love to explore the tunnels they found this spring." Really what he wanted to do was turn around and go back to Missouri. Sit next to Ellie until she could go home. Take care of her as much as she would let him. Then bring her to Montevaro where she could be waited on hand and foot.

Twenty minutes after the plane landed, the royal speedboat pulled up to the dock at the island palace. He hopped off as soon as it came to a stop and found himself wrapped in a hug.

"I am so glad you are well, brother." Adeline held onto him for a long minute before stepping back and smacking him in the chest. "Do not do that to me again. Not only were you missing, but so was Charlie's cousin. He and Lindsey have been frantic."

"How is Father?" Richard kept his arm around his sister's shoulders as they walked through the palace.

"As well as can be expected. Better than he was, not as good as he was years ago." She leaned her head against him as they walked. "I do wish you had been home sooner."

"I know."

"You should not have gone on this last trip. You should have come straight home." The gentle scolding hit its mark. "It is not even the matter of getting lost, but rather that you were not here in the first place."

"I know." He squeezed her shoulders again then dropped his arm, reaching for her hand instead. "Congratulations. I'm glad Charlie used this ring."

Her soft smile told him everything you needed to know. "I am, too. You will love him and Lindsey both."

"I am sure I will, Maddie." She would hate that. He knew it and waited for her response.

"Do not call me that." Addie smacked his arm as they turned toward the medical wing. A thought kept niggling at the back of his mind. "Adeline, is anyone using the plane the next few days?"

"Not that I am aware of."

"What if I flew back with Charlie, Lindsey, and Dan? I would imagine they would like to see Ellie."

Adeline stopped walking and pulled her phone out of her pocket. She tapped the screen a few times. "I am certain they would love to go, but we have a meeting tomorrow regarding the ceremony for Charlie, his parents, and Lindsey."

"Ah, yes. The Marquis title."

"Precisely. Dan and CeCe need to be there as well, though he might be able to return for a day or two after that." She tapped her phone against her chin as she thought.

Richard turned and started walking. Adeline fell in step with him. "I will take him back to Missouri and bring Ellie back with us. I could use her help, and she will not be able to work for some time."

"That sounds like a good plan. We can take care of her here. She has been invited to the ceremony and, from what I have heard, was planning to attend. She will not be able to walk in the parade as planned, but perhaps we can find a coach for her or make some other arrangement. Even if Dan cannot go with you, his sister will return shortly, and that will be good for him."

"Agreed."

"Their parents will be here in a few days as well." Her high heels tapped a staccato rhythm on the ancient stone. The sound both annoyed and comforted him. He hated the sound and how it represented the entrapments of the palace. But he also associated the sound with his mother coming to tuck him in at night as a child. Those were his favorite memories of his childhood.

Richard came to a decision. "We will see Father, and then I will return to the States."

Ellie reached for the wheeled knee scooter. They'd had her practice on it for a bit earlier in the day.

And now she would use it to make her escape.

She had two hospital gowns on. One forward. One backward to cover what the other one didn't. Trent's girlfriend had brought by some clothes for her to wear when she was finally released but her doctor wanted to keep her another night.

She wanted to leave AMA.

Against Medical Advice.

Tucking the clothes under one arm, she put her knee on the pad and scooted her way to the bathroom. She had a pair of loose fitting pajama pants to wear over the boot and a tank top she could get her cast through. Not exactly her first choice but it's what she had. It made sense. The plan was for her to sneak out the back door where her car was already parked. And since it was her left leg, she could still drive. She would sneak herself out a day early and avoid any reporters still hanging around.

It took her fifteen minutes to get herself dressed. That didn't include hair or makeup. She wouldn't mess with either of those. If photogs got a picture of her, they got a picture of her. All she wanted to do was get home.

With one shoe on and the other tied over the handle of her scooter, she pushed her way toward the door. Fortunately, she was near the end of the hallway, near the exit door and the stairs. Thankfully only one flight. The whole hospital was only three floors and not very big ones at that.

But all she had to do was make it past one other room and to the stairs.

Ellie opened the door and peeked out into the hallway. No one to be seen. Thirty seconds later, she shut the door behind her, wincing at the sound of the snick as it closed.

She looked at the stairs below her.

Not even Rocky's stairs seemed so tall.

But she could do this.

She had to.

She couldn't go back.

"Thank you for coming with me."

Dennis rolled his eyes. "Like we had much of a choice."

"Thank you anyway. As much as we have been out of the country, just the three of us, you could have asked someone else to cover and take a few days off."

Steve answered for them. "We both will once we get past the ceremony this weekend. You'll have to put up with someone from the bodyguard pool."

"Maybe I just won't leave the palace," Rick muttered.

"That would be one option."

"He'll go crazy in the first two days," Dennis pointed out as he opened the glass door at the back of the hospital. Fortunately, no reporters anticipated his return, and the personnel at the Allegiance airport were discreet.

Rick walked through the open door and turned to start up the stairs. Instead he stopped, narrowed his eyes, and crossed his arms over his chest.

"Just what do you think you're doing?"

Ellie glared at him from halfway down the half-flight of stairs. "I'm going home."

He cocked an eyebrow at her. "Without permission?"

"So?"

Her knee scooter rested on the stair in front of her and she lowered herself down another step. She moved the scooter with her good arm and went down one more. Dennis took the scooter from her. Rick simply held out his hand.

Ellie took it, and he wanted to take long minutes to memorize every callous, every scar that made her hands different from those of the aristocratic females he normally socialized with. Instead, he helped her stand. She hopped down the last two stairs and reached for her scooter. Dennis and Steve tried to hide their smirks. They knew he would have none of this.

He scooped Ellie into his arms. "Relax."

Her arms looped around his neck and she did just that, letting her head rest on his shoulder.

Then he started up the stairs.

"Rick! Put me down! I'm leaving, not going back upstairs!" She pounded his back with her fist.

Either she'd been too drugged up to remember their phone conversation and still didn't realize who he really was or she simply did not care.

He hoped for the latter.

Dennis was ahead of him and opened the door onto the second floor. A nurse was coming out of one of the rooms, a look of panic on her face. It turned to fury as soon as she saw them.

"Ellie Brewer, I'll be calling your mother," the nurse snapped at her. "Get back in your bed."

"You can't call her," Ellie snapped back. "She and Dad are on a cruise."

"Then I'll be the first one she talks to when they dock. You know how she and your father would feel about you leaving AMA."

Rick could not stop the chuckle. "She will not be leaving again until the doctor releases her."

Chapter Six

You don't get to make that decision for me." She glared at the man holding her in his arms.

He must have decided not to answer because all he did was walk into her recently-vacated room and set her gently on the mussed up bed. "Then let me ask you to stay until the doctor releases you. When he allows you to leave, the Montevarian jet is waiting at the Allegiance Airfield. Your uncle and aunt will be receiving the March this weekend in honor of their service to the country of Montevaro."

She groaned and let her head drop to the bed. Right. The trip to Europe was on her schedule. Had been for over a month. How could it have slipped her mind? The reason her cousin had been her second brother growing up. His parents were always off on some dig or other. But when they discovered the long-lost entrance to a tunnel containing a room filled with Montevarian treasure, they became the recipients of the title Marquis and Marchioness, and would be given the March owned by the last Marquis who died without any heirs. Her cousin, Charlie, would be given knighthood at the same time, for service to the crown when he saved Adeline from an attack by a suitor who wanted to "ruin" her for another man. He would become a Prince once he married Crown Princess Adeline, and a Duke once she took the throne. She'd heard the proposal story through her niece's eyes during her brother's rehearsal dinner a few weeks earlier.

So she would be asked to attend a ball or two and the ceremony - and wasn't there a parade? - all with her foot in a boot and her arm in a cast.

"You will be waited on hand and foot when we return to the palace. Your parents will be going straight from the dock to Montevaro. My sisters and others will help you pick out appropriate attire for the occasions. The dresses and other clothes will be brought to you rather than going shopping while you're injured."

She didn't say anything but wondered if he'd not gotten to know her at all as they sat under the stars. What would make him think she wanted to be waited on hand and foot? She would smile, nod, and go along with it.

And as soon as she could, she'd break away and try to find another one of those hidden passages. Just because she could, not because she thought they might give her some unknown earldom.

Meantime, she pulled the covers up across her chest, folded her arms over the top, and glared at the incompetent-camper-turned-prince. "If you're not going to help me, leave. Go away."

He grinned that annoying grin of his. "No. I will stay right here until it is time for you to leave. Then I will escort you to your home, help you do whatever you need to for a trip to Montevaro until you heal, and take you to the airport. We will fly to my country where your brother, sister-in-law, cousin, his daughter, aunt, uncle, and parents will be most delighted to see you before the ceremony."

Rick planted himself in the hard plastic chair to the side of her bed and pulled out his phone. "I do believe I'll play a few games. Would you like to join me? Perhaps a form of

Pictionary?"

Before she could answer, her doctor walked in, looking angrier than she'd ever seen him.

"Ellie, we need to talk." He looked around at the men gathered in the room. "Would you like them to leave?"

She shook her head. If there were witnesses, maybe he wouldn't be so tough on her.

"What were you thinking?"

"That I want to go home. I hate the hospital. I hate being confined to this bed. I hate all of it."

"You're only twenty-four hours out from surgery and you were planning to drive?"

"I'm twenty-eight hours out from surgery," she tossed back at him. "The restrictions are only for the first day."

"Don't get snippy with me young lady." He crossed his arms over his chest. "I brought you into this world."

Ah. The wonders of a small town. She'd been born in Allegiance, moved to Serenity Landing when she was four, and her cousin moved in with them while his parents were overseas. Ellie moved back after a most boring year in college. She loved her town and her job when she wasn't inundated with pretty boys.

"Sir?" Rick's voice startled her.

"Yes?"

"Is your objection based solely on Miss Brewer being alone?"

"Mainly."

"Perhaps a compromise?"

"What do you have in mind?"

"My friends and I will be escorting Ms. Brewer to Montevaro as soon as she is able to travel. Perhaps we could move up our time line. Once there, she will have the entire staff of my home at her disposal and access to the best in medical care in southern Europe with one phone call." He nodded his head deferentially. "That is certainly not meant as a slight to the care she has received here. I simply mean we have any number of world class physicians who will gladly come to her side as a personal favor. She will not be left alone and she will certainly not be asked to drive or handle other heavy machinery." His mouth twitched.

Was Rick really offering to help get her out of this place early? If so, she just might have to let him. No matter how annoying he could be.

Her doctor nodded slowly. "As long as you can guarantee she'll be taken care of."

"Absolutely. We will be over the Atlantic for part of the trip. But we have a private plane and both of my friends are trained medics."

He thought about it for a minute. "Very well." The doctor turned to Ellie. "Can you agree to behave? Let the gentlemen take care of you and follow instructions of the doctors in Montevaro?"

She nodded. Whatever she had to do to get out of this place.

"I'll get the paperwork started, and you'll be out of here in an hour." He smiled and squeezed her good foot. "You know it's just because we all care about you."

She nodded. "I know." He left and she turned to Rick. "Don't think I'm just going to sit around in some room doing nothing."

"I have no doubt you will be finding your way around the palace more quickly than even Lindsey has." He smiled. "I met her and Charlie for the first time on my trip home. Lovely people. They will be good for my sister."

"I'm sure they will. My cousin is a wonderful dad and a great guy." She picked at the fuzz on the blanket. "I really don't want to be an imposition."

Rick waved her concerns away with a flick of his hand. "Nonsense. No imposition at all. In fact, we are delighted to be of service. After all, this is all my fault."

Two hours later, Rick stood in Ellie's cramped flat. It was one room, far smaller than his bathroom in the palace, with a closet for a small, stacked washer and dryer and a bathroom that made the one on the airplane seem positively roomy.

"What can we help you do?" he asked as Ellie sank onto the daybed.

"Just let me be for a few minutes." She closed her eyes and let her head fall to the pillow.

"Can one of us go pick up your prescription for pain medicine?" He looked around for another place to sit but all he could find was two kitchen chairs. Pulling one away from the table, he swung it around and straddled it.

"I'll call the pharmacy in a few minutes. Otherwise, they won't give it to you. They all know me." She didn't move except to use one hand to pull a blanket from the back of the bed over her.

Dennis leaned awkwardly against the door. Steve looked around and settled for a hip against the counter in the tiny kitchen. The three men held their tongues until finally Ellie held her hand out. "Who has my phone?"

Rick leaned to one side and pulled it out of the pocket of his jeans. Reaching to place it in her hand was easy. The flat could not be more than twelve feet wide.

She opened her eyes long enough to scroll through the contacts on her phone. The conversation was short and casual. Eyes closed again, she told whoever was on the other end of the phone Dennis, Steve, or Rick would be coming by to pick up her Rx - she actually said Rx, not prescription - and then clicked the button on the top of her phone when she ended the call.

Dennis asked for directions then went to get the medicine. Rick and Steve looked at each other and shrugged.

Steve finally broke the silence. "Can we help you pack, Miss?"

Ellie opened one eye. "Miss? Really? After you carried me on a litter for two days?"

Rick rolled his eyes. "We are no longer in the middle of nowhere. It happens to me all the time. As soon as we get back to civilization, they turn proper on me. Call me 'sir' or even 'Your Highness' if they want to get annoying."

She closed her eye. "Thanks for telling me about that, by the way. We sat next to that tree for hours and you never thought to mention, 'Oh, by the way, I'm *royalty* and that's why my family has a Wiki article'?"

He looked at his bodyguard who shrugged then went out the front door to give them a bit of privacy. "I don't get to be myself with very many people. Most people, especially women, see me as only my title, not as a person. I am very protective of that time with a new friend."

"Did I ever give you the impression I would only care about who you are?"

"No. I should have told you, and for that I apologize." He sighed. "I do hope you can appreciate how hard it is to bring up in conversation."

"I suppose."

"Can I help you pack?" Not that he had ever packed himself for a trip. A camping trip, sure. But not an actual trip.

"No, I'll take care of it in a bit. When are we leaving?"

"Whenever you are ready. The Montevarian royal plane awaits at your leisure."

"Then give me my scooter and get out. I'll let you know when I'm ready to go."

Rick hesitated then nodded. He pushed the knee scooter to the side of her bed. "I will be outside when you are ready. Don't hesitate to ask if you need assistance with anything."

He closed the door behind him and leaned against the brick façade. How could he help her if she would not let him? He just hoped she'd let the staff help her when they arrived at the palace.

"Packing a suitcase while rolling around your too-small apartment on a knee scooter with only one good hand may have to be the hardest thing ever," Ellie muttered to herself. She shoved one more pair of socks into the suitcase and leaned on it until she could get the zipper to squeeze shut. She rolled over to the door and flung it open.

In tumbled Rick, knocking her scooter backwards and Ellie to the floor.

Pain shot through her elbow as she hit the thinly-carpeted concrete.

"Are you all right?"

She could hear Rick scramble to his feet as she clutched her elbow with the fingers sticking out of her cast and propped her booted foot on the floor.

"Yes," she managed from between clenched teeth. "Just landed on my funny bone. What were you doing leaning against the door?" She finally opened her eyes to see him looming over her.

"I didn't have anywhere else to be and I thought you would just call out rather than opening the door or that I would hear you." He held out a hand and she took it, gratefully. He helped her to her good foot. "What can I do for you?"

She ignored the warmth spreading from her fingertips and up her arm. "I'm ready to go."

Half an hour later, Ellie managed to hop one-footed up the narrow stairs of the royal plane. The opulence overwhelmed her. Leather seats. Teak wood. Or she guessed it was teak. Wasn't teak the wood of choice for stuff like this? And the seats were butter smooth. Creamy off-white, and the nicest plush carpeting she'd ever seen in real life. A mini-kitchen. Refrigerator. Couches. It was a smaller plane. A Learjet maybe?

They relaxed into the seats. A few minutes before they took off, Rick reached into the fridge and held out a bottle of water.

"How long is the flight?" Ellie had no clue how long it took to fly, basically, to Italy.

"Only a few hours this leg."

"This leg?" She looked over at him, eyebrows pulled together. "We don't fly straight to Montevaro?"

"No. We will refuel in Greenland. Technically, this plane could make it from Allegiance to Montevaro without refueling, but we prefer not to cut it so close."

Right. Because the man sitting across from her came from a family with enough money to just *buy* a Bombardier Challenger 300 Business Jet - at least that's what it was called in the guest packet handed to her by the co-pilot. They had enough money to have it lavishly appointed. The family crest - or what she guessed was the family crest - was on the seats, the cabinet doors, in the carpet pattern. Enough money to fly around the world at a moment's notice. They probably had a yacht that would make the Noah's Ark look like a rowboat - and far less stinky.

Rick leaned his head back and watched her as the plane sped up and took off. The speed was like nothing she'd ever experienced. Her eyes were probably bugged out like a cartoon character.

A minute later a voice came over the intercom. "We'll reach our cruising altitude in a few minutes, sir. Until then, we ask that all of you remain seated. Thank you."

Rick grinned. "He says that every time. Usually, I ignore him, but today I will be good."

Ellie gave him a weak smile. "You should always listen to your pilot." She flipped through the guest flyer packet. "How long will we be in Greenland?"

"I am not sure. It does not take terribly long to refuel."

Steve snorted then tried to cover it with a cough. Ellie peered at Rick through narrowed eyes. He just smiled - a gorgeous smile, but something lurked in his twinkling eyes.

"And after Greenland we'll go to Montevaro?"

"Perhaps. We may stop elsewhere."

He was keeping something from her. She had no idea what, but it was going to irritate her if she dwelt on it.

"If you would like to get some rest - as soon as they turn the light off, we can help you get settled on the divan in the back of the plane. I have taken many a nap there. You should be quite comfortable."

Ellie nodded. "Sounds good." A few minutes later, Steve helped her to the couch, and she slept until Rick woke her up as the plane descended into Greenland.

Rick looked past Ellie and out the window of the helicopter, but mostly he paid attention to her reactions.

"Look," she said into the headset. "See the dog sled?"

They flew above a glacier in Greenland, and he knew she would have a hard time taking it all in, but it was the best he could do with their time constraints and her injuries. "Scott, Dennis, and I did that a couple years ago. We spent about a month hiking and mushing our way around the country."

"That's incredible. I would *love* to do that sometime, but I couldn't take a whole month off work."

Rick just smiled and pointed ahead as the helicopter swooped down over the ocean. "I think that's a humpback whale."

"This is amazing." He didn't think she realized it, but she reached out and took his hand. "I don't know how to thank you for this. Never in my wildest dreams..."

He squeezed her hand lightly. "No thanks needed. It is my pleasure to arrange this. To be truthful, I told Dennis what I wanted to do and he took care of the details."

The rest of the ride - a private tour over large sections of

Greenland as Rick had mapped them out - took another two hours. They stopped on top of a glacier. They watched as icebergs broke off into the ocean. They followed the humpbacks. They watched dog sledders as they flew past. Wild reindeer ran along with the helicopter for a few yards until they could no longer keep up.

Rick was first out the door when it landed. He turned and reached up for Ellie. Dennis held her steady until Rick could get a hold of her waist. She propped her hands on his shoulders, and he lowered her to the ground.

Or he started to.

Instead, she threw her good arm around his neck while her casted one rested on his shoulder. "Thank you," she murmured. "That was incredible. I just wish I'd thought to take pictures."

He wrapped his arms around her waist, happy to hold her in place against him. "Steve took plenty. I will make sure you get copies."

Her hiking boot and walking boot with a large wool sock pulled over it still dangled above the ground. Something stirred deep inside him. Had he ever held a woman like this? If he had, none had made him feel like Ellie did. He wanted not only to protect her from further pain but to do things that would make her want to hug him like this more often.

A sleek limousine pulled up a few feet away. Rick set Ellie on the ground, but as soon as she had her feet under her, he picked her up into his arms and carried her to it where the driver held the door open for them. He set her down, and she turned to ease her way in. It was getting easier for her to do so, though she had nearly yelled at him when he carried her away from the plane.

Dennis rode in the front with the driver while Steve sat in the rear facing seat across from them.

"Are we going to eat dinner?"

Rick shook his head. "We are, but we will be staying in Ilulisaat overnight. We have reservations at the Hotel Arctic."

"Have the pilots been flying too long to keep going?"

"That is part of the reason, yes."

"What's other reason could there be?"

Rick leaned close to her until he could whisper in her ear. "Trust me."

"I don't like surprises." She crossed her arms and leaned away from him.

"I think you just don't like others knowing things you don't."

"That, too."

Something in her voice made Rick look a little more closely at her. Did she not like people knowing things she didn't, or was there more to it than that? He would have to think about it. Perhaps go over their conversations from the trail in his head and see if he could figure out what bothered her.

"When will we be in Montevaro?"

He shifted away from her, but turned his body her direction so he could watch her face more closely. "We will spend tomorrow night there."

"How long is the flight?" Her voice conveyed her incredulity.

"We will be making one other stop tomorrow." He watched for any sign that might betray her feelings.

Her face remained impassive. For a moment, he considered canceling the plans for the next day, but the memory of her face as they flew over the reindeer changed his mind. A stop in Iceland for a long helicopter tour of volcanoes, majestic waterfalls, and more glaciers would likely bring that same look. He liked being the one who caused the look of awestruck wonder.

No. Not him. The Creator. But he liked being the one to show her the majesty the Creator put in place. And the world's largest puffin colony was a sight to behold. Ten million puffins in one place? She had never seen anything like it and given her comments over the last week, it was unlikely she would ever be able to take herself.

A few minutes later, they pulled to a stop in front of the Hotel Arctic. Dennis would handle the check-in.

"You will have your own room," he assured her. "Tomorrow morning, we will take a helicopter back to Kangerlussuaq and from there fly to our next destination. We will arrive in Montevaro tomorrow evening in time for you to see your brother, cousin, and his daughter. You will likely also have the chance to meet my family."

"Great. I'm fresh off two days of flying and I get to meet the king and queen." She closed her eyes and whimpered a bit.

Rick frowned. He did not expect her to be overcome with gratitude or anything of the sort, but she seemed annoyed. What could he have done to annoy her? Just by deciding to take her on a bit of a site-seeing trip on the way home? He just wanted to give her the chance to experience things she thought she would never have the opportunity to do.

When she stepped out of the car, Ellie took her crutch and moved away from him as fast as she could.

Rick watched her go. "What did I do?" he asked Steve.

"I'm not sure, sir."

Therein lay the problem. Rick really did not know either.

But whatever he had done, he had a feeling that, unless he sought her out, he wouldn't see Ellie again until it was time to leave for the airport.

Chapter Seven

*E*llie sat in her suite. A deluxe Umiaq suite. She'd asked six times how it to pronounce it, and she still hadn't gotten it right. Unless she was very mistaken about what a palace would look like, Rick was used to much nicer rooms.

But one glance out the window told her the view was unsurpassed.

A view of the sea *and* the icebergs floating around. A plume of spray not too far out confirmed her other thought. Whales were nearby.

Had she ever been so close to a whale in the wild as she had been when the helicopter flew over a pod of humpbacks? Sure, she'd sat in the front row at Sea World with Charlie and Lindsey that time, but that couldn't be compared to the incredible view of being nearly close enough to reach out and touch one. A row of igloos sat not too far away from them. What she wouldn't give to stay in one of them.

Rick had told her he would be happy to come back sometime and take her on a boat tour.

Like she could afford that.

The dream was nice, but the bubble had burst in the car on the way to the hotel. She could never have the money to do all of this, and Rick was only taking her on helicopter tours over icebergs and glaciers and wild reindeer because he felt badly about her broken arm. Once they reached Montevaro, he would turn her over to her family, and she'd be lucky if she saw him outside of the ball being held in honor of her aunt and uncle and their new March.

She used her crutch to hobble to the door leading to the balcony. Sliding it open, she hopped out and leaned her forearms against the railing.

For whatever else she thought about Rick, he'd thought about her comfort and needs. A very nice, heavy coat and woolen sock to protect her toes had been waiting for them when they reached Kangerlussuaq Airport. She had packed a wind breaker, but she had no idea they'd be headed this far north and hadn't packed her winter gear.

Or had Dennis handled that when he'd made the arrangements?

She had spent an innumerable amount of time contemplating the icebergs floating not too far from her when a knock on the door shook her out of her thoughts.

"Come in," she called.

Rick walked through the door and out on to the balcony. He leaned against the railing next to her and stared at the water without saying a word. Finally, he broke the silence. "Have I offended you, Ellie?"

"No."

"May I ask what is wrong?"

"Nothing, really. Just wish my leg and arm were better."

"Was I wrong to arrange the tour today? Would you have preferred to fly straight to Montevaro?"

For a prince, he seemed pretty insecure. From what she'd

gathered during their few conversations, it seemed he'd spent most of the last few years traipsing around the world. It didn't seem very likely that he'd spent a whole lot of time with women he might - or might not - want to impress.

Ellie turned the question over in her head as she saw another spout followed by the breach of an Orca nearby. "Physically, I would have preferred it. My body isn't nearly recovered from the fall, and it hasn't been much more than forty-eight hours since we made it out of the woods with me on a stretcher. But otherwise, it's beyond anything I could have imagined. Reindeer? Whales?" Ellie stretched out a hand and pointed as an Orca breached, followed by another. "Staying this far north? If my arm wasn't broken and my ankle out of commission, it would be a dream. And when I think that you spent a month traipsing around here? I can't help but be a bit jealous then wonder what it would be like to stay in one of those igloos over there."

"I tried to convince Steve and Dennis to stay out there, but there were only two available tonight and they only sleep two. If we could have arranged for three, we would have. Perhaps some other time, when we have more than fifteen hours to make the arrangements."

Some other time.

That implied he thought they might see each other after she left Montevaro.

Likely another empty promise. A platitude.

Nothing more.

It was never anything more.

And, if her mind had anything to say about it, it never would be.

What was going through her mind?

Rick turned away from the incomparable view to watch a

different one. This view, though, was a play of emotions crossing Ellie's face. Emotions he could not define, much less understand.

He reached out and brushed a bit of hair off her cheek and tucked it behind her ear.

Whatever possessed him to do such a thing, he would never know, but when she turned and looked up at him with tears in those big hazel eyes of hers, he did something quite unexpected.

He kissed her.

He leaned right in and cradled her face in his hand and bent over enough that he could brush his lips against hers. For a second, there was no response, but then she melted against him. His free hand wrapped around her waist, pulling her closer to him as the kiss deepened. Her arms slid around him, holding tight to his back as she trusted him to help her continue standing on one foot.

Emotions he had no experience with swirled just beneath the surface. His fingers slid into her hair and his arm tightened around her. One hand and the other fingertips clutched at the back of his shoulders. The maelstrom threatened to overwhelm him. One part of his mind told Rick he needed to back away, to give them both some space, but the rest of him knew he had found one thing he never had in all his travels around the globe.

Home.

It was not on an island in the middle of a clear Alpine lake in one of the world's most beautiful palaces.

It was not in the shadow of the Everest he would never climb.

He had not found it on the top of Mt. Fuji or the depths of the world's largest cave.

Richard Jedidiah David Nicklaus of Montevaro, second in line for the throne, found home in the arms of a petite brunette who turned his world upside down.

A throat clearing behind him caused him to break away long before he was ready to.

"My apologies for interrupting, Your Highness." Dennis knew how much Rick hated it when they called him that. He supposed it was Dennis's way of reminding him who he was. Who Ellie was.

And it was likely very wrong for them to be kissing like God had made them for each other.

"Yes, Dennis?" Rick didn't take his eyes off Ellie. Her eyes had gone wide and stayed fixed on his.

"The king is calling in a few minutes. He needs to go over a few things with you before you retire for the evening."

Not "your father is calling" but "the king." Another reminder of how a romance with the woman in his arms would likely be found unacceptable in the halls of Parliament. He was not the heir, but it had been made quite clear to him that until such time as Crown Princess Adeline had heirs of her own, his life was subject to their approval.

He kept his hand on Ellie's waist until he saw she had gripped the railing next to her and would not fall when he let go of her. Rick took a step back and bowed slightly at the waist. "Sleep well, Ellie. Someone will knock or call approximately half an hour before we need to leave for the airport. Your things should be in the closet."

She nodded.

"Good night."

Dennis waited for him to pass before falling in behind him. His friend-turned-bodyguard shut the door and clicked the lock. Rick turned to see Dennis watching him, stone-faced.

"What?" Steve was confused by the sudden tension between them.

"I will let His Highness tell you." Dennis's countenance did not change.

Rick saw Steve wince. "What happened, sir?"

"I kissed Ellie. And if you were not both my friends as well as my security detail, I would not tell you that much." Richard crossed his arms over his chest. Rarely did he pull rank on his team - and even less rarely did they pull rank on him.

"Parliament will never approve, sir." Dennis did not back down.

"I am not the heir. What Parliament says does not matter. And her cousin will be marrying the queen. Why is Charlie good enough for Adeline but Ellie an unacceptable choice for me?" Dennis opened his mouth, but Richard stopped him with a hand in the air. "I am not saying I wish to propose to the girl tomorrow, I am saying why should it matter what Parliament thinks?"

"Because as soon as your sister is crowned, you *are* the heir, sir. They will be quite willing to interfere and divest you of your status."

"So her aunt and uncle can be given the March, her cousin can be knighted for service to the Crown, and Parliament would force my sister to disown me over their prejudices?"

"It is quite possible, sir. You know that as well as I do."

Rick sighed and his shoulders slumped, one hand rubbing the back of his neck. He did know that as well as they did. The weight of the world settled on his shoulders. "You are not incorrect, but whether I choose to spend my life with Ellie or someone else, I will not put my position above the one person I care more about than anyone else in the world."

"I hope it does not come to that choice, sir."

At that moment, his phone rang and Rick excused himself to the other side of the room to talk to his father.

The flight from Kangerlussuaq, Greenland to their next destination was quiet. Ellie couldn't put her finger on where the tension was coming from, but it likely had something to do with her. Rick had been most solicitous since leaving Allegiance, but not today. This time, Steve seemed to be tasked with helping her in and out of cars and up the stairs in and out of helicopters and airplanes.

In fact, the relationship between the three men had cooled considerably since the day before. They treated Rick with a deference she hadn't noticed previously. Rick was first into the car, first out. First onto the helicopter, first out. First onto the plane. In fact, Steve and Dennis seemed to almost wait for Rick's permission to do anything, though their eyes were always scanning for any potential, but unseen, threat. They called him "sir" or "Your Highness", something she'd only heard from them a handful of times all together, and never when it was just the four of them - only in the presence of others.

What was going on?

Their plane touched down... somewhere. Ellie still didn't know where they were going, but the flight had only been about three hours. She could count on one hand the words that had been uttered.

Rick had given her a tablet computer to play with. He held one of his own and seemed to scroll through and read pages of something. He tapped on it as though he was typing a few times. Steve slept. Dennis stared into space or talked with the pilots or worked on his own tablet the whole time.

"Where are we?" she asked as the door opened.

"Keflavik Airport in Reykjavik, Iceland, Miss." Dennis's voice lacked the warmth it had once held.

"Iceland?" She looked at Rick, whose face betrayed nothing.

"You can both stay here. We will not need either of you for this excursion," he told them.

"That is unacceptable, sir." Steve stood. "You know we'll both accompany you."

"You will be seated as far away as possible. We are the only ones on the charter. There will be plenty of room."

Charter? A boat? Another helicopter ride?

Dennis trotted down the stairs to the waiting car and held the door open. Rick followed more slowly. Steve helped her. The car ride was short and silent. A large helicopter waited for them at the other end.

It was large enough for there to be some separation between her and Rick and the other two men, and she was glad of it.

"Can you tell me what's going on?" she asked before the rotors sped up enough they would have to use the headsets.

Rick smiled at her, though it lacked the warmth from the day before. Did he regret the kiss? The one perfect kiss she'd ever experienced in her life. One that put the one between Westley and Buttercup's in *The Princess Bride* to shame.

"It is nothing, Ellie. We will just enjoy this tour, all right?"

She nodded and put the headset on. Whatever was going on between the men, she would never have a chance like this again, and she wasn't going to waste a minute of it. They soared over Reykjavik. Ellie tried to take it all in, but it was near impossible. "Where are we going?"

"We will be flying to a volcano, over a glacier, to see Orcas and the world's largest population of puffins."

"All in one flight?" She turned wide eyes toward Rick. "Seriously?"

"We may need to stop and refuel at some point. I told them what we wanted to do, and they said they would arrange it." Rick leaned in toward her and pointed out the window. Ellie returned her attention to the scenery, in awe of the amazing views.

An hour and a half later, Rick helped her out of the helicopter, carrying her in his arms toward the volcano. She leaned her head on his chest as he carried her away from his ever-present shadows. They wouldn't be out of sight, but they would be far enough away Steve and Dennis wouldn't be able to hear whatever Rick would say to her.

What did she want Rick to say?

She'd promised herself she wouldn't fall for him or any other man. Her "no pretty boys" policy was still in place. And he was responsible for her broken arm. Though, she admitted, he took full responsibility for his own actions and had done more than enough to make up for what happened in the cave. Her eyes closed until he whispered.

"We're here."

He set her down in front of him and wrapped his arms around her waist. To support her, she told herself. The back of her head rested against his chest as she looked around.

If only...No. She wouldn't go there. Her past hadn't changed. Her goals in life were the same as they had been two weeks ago. And none of that involved falling in love with a prince.

Rick tightened his hold on Ellie. He'd seen the volcano before. This time he looked without seeing. Her hair blew back in the breeze, tickling his cheek. He turned into her, burying his face in her hair. He could smell the papaya and guava that must have come from her shampoo.

"What is it, Rick?" her voice drifted back to him.

"I wish..." He hesitated, unsure whether to voice what stirred deep inside.

Whatever he would have said was interrupted by Dennis calling to him. "Sir, the pilot says it's time to go."

"What do you wish, Rick?" Ellie turned to look up him, her gorgeous eyes unsure and hesitant.

He pressed a kiss to the side of her hair. "Unfortunately, it does not matter what I wish. Sometimes we simply must accept what must be."

"What must be?" Her brows knit together in confusion. "What do you mean?"

Rick shook his head. "Nothing for you to worry about today."

Dennis called again, more insistent this time, and Rick released Ellie before scooping her back into his arms. He would miss her out-of-commission ankle. He would not have a reason to carry her and have her sink into his hold. Her head burrowed into his shoulder. It felt so perfect - so right. But he knew others would believe a relationship would be so wrong.

He wanted to tell her he was sorry for kissing her the night before, but the words would not come before they reached the helicopter. Moments later, they were airborne once again.

By the time they made it back to Reykjavik, he knew one thing for certain.

One day, he wanted to return with Ellie.

And, standing on a glacier in the middle of Greenland, he wanted to propose.

Chapter
Eight

The flight from Reykjavik to Montevaro was as silent as the one from Greenland. This time, though, Ellie sat on the couch in the back of the plane with her booted foot propped up along it. She did her best to nap, but every time she closed her eyes, she saw Rick, looking down at her then leaning in for a kiss.

She had to get him out of her head.

The next few days in Montevaro would be busy ones. They would land after dinner, but a meal of some kind would be waiting for her.

She wondered if it included Ben and Jerry's.

Somehow, she didn't think so. There would be enough time for her to see her family before it got too late. She would be staying in Adeline's apartment along with Charlie, Lindsey, Charlie's parents, her parents, her brother, and sister-in-law. She didn't know if Adeline would be there as well. Rick had his own apartment he shared with his slightly younger twin sister. Ellie couldn't remember what her name was.

The plane landed in Montero, the capital city of Montevaro.

They were met by a large black SUV. Steve and Dennis disappeared. Rick shared the second seat with her while two men she didn't know sat in the front. He reached over and took her hand in his, lacing their fingers together.

"I will likely not see you again tonight and possibly not tomorrow. There are obligations I have shirked for too long. Instead of going on the hike in the Ozarks, I should have returned home and taken care of some business. Between taking that trip and this one, I am at least two weeks behind on things I need to take care of." He had been looking at their hands but now he looked at her.

Ellie could see disappointment and sadness in his eyes, though she couldn't be sure why.

"You will be taken care of. The tablet is yours for the duration of your stay. Your schedule is loaded into it. Adeline or Charlie will make sure your assistant knows about the additional time it will take you to get anywhere in the palace."

"My assistant?" she managed to croak out.

"Yes. There will be someone assigned to help you with anything you need. Whether it is shopping or your hair or finding your way around or anything else, just ask. I am not sure who Adeline chose for the task, but I am certain whoever it is will be well-qualified."

"I'm sure she will be." Her mind swirled with thoughts she didn't want to give voice to. Rick would be leaving her. He wouldn't be leaving her *alone*, but Charlie, his parents, and Lindsey would all be very busy. Dan and CeCe probably would be, too. Her parents had been trying to get her to stop her hiking and backpacking trips for years. This would be just the excuse they needed to push her even harder.

And she wouldn't even be able to escape into the mountains. She'd be marooned in a palace on an island in the middle of one of the most beautiful Alpine lakes around. Even if she could get to the mainland, she couldn't hike. She was helpless.

The vehicle entered the gates of a garrison and came to a stop in the middle of an open area. Before Rick could turn to help her out of the SUV, a man pulled him aside. Her door opened and her knee scooter waited for her.

"This way, Miss." The man who had been sitting in front of her led the way through massive double doors on one end. "For many years, troops were stationed here to protect access to the palace," he explained. Down a hall and through another set of doors, a gangplank waited. This was plenty wide enough for her to maneuver up by herself.

This boat wouldn't put Noah's Ark to shame, but it was a far cry nicer than any she'd ever been on.

A steward met her. "This way, Miss."

If everyone kept calling her that, she'd scream.

Loudly.

"Would you prefer to sit on the deck or inside?" he asked.

"Where will Rick be?" Did she want to be near him or not?

"Rick, Miss?"

Right. "Sorry. Prince Richard."

"His Highness will be inside conducting some business, I believe."

He had business that couldn't wait the four minutes it would take to get across half the lake?

"No, Garrett. I would like Miss Brewer to ride up front with me." Rick walked onto the boat, wearing the same thing he had been moments earlier, but somehow he looked more... royal.

"Very well, Your Highness. As you wish."

Rick smiled at her. "I will meet you there before we get underway. They are loading our luggage now." He turned back to the same man who had met him at the car.

"This way, Miss." Garrett led her through a series of passages and helped her hop up a narrow staircase.

It seemed an eternity before she collapsed onto the seat at the bow of the boat.

"Going down will be much easier, Miss." Garrett gave her a sympathetic smile. "We will be departing in about five minutes. His Highness will arrive before then, I'm sure. If, for some reason, he does not, I will be back to make sure you have everything you need when we arrive at the palace dock."

She gave him a weak smile. "Thank you." What else was there to say?

Ellie situated herself so she could watch through the Plexiglass shield, but she couldn't see the palace. She couldn't see much of anything but darkness off the bow. Either the palace had no lights at all on this side, or they were facing the wrong way. She guessed the latter.

The engines shuddered and the boat began to move. Rick still hadn't arrived. A whisper of disappointment surged through her, but she clamped it down. She didn't need him around, and she'd do her best not to miss him.

"I am sorry to be late." Rick's smiling face appeared as he climbed up the stairs. "I do not want to miss your first glimpse of the palace."

He sat behind her, one arm extending along the back of the seat, and the other reaching around to pull her toward him. She rested her back against his chest, remembering the feel of his strong back under her fingers the night before. Had it really been only twenty-four hours since he'd kissed her in Greenland? He laced his fingers through hers.

"It is likely quite conceited for me to say since it is my family's palace, but there is none quite like it in the world."

His breath warmed her ear as he spoke into it. Though the engine noise wasn't loud, the wind whipping around them would have made it hard for her to hear him otherwise. She just nodded. The boat turned and there it was.

A gasp ripped from her.

She'd looked up pictures after Charlie and Adeline had gotten together, but nothing could prepare her for seeing it in person.

It looked like the one Disney World's Cinderella's castle had to be based on. Spires. Turrets. Lit up on all sides. The stonework was incredible. It must have taken a century or more to build - especially given its lake location.

"It's amazing." She would have whispered, but the words would have been lost in the wind.

"Yes, it is."

Ellie twisted to look up at him, but he wasn't looking at the palace.

He looked straight at her.

Rick held everything he wanted in his arms, but she would be ripped away all too soon.

Once they reached the palace, he would no longer be Rick. He would, instead, be His Royal Highness, Prince Richard. Everything from his clothing to his diction to his time management would be different. He hated it, but it could be no other way. It would likely be at least a day, and probably two, before he saw Ellie again. And so he had instructed the captain of the boat to go the long way, to circle the palace. Ellie could see it from all sides, but it would also give them a few more moments together before things changed.

If he was honest with himself, he had no idea if she craved this last bit of time as much as he did. He could hope, but without asking he could not know. And the last thing he wanted to do was ruin the moment by asking.

Instead, he watched her face in the Plexiglass. It lost something in the reflection, but the other option would have been to sit across from her, and he found that to be unacceptable.

Even taking the long way, the ride was far too short and the boat pulled up to the dock on the palace island before he was ready to let her go.

"I will help you down the stairs," he told her, standing up and holding out a hand. "Your scooter will be waiting for you at the bottom. I am afraid that is where I must say good night. I need to speak with the captain for a moment and my assistant is waiting for me to disembark."

She nodded. "I see."

There was not enough room for them to go down the stairs side by side, so he went first, backwards, keeping a hand on her waist to steady her. Relief flooded her face as she rested her knee on the scooter. Despite his efforts to make the trip easy on her, it had been too much. He had expected it might be, but he hoped the trip itself was worth it for her.

Raising her hand to his lips, he kissed it gently, never taking his eyes off hers. "Good night, fair maiden."

She snorted. "Fair maiden? Really? Does that make you my knight in shining armor?"

Richard smiled. "No. If you were damsel in distress, then yes. Fair maiden you may be, but distress? I have no doubt you are quite capable of saving yourself."

Before she could respond, footsteps interrupted. Garrett approached, stopping some distance away but obviously waiting for Ellie.

"I do not know when I will see you, but promise me you will make your needs known? If you need anything at all, the staff is here to help, especially your assistant."

She nodded, but did not say a word.

"Then I will bid you good night here and hope I will see you tomorrow."

"Good night, Your Highness." She gave him a small smile and pushed off with her good foot, rolling toward Garrett.

He had never liked the title much, though he liked the privileges it afforded him.

But Prince Richard found he liked it even less coming from her. If only...

Rick shook his head before he could finish the thought. If onlys would get him nowhere. If wishes were horses, beggars would ride.

There were not enough horses in all of Montevaro for him to escape his responsibilities. As much as he wished there were another way, he knew he would not trade his life for anything.

Except maybe a life with the beautiful woman who just left.

Ellie was overwhelmed by the palace. She'd expected to be, but nothing in her expectations compared with the reality. The tapestries. The coats of arms. The paintings of people she guessed where Rick's ancestors. The furniture.

The sheer scale of everything.

Her assistant - something she had a hard time accepting - met her as she rolled her way onto solid ground. The woman, Danica, led her through the hallways, past ornate staircases and through doors that likely weighed more than her first car. A small elevator, not much bigger than a couple of phone booths, took them up three floors.

"This is an apartment for guests," Danica explained. "Your family has been moved from Princess Adeline's apartment and is staying here for the time being. Once the ceremonies are over this weekend, Charlie and Lindsey will be moving into his parents' new home until Crown Princess Adeline and Charlie's wedding."

Ellie's eyes went wide. "Have they set a date?"

Danica smiled. "Yes, Miss Brewer. The wedding will be in late August, the week before Princess Adeline's coronation."

She shook her head to clear the shock out. "That's a busy

week."

"It will be. The wedding, balls, family soirees, and fundraisers. Princess Adeline will spend part of that week in meetings with Parliament and the Council, but she and your cousin were quite adamant they wanted the wedding first."

Ellie did the math in her head. Less than two months. By the time her ankle healed, it would be time for her to return to Montevaro. She may as well just stay - if her aunt and uncle would let her crash at their new home with them. Maybe she could help Rick start up his outdoor company here. If he wanted her help. He'd said he did, but could she trust what he said?

The living room of the apartment was empty. Her little loft could have fit into it about six times over. Danica led her down the hall and to a door on the left.

"Here is your room."

As Ellie followed her in, her stomach dropped. This wasn't a room. It was a suite. A sitting room, with an archway into the largest bedroom she'd ever seen. And unless she missed her guess, one of the doors would lead to a well-appointed bathroom. Maybe it would have a big soaker tub. She'd have to be careful with her ankle and make sure her cast didn't get wet, but a long soak would be wonderful.

"Your family is having dinner with Princess Adeline this evening, but they should be back momentarily. Prince Richard asked that you be shown directly here, saying you would likely want to rest rather than meet his family at the moment."

"Thank you."

"You have the tablet Prince Richard gave you?" Danica asked.

"Yes." Ellie wanted nothing more than to either sink into one of the chairs or find out about that tub.

"There is a schedule app on the top right of the home page. Please peruse it this evening before you go to bed. There is a key in there for you to help define the different events and what sort of attire would be required. If you have any questions, please ask me. My information is programmed into the contacts under 'Danica, Assistant.' You can text me from the tablet or call me from any phone in the palace."

The phone in Danica's hand buzzed and she checked it. "This is something I need to take care of. Do you need anything from me first?"

Ellie shook her head. "No, thank you."

Danica said good-bye and let herself out of the room, shutting the door behind her. Rather than giving in to the comfortable looking chair that beckoned her, Ellie made her way across the bedroom and through the open door into the bathroom. Just as she suspected. Reaching to the other side of the tub, she turned on the waterfall faucet and sat on the edge with the tablet in her hand.

No time like the present to check out the schedule. The trip to Iceland wasn't listed but their arrival at the palace was. She tapped the arrow for the next day. Her eyes bugged out. Every line was colored in. Blues. Yellows. Greens. Purples. Reds. Pinks. Oranges. The first event looked to be at seven-thirty. She tapped it.

"Breakfast with the entire Montevarian royal family and the entire Brewer clan," she read. "You are expected to attend the orange, yellow and red events, beginning with this one." Ellie went back and checked all the events of those colors. They seemed to be meals with the colors indicating who would be attending. Orange for both families, yellow for all of the Brewers and red for her, Dan, and their parents.

Fair enough.

What were green events? They seemed to involve the royal family in some sort of official capacity. Princess Adeline reading to children at a local hospital. Ellie was not expected to attend the things color-coded green. That explained why multiple things were scheduled at once. All of them at that time were different colors of green - a different shade for each family member? Rick would be meeting with members of the Council, but it didn't say what about.

A feeling of being overwhelmed started in her eyes and sank through her mind and into her belly. Every moment of the day she had somewhere to be. Something she was expected to do. Well, technically, she wasn't required to do all of them, but the way it was worded...

It reminded her of a trip she had taken as a preteen. She, her parents, Dan, and Charlie had gone to Washington, D.C. and while they were there, they attended a changing of the guard at the Tomb of the Unknown Soldier. The soldier in charge bellowed, "It is requested that you stand during the changing of the guard." Most everyone already stood, but one guy - on the other side of her dad - remained sitting on the concrete.

The soldier bellowed again. "It is *requested* that you stand during the changing of the guard."

The guy still sat there.

The soldier marched in the stiff, formal way the guards at the Tomb did until he stood directly in front of the guy on the ground. "It is *requested* that you *stand* during the changing of the guard."

Embarrassed, the fully able-bodied man finally stood, as he should have from the beginning, and the ceremony commenced.

Requests weren't always requests. Sometimes they were commands. Sure, the guy at Arlington was being disrespectful at best, but what would the royal family think if she didn't show up at breakfast? What would Rick think? Would she be in trouble?

Or would he even care?

Chapter Nine

Richard walked into the dining room, his step light. He had not thought he would get to see Ellie, but had been pleasantly surprised to see a three-family breakfast planned.

"Richard." His mother's voice carried across the room above the din. "So glad you are here."

He crossed to her side and kissed her cheek. "Good morning, Mother."

"It is about time you made it home."

"I was here the other day."

"For only a few hours and I did not see you."

"Someone needed to make sure Miss Brewer made it here safely. There was no reason for her to take commercial planes given her injuries and the cause for them." He scanned the room. "Where is she?"

"She has not arrived yet." His mother rested her carefully manicured hand on his arm. "I am certain she will arrive shortly."

Concern began to niggle at the edge of his mind, and he resisted the urge to glance at his watch. Could jet lag be bothering her as well? Likely, he was more used to it than Ellie.

"I have seated you next to Charlie's mother and Lindsey. Ana will be across from you."

He narrowed his eyes. What was she up to? Why did she not seat Ellie near him? Granted, his mother likely put her next to her own family, but a subtle undertone unnerved him.

"Prince Richard?"

Richard turned to see his assistant walking toward him. "Pardon me a moment, Mother. I will return shortly." Richard and Lucas walked to the side of the room where Lucas pulled out a leather portfolio.

"Sir, you have a meeting with the Council today."

"We cannot put it off a few more days?"

Lucas shook his head. "Sir, I've done my best to keep them apprised of what you're doing and why, but I am afraid they want to hear it from you."

"Why I have been traipsing around the backsides of nowhere instead of attending University or some other more noble pursuit?" Richard felt the tension mounting in his neck muscles.

"Something along those lines, I would imagine." He slid that paper back into the folder side of the portfolio and pulled out another. "Tonight, you will be having dinner and an after-dinner meeting with your father, Princess Adeline, and the leaders of Parliament."

"Why do I need to be there, exactly? I am not the heir."

"No," Lucas reminded him patiently. "But until Princess Adeline has a child you will be the heir, so you are required to attend some meetings."

"Very well." The noise behind him changed to that of chairs being pulled away from the table. "I will be there."

"Tomorrow, you have meetings all day."

Richard pinched the bridge of his nose. He would do his duty and do it to the best of his ability, but he wished he could simply escape into the mountains for a few days. Or to northern Greenland with a pretty woman and appropriate chaperones. Or two gold bands and no chaperones. The official duties of being a prince grated on him. God had designed him for the great outdoors.

"All right. My mother will not be pleased if I hold up breakfast any longer. I will meet you in my office a few minutes after I am done here."

Lucas left as Richard turned back to the table. Everyone was seated except him. Odd. Perhaps because his father was not feeling well enough to remain standing and other people sit when the king does. He took his seat and saw Ellie was as far away from him as she could possibly be. It took everything in him not to frown and ask everyone to move around.

He pasted a smile on his face and made small talk with those around him, learning more about Charlie and Ellie's family. Whenever he could, he glanced toward Ellie, a bit concerned that she seemed so quiet. He would have to find a few minutes to talk to her before he went to his office and got this day started.

By the time the king stood, indicating the end of the meal, Richard had determined he would do just that. Chairs scraped back and everyone else rose. He nodded his good-bye to those around him, turning toward the other end of the table.

"Richard." His father's voice stopped him. "Would you walk with me, please?"

With no choice in the matter, he followed his father out of the room, wondering when he would get to talk Ellie again.

Rick walked away from her without a backward glance.

Ellie hadn't had a chance to talk to him during breakfast

since he'd been seated so far away. Beforehand, she'd seen him talking with some guy who left as everyone else was seated. His assistant maybe? Rick looked at her a few times during breakfast, but to just walk off?

She had remained seated even when everyone else stood so he'd be able to get to her a bit more easily and because her ankle ached. If it was some horrible breech of protocol, no one said anything to her.

"Ellie?" The cultured voice could only belong to one person.

Breathing a prayer, she looked up. "Good morning, Princess Adeline."

Princess Adeline wrinkled her nose. "Please. We will be family by summer's end. Call me Addie in private." Her mouth turned into a bit of a sneer. That was the only way Ellie could describe it, though there wasn't any malice behind it. "When we're in public, or even around some of the staff that's not one of our personal staff members, I am afraid we will have to be a bit more formal, but family is one place I can be myself and not the Crown Princess."

Ellie smiled. "Then good morning, Addie."

"Much better." The princess sat next to Ellie. "How are you feeling?"

"I'm fine. My ankle is still bothering me quite a bit, and I can't put much weight on it yet but, overall, I feel much better."

"I am glad." Someone cleared their throat nearby. "I have a meeting to get to, but I look forward to getting to know you."

Addie placed a hand on Ellie's shoulder and squeezed as she walked off. Someone else came to stand next to her. Ellie looked up to see Danica standing there. "Where to now?" Even to her own ears, her voice sounded resigned.

"There is a gathering for your aunt and uncle. While I will make certain you have somewhere to sit should you want to, it would be best to get over there as soon as possible as there is limited seating in the room."

Ellie nodded, stood on her good foot and took her knee scooter from the guy who brought it over for her. Rolling off, she wondered if *everything* would be this scheduled.

Richard had not seen Ellie in two days. Well, he had *seen* her but he had not spoken to her, and it was driving him crazy. He wanted just a few minutes, only the two of them, to talk to her, maybe hold her in his arms. And if he went really crazy - kiss her.

But that would not happen, so he waited in an anteroom near the door to the apartment her family was staying in. He read through a document on his tablet while he waited for the sounds of people. Walking out of the room, he saw her family heading toward a staircase. Ellie, though, still used her scooter and would go right by him.

Her assistant walked next to her until he stepped out from behind the coat of armor. "Good morning, Ellie."

Her smile brightened his day. "Rick!" Then her face fell. "Sorry. Prince Richard. Old habits and all."

Rick looked at her assistant. "Danica, I will escort Ms. Brewer from here. You can meet her downstairs?"

Danica bit her bottom lip then nodded, turned, and followed Ellie's family.

With his hands clasped behind his back and holding his tablet, Rick walked next to Ellie as she rolled toward the elevator. "How are you?" he asked after a moment of silence.

"Scheduled to death." Bitterness colored her voice.

"Pardon?"

"Wondering when they're going start scheduling bathroom breaks."

"Today, I fear."

She glanced up at him, annoyance clearly coloring her features. "Seriously?"

"Yes. Today is one of those days where everything needs to go like clockwork. Breakfast will be served in fifteen minutes. As soon as we are done there, we will go to the throne room for the investiture of the title onto your aunt and uncle, as well as Charlie's knighting. Then a parade through town and a motorcade to the March for a formal turning over of the house and grounds." Rick pressed the down button. "A luncheon will be served there followed by a tour of the grounds for invited guests. You will not be able to go through the entire tour as there is not an elevator at the house, so you will not be quite as constrained as the rest of us. We will return to the palace about two hours before dinner and the ball to give everyone time to get dressed. A gown has been set aside for you."

The ding signaled the arrival of the elevator. Rick put his hand in front of the sliding door until Ellie rolled in. He hoped she would like the dress he picked out. His conversation with her brother led him to believe she was concerned about her attire for the evening. Rick had asked his assistant to get with Danica and come up with a few options. He picked the one he thought she would like best, though the others were still on the premises, just in case.

"Great," she mumbled.

"I would imagine you have the same feeling toward rigid schedules as I do. You would much rather be outdoors doing whatever you want." Rick leaned against the wall of the elevator.

Ellie gave a half-shrug. "Even if we didn't have this ridiculous schedule, I wouldn't be able to go hiking."

"I am sorry."

"I know. And you're doing your best to make it up to me and I know that." The bell dinged and the door slid open. "But I still don't get to hike the Alps."

"You will. You can come visit another time, and I will take

you to the highest peak in Montevaro." He grinned at her. "I will show it to you this afternoon. It is not far from your aunt and uncle's new home. My family has a home on the other side of the mountain from the March, though there are really no direct roads between the two." He gave her an amused grin. "It would be more fun to hike anyway." They started down the hallway toward the sound of voices. "While you are here, I would like to discuss the possibility I mentioned of starting something similar to Outdoor Ozarks here in Montevaro."

She stopped and looked up at him. "You really want to discuss that with *me*? Why?" Sure he'd mentioned it once before but he hadn't *really* meant it. Had he?

"Because you know far more about it than I do."

"Me? Aren't you the one who's hiked pretty much the whole world?"

"Well, yes," he conceded. "But I show up when I am scheduled to and leave when the excursion is over. I know nothing of how to plan multiple trips and how many employees or what kind of supplies I need to keep on hand."

They started moving again. "I do know about that kind of thing. At least for the Ozarks, but the needs might be different here."

"The basics will be the same. I am working to put together a business plan to present to my sister after the coronation. I believe she will be more open to it than my father. Or at least to the idea of me running it. Father would never approve."

They emerged into the hall outside the dining room. His father was seated on one of the horrendously uncomfortable couches. As soon as he saw Rick and Ellie, he stood and started walking toward the open doors. Everyone fell in behind him. Rick knew he would be expected to sit in the same place he had the last two days during meals with all of the families, but he wanted to break with his mother's instructions and sit next to

Ellie. His mother's glare dared him to try. He held Ellie's chair for her, intending to not rock the boat but go to the other end of the table.

Ellie's father surprised him, though. He sat in Rick's seat from the last two days and sent a quick wink Rick's way. It took everything in him not to grin, but instead he gave a small half smile and took the seat next to Ellie. His mother would be mad, but it would be worth it.

Chapter Ten

*H*e *what*?!" Ellie yelled, not caring who heard her. Danica just stood there, holding the hanger above her head. "Prince Richard picked out the dress for you."

She stared at the vinyl covering the dress she hadn't even seen yet. Had he mentioned earlier that he'd *picked* it or that he'd make sure she had options? An unwelcome memory threatened to rear its ugly head, but she turned to Danica instead.

"At least let me show it to you, Miss." Danica reached for the zipper.

Ellie took a deep breath in, blew it out slowly and told herself to relax. Finally, she nodded.

Danica unzipped the bag and pulled the dress out. It was nice, though she hadn't really expected anything less. A very pretty purple color. She rubbed a bit of the fabric between her thumb and forefinger. A strap with some kind of applique on it went over only one shoulder. That would be kind of nice. She wouldn't have to worry about fitting her cast through a sleeve. The bust line went straight across and looked to be high enough she'd feel completely covered.

"It's not horrible," she told the other woman.

"It's by a local designer, one of the best in Europe, but she's from Montevaro and always helps with events like this." Danica removed the dress from the bag and showed Ellie the back. The strap that went over the shoulder met at about her shoulder blade with one coming from the waist and then flowed down the full length of the dress to join with the court train on the floor.

She reached out and let the separate swath of fabric flow through her hands. The nicest dress she'd brought didn't begin to compare to this one, but something still didn't sit quite right with her. Rick choosing her clothes? Telling her what to wear?

But as much as she loved the outdoors, sometimes she liked feeling like a woman and right now, she wanted to see how she looked and felt in the purple chiffon. "I'll try it on."

"There are several pairs of shoes waiting for you as well."

Of course there were. Ellie hated needing help, but she had no choice. Ten minutes later, Danica had helped her slip the dress on. It fit well.

In fact, it was perfect.

Ellie hated to admit it but, as she stared at her reflection in the full length mirror, she did. Rick had picked the perfect dress.

She sat on the bed as Danica brought out a selection of shoes for her left foot. One pair matched the dress. The other two were strappy, silver sandals. "Um... I didn't have time for a pedicure. Open toe is not the way to go."

Danica nodded. "Very well. We don't have time for a full pedicure, but we could do the nails, if you like?"

Ellie stuck her foot straight out and twisted it one way, then the other. Just as well she'd had one for her brother's wedding a few weeks earlier. She'd opted for clear polish, but that could be fixed in just a few minutes even if it wasn't perfect. Danica reached for a bag sitting off to the side and pulled out several nail polish options.

"Which one?"

Ellie pointed at a shiny purple that matched the dress. Danica helped her change back into a robe then went to work.

"Someone will be here to do your hair in a minute. We'll do another coat after that."

Had she ever been so pampered? She knew someone else would be there to do her make-up and Danica would help her get dressed.

An hour and a half later, she'd been primped and pampered. When she put her knee on the scooter, she realized the left side of the skirt had a slit in it up to her thigh. Closer inspection showed that the slit had gone several inches higher but had been sewn shut. It still showed a fair bit of leg but less than she would have wearing shorts. Had Rick picked it to make it easier for her to roll around, but known she wouldn't want it too high? He was right, but the discomfort continued to plague her.

"Your parents are waiting outside, Miss." Danica tapped on her tablet. "Are you ready?"

Ellie rolled carefully toward the door. She could take crutches but she wasn't very good on them and the distance was too great. Too bad her boot was black, but at least it wasn't puce.

Mom, Dad, Dan, and CeCe stood in the living area of the apartment that was theirs for the time being. Dad and Dan looked quite handsome in their tuxedos. Mom and CeCe both wore ball gowns - Mom's in silver and CeCe's in dark green.

Dad gave her a big, if one-armed from the side, hug. "You look beautiful, princess."

"Even though I have to roll around on this thing?" It would ruin her night. Not that she liked dancing all that much most of the time, but there was no chance she'd get to dance with Rick with her foot in a boot. She should make him sit with her the whole time since it was all his fault.

Even as she thought it, she knew it wouldn't happen. He'd be dancing with real princesses and countesses and debutantes and actual ladies. There would be no time for him to sit it out with her.

Danica returned to walk with Ellie to the elevator and then to the ballroom. She'd been told this wasn't nearly as formal as the Coronation Ball would be. They were announced and there was a receiving line, but it was only her aunt, uncle, Lindsey, and the king and queen. Ellie moved quickly through the line. She'd already congratulated her extended family and would be moving to the house in the morning. The king and queen made her nervous so she breezed past them as fast as she could without being rude.

She planned to find a place to sit down - there were a few chairs, tables, and settees scattered around the perimeter of the room - but before she could skin brushed against her bare back.

Rick could not stop from smiling as she jumped, just slightly. She looked as wonderful as he thought she would. "This way, Ms. Brewer." He held out an arm and rested his other hand on her back. "I would like to ask you for the first dance of the evening, but since you cannot dance, I will sit it out with you."

"No, I can't ask you to do that." She rolled along toward the side of the room.

"I wish I could promise to stay with you for the duration of the evening, but I cannot."

"Just as well. Everyone is looking at me."

"Of course they are. You look amazing this evening." He helped her move off the scooter and onto a settee. Her scooter was moved out of sight by an attendant who then offered them both a drink.

Ellie asked for some water and the attendant promised to return momentarily. The string quartet could be heard warming up in the background.

"The first dance is about to begin." He stretched an arm out along the back of the small couch.

"They don't expect you out there?" Rick noticed how she thanked the attendant who returned with a wine glass of ice water for her.

"My parents do, but I told them if I could not have the first dance with you, I would sit it out. I would have commandeered my sister but she already has a partner."

"Charlie."

"Well, yes, Adeline and Charlie, but I meant Ana."

"She's your twin, right?"

"Yes." He leaned closer to her. "But I am four minutes older."

"Does she have a boyfriend?"

"No, but my mother has her dancing with one of Addie's castoffs."

Ellie arched an eyebrow at him. "Addie's castoffs?"

"My mother set Adeline up with several men as soon as she returned from the States. One of them has been invited in the hopes that he and Ana will discover they are the perfect couple." Rick took an appetizer from another attendant. They would stop serving for the first few dances and he had not had a chance to get a bite to eat like he normally would. Before biting into the hors d'oeuvre, he leaned over. "Save the last dance for me, too, would you?"

"I don't think you're in any danger of me running off to dance with anyone else." She thanked another attendant for a bit of cheese and crackers.

His parents walked out to the middle of the dance floor. A few minutes later, the floor was full as the first dance ended. Rick stood and bowed slightly Ellie's direction. "I will return whenever I can. Let one of the attendants know if you need anything?"

She nodded.

He quirked an eyebrow at her. "Promise me."

That got him rolled eyes. "Fine. I will ask if I need anything."

"Good." He took her hand in his, bowed again until he could kiss it. "I will count the minutes until our last dance." Giving her another smile, he turned and walked toward the dance floor. Whichever young lady his mother had arranged for him to dance with would find him.

Jonathan William Langley-Cranston IV kept a very respectable distance between himself and Princess Ana as they twirled around the dance floor. His first ball at the palace, he'd escorted the Crown Princess and conspired with Lindsey to get her dad and Addie out onto the balcony at the same time. He'd stayed hidden, but saw the kiss they shared. Now, they were engaged and the wedding was coming up quick.

And he was here with a different princess.

Another one he was attracted to but still felt nothing but friendship for.

"Are you okay, Jon?" Princess Ana was the only person who got away with calling him that. No one else ever dared try. Except Phil, but his brother wasn't speaking to Jonathan at the moment.

Jonathan pasted on the best smile he could and spun her around again. "I'm fine."

"I know better. What is it?" When he didn't answer, she filled in the blanks. "Do you wish you were with Addie? I never knew what happened between you two, but did you feel a lot more for her than she did for you?"

He shook his head and spoke softly, so the other couples dancing around them wouldn't overhear. "No. Neither one of us were in love with the other. She was already in love with Charlie and I knew that. Both of our parents expected it from us. Even before she knew they'd approve of Charlie, we ended things privately." He'd kissed the Crown Princess. Once. No one else needed to know that. He didn't even know if Charlie knew about that kiss in the Alpine meadow.

"So you were just a distraction for my mother?"

"Count Bladvile had already been here and made vague threats against your sister. We really did try to see if we could work things out, knowing what we knew. We simply didn't tell your mother when we knew it wasn't going to happen. It took us a while longer to do that."

Ana looked up at him from under lowered lashes. "And now she's trying to set you up with me."

He hesitated. Long enough that she looked him straight in the eye with a big grin crossing her face.

"Oh, don't be such a grumpy Gus. There's nothing between us, and you and I both know it. My mother probably knows it. But as long as you're around, I like hanging out with you a lot better than some of the other men my mother has tried to set me up with. At least the whole thing with the attack on Addie by the count seems to have slowed her down some."

He smiled at her. "I'm glad."

The dance came to an end and Richard nodded toward the side of the room. Jonathan backed away from the princess and handed her over to another man who walked up. He tugged down on the emerald vest he wore under his tuxedo jacket and ambled over to the bench where a lovely brunette sat. Without waiting for an invitation, he took the seat next to her on the bench. "Good evening. I'm Jonathan."

She glanced at him, a bit nervous. "Ellie."

"Charlie's cousin, right?"

"Yes."

Jonathan leaned back and relaxed, stretching his legs out in front of him as he surveyed the ballroom. "Your first ball?"

"Yes."

Was he only going to get one word answers from her. "What

do you think?"

She gave a slight shrug. "I'm not sure. I'm stuck over here."

"I heard about what happened. How're you doing?"

"A bit better."

"I bet you really wanted to slug Rick with that cast of yours."

Ellie's face colored. "I might have."

"But you didn't because you were afraid you might somehow, inadvertently, start a war or something?"

"Pretty much."

"When are you headed back to the States?"

"I'm not sure." She held up her cast. "I can't really work until my arm's healed. Not just the cast off but the muscle mass rebuilt."

"So it'll be awhile?"

"Yes."

Back to the single syllables. "Maybe we'll run into each other again while we're both here. I'm taking the summer off from school, so I told Addie I'd hang around." Ellie seemed like a nice enough girl and, though he was conducting some business for the family, he really didn't have much to do but sit around and read at the Lydia House. The house, near the garrison that housed vehicles for use on land and the boats that traveled the lake to the palace, was his home away from home for the next few months. At least when Charlie and Lindsey had been staying there, he had some company occasionally.

They talked for another minute before the dance ended. A man he recognized as Charlie's father walked toward them and Jonathan stood. "Thank you for keeping me company, Miss Brewer."

"I had nothing else to do." A smile softened her words. "It was nice talking with you." And that, right there, was the most he'd gotten from her.

A spoiled debutante sauntered up to him, bold as you please. She held out one limp-at-the-wrist-so-he-could-kiss-it-he-supposed hand. "I'm Lizbeth Bence of Mevendia. I don't suppose you'd ask me to dance."

Jonathan's smile was even more forced than when he tried to convince Ana he was fine. "Of course. May I have this dance, Miss Bence?"

Her lashes fluttered at him. "I thought you'd never ask."

Someone, probably Rick, had made sure she would not be left alone to wallow in her injured status. With each dance a new man sat next to her, almost as though she actually did have a dance card. Dukes. Lords. Jonathan William Langley-Cranston the Fourth. As close as the United States came to royalty. She hadn't recognized him until after their conversation. Probably just as well.

All of the gentlemen were very nice, but none of them were the pretty boy. Even as she chatted with the men, she kept an eye out for Rick. He looked quite dashing in his tuxedo. She wasn't wearing a watch, but it had to be nearing the end of the night. The next man said his good byes, and Ellie closed her eyes for a moment. Even if she'd been in top form, this would have been a long night.

When she opened them again, she tried not to double take when she saw who was sitting next to her.

King Jedidiah chuckled. "I am not an ogre, Miss Brewer."

"I'm sure you're not, Your Majesty." She wove her fingers together and squeezed them tightly.

"There is no reason to be frightened or nervous."

"I know, sir." She took another sip of the water one of the attendants kept filled for her. "How are you feeling? Are you recovered from your skiing accident?"

The king sighed. "For the most part. I cannot do everything I used to. You likely did not notice that I only danced a few times this evening. A few years ago, I would have been all over the dance floor." His eyes took on a faraway look. "I know it is not quite manly to say, but I have always loved dancing with a good partner. Perhaps at the wedding or coronation balls, you will do me the honor of joining me for a waltz."

"I'm afraid I don't qualify as a good partner, sir." She watched as he reached for a glass of water from the attendant who seemed to anticipate his every need. As he did, she noted the telltale shake of Parkinson's in his hand. Not much, but a bit. So that's what else was really going on.

He just looked at her as though measuring her for something. She knew, whatever it was, he would find her lacking. But then he gave one slight nod. "I see the way my son looks at you, Ms. Brewer. I believe you will be good for him."

For several seconds, she struggled to process his words, but then she took a chance, knowing this would likely be her only opportunity. "You know he would like to start an outdoor excursion company here. Bring people from all over the world to experience your part of the Alps."

"I know."

"He would like to run it."

The king gave her that knowing look again. "I know."

"Will you let him?"

He stared at his water glass for a moment. "In two months, it will not be my decision. As his father, I suppose he might still want my blessing, but it will be up to Adeline. I have never been opposed to him doing what he loves. I *would* like for him to have an education to go with it. I know not everyone needs a business degree to run a successful business and I know he can surround himself with people who know what they are doing. But I would like to see him get a degree so he will know they are doing what they are supposed to and not subverting him or stealing from him."

Ellie mulled that over for a moment. "I guess I can

understand that. I'm sure my parents would agree with you."

The king looked like he was going to say something else, but the queen and Rick chose that moment to walk up. He looked over at Ellie, his eyes kind. "It has been a pleasure talking with you, my dear. I look forward to getting to know you better over the next few months, but now, it is time for me to take my bride back to the dance floor."

His bride? She saw the way the king smiled at his wife and knew that he loved her more than he must have the day they married.

Rick held a hand out to her. "Come on. I have something I want to show you."

Chapter
Eleven

Rick kept one hand on Ellie's back as he steered her out of the ballroom and onto the balcony outside. Though the ballroom was on the bottom floor of the palace, it was still quite a distance above the ground below. The benefits of building on top of a hill on an island. It had protected his ancestors for centuries.

"This is beautiful." Ellie rolled to a stop at the stone railing.

He stood next to her and looked out over the lake toward the mountains on the other side. The moon hung low over the top peak.

"My room as a child looked this direction," he told her, resting his forearms on the top rail. "I would stare at them for hours and wonder what it was like to live there, in the woods, off the land. I have had a chance to do that in some of the most amazing places on Earth, but there is still nothing quite like this view." Rick turned to look at her, moonlight dancing off her hair. He reached out and brushed a bit of it back. "There is no one I would rather be standing here with."

Ellie dipped her head, and he saw a blush creeping up her

neck.

"May I have this dance?"

She looked up at him, disbelief on her face. "I can't dance, Rick. My ankle is still not..."

He stopped her with a finger on her lips. "May I have this dance?" he asked again.

She hesitated then nodded against his finger.

Rick helped her move the scooter. He slid his right arm around her waist and took her other hand in his. "Lean on me. We're not going far."

She rested her cast against his arm as they swayed slightly to the music.

"When your foot is better, may I have your first dance?" He tucked her hand against his chest as she looked up at him.

"I promised your father a dance."

Rick grinned at her. "You can dance with my father all you want, but I would be honored if you would save your *first* dance at the wedding ball for me." He made himself stay focused on her eyes. If he let himself look at her lips he would not be able to stop himself from kissing her again.

She nodded. "Very well. I'll save the first dance for you."

He could not help it. Before he could talk himself out of it, he leaned down and brushed his lips against hers, tightening his hold on her. As intense as the first kiss in Greenland had been, this one was different. Soft. Tender. Full of the hopes and dreams he had let himself feel for the first time.

When they both pulled back, Ellie rested her cheek against his chest. She was the perfect height to lean his chin against her head.

"This is nice," she murmured. "Thank you."

His fingers traced little circles on the skin in the middle of her back. "I cannot say as I have ever enjoyed a dance quite so much."

"Me either." They continued for another minute before she

spoke again. "We are going with your family to your church in the morning?"

He breathed in deeply. "I had hoped to wait until later to tell you, but I am leaving in the morning. I will be gone for several weeks on business for my family."

Their movement stopped as Ellie pulled back to look up at him. "How long do you think it will be?"

"I do not know what your plans are, but I know your family is planning to be here for the wedding and coronation. You are more than welcome to remain here at the palace if you would like to."

"I'm moving to my aunt and uncle's new house tomorrow, but I'll miss you." What was it about this man that made her want to stay here forever? In his arms. Despite her broken arm and sprained ankle, he made her feel safe in a way she had never felt before.

She hadn't dated a lot. Just enough to have her heart broken a couple of times, but never enough to feel safe like this. Was it that he was taller and better built than the other guys she'd dated? His arms more muscular? Or was it that she felt herself, despite her best intentions, falling for him?

And now he would be gone for several weeks. At least she would have her family around. Her brother and sister-in-law would be returning to the States for work until time for the wedding and coronation, but her parents were staying most of the summer, and she couldn't work anyway - not with a broken arm. She *could,* but everything was so much more difficult and she had no desire to mess with camping one-armed. Ed would probably put her on desk duty in the office, but she would rather spend a year teaching math than a week answering phones there.

"I will miss you, too. I do not know that I will be able to call as much as I would like, with the time zone separations, traveling, and assorted commitments."

"I understand." What she really wanted was another kiss before he left, but applause was sounding in the other room. "I guess the ball is over."

Rick reached up with his free hand to trail his finger down the side of her face, sending a delicious thrill running through her. "I will be leaving quite early in the morning, so I must say my good-byes now."

She nodded and was about to say something else when several people streamed out onto the balcony. Rick backed away and helped her put her knee on her scooter. Maybe he would walk her to her room. It seemed like he intended to, but before he could, his assistant motioned to him.

"I am sorry. I will call when I can and email when I cannot."

Ellie gave one quick bob of her head as he took her uncasted hand in his and bent low to kiss her fingers. "Sleep well, beautiful lady." He walked off without looking back.

"Sleep well, handsome prince," she whispered. Even as she did, even as her heart ached for him to stay, her mind rebelled. She had promised herself she would never let another man get close to her again. But here she was, less than two weeks after meeting this man, and already she knew she would miss seeing him every day.

Ellie gripped the handlebars of her scooter and made her way toward the well-camouflaged elevator. She needed a plan. As she waited for the car to arrive at her floor, it came to her. Would Rick appreciate it? Was it worth her time?

Only one way to find out.

Richard strode into the palace. Not his palace, but a palace nonetheless. The king and crown prince would be waiting for him in the office, or so he had been told. King Antonio and Prince William, but not *that* Prince William as his friend was fond of saying, wanted to renew a deal exporting wine and other grape products from Mevendia to Montevaro.

The two men stood as Richard walked in. He didn't bow but held out his hand to the king.

"How is your father?" the king asked as they settled into their seats.

"Recovering from his injuries." The skiing accident had been news worldwide since King Jedidiah had been with the American First Family when it happened. Richard hesitated, unsure whether to say more. It was common knowledge his father was abdicating, but not the reason why. Not yet.

"He told me about the Parkinson's a few weeks ago." King Antonio leaned back in his plush leather chair. "I don't know what we might be able to do to help, but please let us know if we can be of assistance."

"Of course. He will appreciate that."

The king chuckled. "He is my cousin, after all."

Richard grinned. "About a thousand years back."

"More than that since the brothers split the land." He leaned forward and rested his forearms on the desktop. "Have you spoken with Christiana lately?"

Christiana. The first of the younger generation to take the throne in their trio of countries. Not the way any of them would have wished after her parents and younger brother were killed in a tragic car accident when she was only five. Rick shook his head. "No. I will be in Ravenzario on this trip, though. I hope to speak with her alone at some point."

Something was not quite right in her island nation, but Richard could not put his finger on what it was. Neither could anyone else.

"Please give her our regards." He leaned back again. "William is getting his feet wet in diplomatic relations, dealing with everything related to Mevendia's relationship with Montevaro and Ravenzario. All subject to my approval, of course, but it's time."

Twenty-two year old William shook his head. "I am not completely incompetent, but yes, it is time for me to start taking over a few things here and there. Since I am still at university, our trio is a good way for me to begin participating while not inadvertently starting World War III."

Richard chuckled along with the king. "This is the first trip where I am on my own. I have done a few things, but not too many."

"They still won't let you climb Everest?" The king quirked an eyebrow at him.

"No. Maybe once Adeline has a couple heirs, then I will no longer be 'the spare.'" He turned to look at the younger man. "There is something I would like to discuss with you soon, William. Both of you most likely, but I think you'll catch my vision faster." He launched into a brief explanation of what he wanted to do. "And if we can tie it in to trips in Mevendia or hikes from one country to the other, feature each other's products whenever possible, I think it could be good for both of us."

William had leaned forward, an eager look on his face, while the king tapped his pen. "I love the idea, but that should not surprise you."

It did not. He knew William envied Richard his opportunities to traipse the globe, but here, William was the heir and as such, had duties to attend to rather than a survival trip through the Sahara. Rick turned to the king.

"I see possibilities. Once you have more details sorted, send us a proposal. Perhaps we could also work with Christiana and put together some Commonwealth of Bellas Montagnes combination vacation packages. In fact, I'm not sure why we haven't thought of it before." He nodded toward Rick. "I know your goal is the more adventurous side of things and we could surely add some diving off Ravenzario. The ski slopes are better here, but we're the Alps, not a couple of islands in the Mediterranean."

Richard turned that over in his mind. His father and Addie would be more likely to go for it if it was part of a larger package to increase tourism and spending in Montevaro in general and not just specifically for his venture. "I think it could work. I will get something together and send it to you sometime soon. It probably will not be until after the wedding and coronation, but definitely something to look into." He set his leather portfolio on the desk in front of him. "But I think we better get down to the business at hand. Your assistant said we have a limited time, and we should make the best of it."

Lunch with Princess Adeline and Charlie Brewer. Ellie looked at the note on the tablet and she breathed a sigh of relief. Lunch with her cousin and his fiancé she could handle. She gratefully slid both feet into a pair of shoes and prayed she wouldn't get lost. With her luck, she'd wind up in some off-limits part of the palace and break some irreplaceable artifact, while wearing tennis shoes that didn't match her outfit but were the only thing she could wear with her not-quite-recovered ankle. Wrapping it seemed to be working. Anything to get out of that stupid boot.

Fortunately, a maid was cleaning right outside the apartment when she left, and she asked directions. A few minutes later, she walked into the relatively informal dining room. Still fancier than anyplace she'd ever been at home, this room paled in comparison to some of the other rooms in the building.

Across the room stood her cousin, with his back to her. Before she could say "hello", she realized what he was doing.

Making out with his fiancé.

Well, that might be a bit strong, but it was definitely an intimate moment she didn't want to interrupt. They had little enough time together as it was. At least after the wedding, they'd spend their nights together, and he wouldn't be commuting to his parents' home nearly an hour away.

So she turned and walked back out the door, giving them a few minutes alone.

"They're a bit disgusting, aren't they?" She turned to see a man sitting in one of the chairs nearby. How had she not seen him when she walked up?

"I don't know about that," she hedged, not wanting to disparage her cousin.

He stood, putting his tablet down on the chair beside him. The grin on his face should have put her at ease but something about him seemed familiar. "Addie and Charlie don't get much time together. I'm glad you let them be, too. They were like that when I got here almost ten minutes ago."

Addie? Not many people called her that. At least Ellie didn't think many people did. And this guy had an American accent she couldn't place. Trying not to show her discomfort, she held out a hand. "I'm Ellie Brewer, Charlie's cousin."

He shook it, holding just a couple seconds too long as his grin spread. "Jonathan Langley-Cranston, lately of Serenity Landing, Missouri."

She felt her eyes widen. Jonathan Langley-Cranston? The third? Fourth? Fifth? She knew he wasn't the first with that name.

He crossed his arms over his chest, drawing her attention to his well-defined upper body. "It's nice to see you again."

Ellie managed to shake herself out of her stupor, though all she could say was, "Again?"

"I was your second 'dance' at the ball."

"Right." She knew that. Now that she recognized him.

He pointed to his face. "The glasses throw everyone off."

She gave a small smile. "As long as you're not really Superman, I promise to recognize you next time."

Jonathan laughed then pointed over his shoulder with one thumb. "How long should we let them play tonsil hockey?"

Ellie found her voice. "Charlie doesn't have his tonsils." Because *that* was the point. The guy came from the family about as close to royalty as America ever got, and she was quibbling over her cousin's surgical history?

Jonathan laughed. "Right." He picked up his tablet and turned, offering her his arm. "It seems you and I are joining them for lunch today. May I have the honor of escorting you?"

Ellie shook herself. Internally. Not for real. "Um, sure." She slid her good hand through his elbow, noticing his height compared to hers and the muscles under her hand as they started to walk. She also realized he wasn't as tall as Rick, nor did he make her heart pound with a mere glance.

They walked in to see Charlie and Addie still in each other's arms, but this time Jonathan cleared his throat, pulling their attention from each other. When they turned, Charlie had a silly grin on his face, but Ellie noticed the blush creeping up Addie's neck.

Addie slid around Charlie, trying to regain her composure. "I see you already met my dear friend, Jonathan."

Jonathan patted Ellie's hand. "Yep. We 'danced' at the ball and had a chance to talk for a few minutes just now. But I'm hungry. Can we eat?"

Addie and Charlie laughed while Ellie wasn't sure how to take it. Likely, Jonathan was much more used to being waited on hand and foot, to having lunch served when he was ready and not making it himself.

With a wave of her hand toward a smaller table Ellie hadn't seen, Addie moved toward it, Charlie's hand resting on her back. "I had them set us up over here. That other table is simply too big to have a nice meal with such a small group."

Jonathan held Ellie's chair for her, pushing it in as she sat. Was this a date? Were Charlie and Addie setting her up without telling her she was going on a blind date? If Jonathan was uncomfortable with the situation, he didn't show it. Ellie would guess he got set up more often than she did, by parents or well-meaning friends or whatever. Likely he was just more at ease in just about any setting than she ever would be. Years of practice?

Conversation flowed around her, not excluding her but she didn't make an effort to be included either, unless they asked her something specifically.

"How much longer do you have to have the cast?" Like that one from Jonathan.

She lifted it up. "Three weeks, I think. I should be able to get it off in four weeks instead of six. The breaks weren't as bad as they initially thought."

"You were really carried out of the woods by Prince Rick?"

She'd never heard anyone call him that, but she'd bet he hated it. "Rick, Dennis, and Steve took turns carrying a homemade stretcher with me on it."

Jonathan shook his head. "I don't get it. I mean, I like a hike as much as the next guy, but to go out without much of anything on purpose? I don't understand that mentality." He didn't seem to be degrading what she did, just curious and didn't understand. Better than most people. Including her parents.

Charlie made a comment Ellie didn't quite catch, but it was enough to draw the attention away from her and for that she was grateful. When Charlie caught her eye a minute later, he gave her a wink. Always coming to her rescue, even more than her own brother ever did.

The rest of the meal passed quickly, but near the end, Charlie turned on her. "My cousin would love to explore the mountains, but hiking might be a bit much. I don't have the time or experience to take her on a horseback tour. Do you think you'd be able to, Jonathan?"

Jonathan grinned. "Of course. It's a date."

Chapter Twelve

*J*onathan waited in one of the many anterooms in the Montevarian palace. He'd been summoned, but didn't know why. And when the royal family called, you came. Especially when the Crown Princess was a friend.

The queen appeared in the doorway that led into the hall, sweeping past him and into the office beyond. "Do come in, Jonathan."

He stood, wishing he'd worn a tie but since he'd thought he was meeting with Ana after lunch, he hadn't. "How can I help you, ma'am?" He was never sure if you called a non-monarch queen "your royal highness", or "your majesty", but she wasn't his queen, so he stuck with "ma'am."

She motioned to the plush-looking-but-he-knew-would-be-uncomfortable chairs across from her desk. "Have a seat." Queen Alexandra sat behind her desk. "Let me get straight to the point. You are attending Adeline's wedding and coronation, correct?"

"Yes, ma'am." He would RSVP as soon as he received his official invitations.

"Anastasia needs an escort."

Blunt. "I'm sure there's someone the princess would rather go with than me." She'd as much as told him there was.

The queen gave him a disapproving look that would have made his grandmother proud. "No one Anastasia wants to accompany her is acceptable."

Jonathan bit his tongue. Words like *Someone like Charlie?* desperately wanted to sneak out, but they didn't. Charlie, someone both the queen and Parliament had deemed unacceptable, had saved the Crown Princess from being violated by a man the queen *had* approved of.

Instead, Jonathan just nodded. "I would be happy to be Ana's escort." Her glare stopped him. "Princess Anastasia is a lovely girl."

"Good. I will make sure a stylist gets your clothing coordinated with hers."

"I will be waiting with bated breath." He didn't wilt under her gaze, but stood. "Thank you for thinking of me."

She dismissed him with a wave of her hand. As he walked toward the dock, a text came in from Ana, asking to see him after all. He changed direction and spoke with one of the guards he'd come to know just a bit as he returned to the more private areas of the palace. The whole palace was literally surrounded by an Alpine lake, but some areas were more accessible to guests than others.

A few minutes later, he walked into the apartment Ana occupied. She closed the door behind him, gesturing to the couch. "My mother got to you?"

He sat, leaning his elbows on his knees. "Yep. You're stuck with me for the wedding, ball, and the coronation and probably everything in between."

She sighed. "The press will have us engaged before the crown hits Addie's head."

"Most likely."

"That doesn't bother you?"

Jonathan sat back and crossed one ankle over the other knee. "I know better. You know better. I think even your mother knows better, but is either hoping for us to change our minds or that I'll keep you occupied until you move on from whoever it is she doesn't want you to go with."

Ana rolled her eyes. "She tried to set Addie up with him, but apparently he's not right for me."

"I'm sorry, Ana."

She shrugged. "I'm used to my mother's interference. I'll likely be going back to university soon and by the time I get back for good, Addie will have been queen for a while and maybe Mother will have calmed down some."

A chuckled rolled out before he could stop it. "You don't really believe that, do you?"

"No. But at least she seems to be leaving Rick and Ellie alone."

Jonathan raised a brow. "You don't really believe that either, do you?"

Sadly, Ana shook her head. "No. I don't. It's only a matter of time before she separates them, too."

Another day. Another palace.

After spending some time with the Mevendian royal family over dinner the night before, Richard flew to Ravenzario. He spent the night at one of the local resorts, not at the palace. It struck him as odd that Christiana hadn't invited him to stay with her. She had essentially been his foster sister for many years. They'd gotten on well all of those years. So why the distance? She stayed with Addie when she was in Montevaro. Maybe because she and his sister were much closer than he and Christiana were.

He waited in an ante room, struck again by the differences

between this visit and the one the day before. Though he was a guest at both palaces, he felt infinitely more welcome in Mevendia. Odd. He clasped his hands behind him, leather portfolio with his tablet in it clutched in one. In front of him was a painting of Christiana's Uncle Henry. Henry Eit, her mother's brother, had been regent until she came of age, but that wasn't what struck Rick as odd. The size did. It was a rather large painting. Across from it, a much smaller one of Christiana when she was still a child.

Unclear thoughts tumbled over and over in his mind, but before he could reach any conclusions, the door opened.

"Good afternoon, Rick." The older man didn't hold out his hand, didn't show any of the deference Richard would have expected. In fact, the mere use of the name "Rick" rankled, something that rarely happened. It wasn't that Richard expected people to bow at his feet, but there was something in the man's attitude that bothered him.

"Good afternoon." Henry turned and walked into the conference room without a second glance his way. Richard followed and took the seat indicated, doing his best to hide his frown. No "please come in." No "apologies for pushing the meeting back by six hours at the last minute." Henry took the seat at the head of the table and opened a padfolio with notes scribbled on it.

"Let's get started."

Before he could say anything else, Rick interrupted. "Where's Christiana?"

Henry's eyebrow shot up. "You mean Queen Christiana?"

Richard shrugged. The guy could call him by a familiar nickname when he wasn't a relation to the royal family by more than marriage but would insist Richard call Christiana by her title?

"She will not be joining us. I have full authority to negotiate on her behalf."

Once again, Richard interrupted. "Is she ill?"

"No." He flipped the page over. "Now, about free travel between Ravenzario and Montevaro. While we're more than willing to allow our residents to travel to Montevaro under whatever minimal conditions your father or Addie would require, we're changing our requirements."

That hadn't been on the agenda. "A passport is already required when traveling either direction."

"Yes, and it will continue to be required for entrance to Ravenzario. However, beginning August first, we will also require a visa issued at least sixty days before planned travel and will be valid for no more than two weeks, except under exigent circumstances. We recommend applying for said visa at least six months in advance of the travel dates."

Richard frowned. "Since this was not on our agenda, I do not have the full authority to speak on my father's behalf, but I am certain he and Crown Princess Adeline will find these requirements unacceptable. Completely unacceptable in general terms, but especially in light of the short time frame. If a Montevarian family planned to come for holiday in August, they would be unable to, even if they applied for the visa today and it was granted immediately."

Henry just stared at him. "That is not my problem." He pushed back from the table. "You will be escorted off the premises. Your pilots have been told that you will be leaving shortly."

Richard frowned again. What about the rest of the things on his father's agenda? But Henry was already gone. A guard waited for him, escorting him out of the building as Henry indicated. By the time his car pulled out of the palace gates, Richard was on the phone with his father and Addie. Something in Ravenzario wasn't right. He couldn't put his finger on it, but whatever it was, his distant cousin might need their help.

Jonathan walked down the street alongside the kind of person he seldom met. A friend who saw beyond his name and political connections and saw *him*.

"So what's your favorite thing about Serenity Landing?" Ellie's sling supported her cast while her other hand swung free as they wandered through the streets.

He took a sip of the to-go soda he'd gotten from a street vendor. "Probably the people. Overall, they're really much nicer than many of the other cities in the US. Can you imagine what would happen in NYC if the power was out for three days, like after that ice storm last spring? Sure, local areas, neighborhoods, would have banded together, but whole counties? So many radio stations devoting all of their programing to helping people find batteries for machines they needed or medications?"

"It did bring out the best in people," Ellie agreed. "Except for the news coverage of that one couple that got stranded in the comedy club."

Jonathan laughed. "I know Josh Wilson. Not well, but well enough. That news coverage was probably the best thing that could have happened to him."

Before she could ask why, his phone rang. The ring tone made him close his eyes and pray for patience. "I need to take this." He stepped to the side. "What is it, Phil?" His brother only called when he needed something. Usually money.

This time was no different. He listened to his brother explain why he needed tens of thousands of dollars. Again. He didn't know who had given his brother money earlier in the year but someone must have. "No." Jonathan ran a weary hand over his face. "I told you at Christmas and again when you called me in January. No more money." He moved further away from Ellie, his other hand slipping into his pocket to feel his token of sobriety. "I'll pay for rehab. That's it. When you're ready to go, call me.".

With his brother's protests ringing in his ears, he pressed the "end" button on the screen. With his head hung and eyes closed, he whispered the same prayer he had for months. *Let him be alive to recover after he hits rock bottom. Please, God.*

Taking a deep breath, and pasting a smile on his face, he turned back to Ellie. "Ready?"

She smiled and linked her arm through his. "I think we need ice cream. What do you think?"

His smile became genuine. "I think that's a great idea."

"Are you sure you don't want to come in?" Ellie rested her hand on the car door handle as they sat in front of her aunt and uncle's house.

Jonathan shook his head. "No. I don't want to intrude. Besides..."

Ellie rolled her eyes. "You're not intruding. You're a friend of Addie's which makes you a friend of ours. And, honestly, my aunt and uncle kind of rattle around in this place. I know they're looking forward to the wedding and coronation being over so they can get back out on a dig."

He seemed to consider it. "I really don't have anywhere else to be and this house looks pretty cool. Can you give me a tour?" As she nodded, he pulled over to the side of the house. She cracked the door and reached down to get her purse, but before she could get everything situated, Jonathan was there, holding the door open.

"Thank you." She spent the next hour telling him what she knew as they walked around the house and the garden. He declined staying for dinner, saying he had a prior engagement but before he left, he surprised her.

If anything, he looked nervous. "Listen, I know you and the

prince are kind of a thing or whatever, but I have a fundraiser to go to Friday night, and I don't have a date. I'm not asking you on one," he hurried to clarify, "but if you would join me, I'd appreciate it. I really don't want to go alone. The queen is trying to set me and Ana up, but neither of us is interested." Jonathan scrunched his face up. "I hinted that I already had someone to go with to get out of it. Ana didn't want to go at all and used it as her excuse."

Ellie hesitated before nodding. "Sure. Sounds fun." She knew she didn't sound convinced.

Jonathan chuckled. "I don't know about fun, but it'll be a lot nicer with someone I like instead of someone my mom set me up with."

He liked her? But it wasn't a date? Right?

"I'll be here around three-thirty. I know it's a bit early but it'll take a while to get there and it starts at six. There'll be a place for you to freshen up when we get there."

"Sounds good." What would she wear? "I'm guessing this is a dressy thing?"

A grin crossed his face. "Nope. It's in a barn. A good old fashioned hoedown." He winked at her. "Line dancing and barbecue." He trotted down the stairs and turned, walking backwards toward his car. "Jeans, boots if you got 'em." She nodded. He reached the vehicle. "And your passport."

Before she could ask what that was all about, he took off. The rest of the week went quickly. Ellie spent some time with her cousin, the princess, and Jonathan. The four of them went out for dinner one night. She hadn't heard from Rick outside of a couple of very short text messages, but she knew he was busy.

Friday afternoon, Ellie had on her favorite jeans. They weren't her nicest, but they looked the best. She already had her cowgirl boots on. The good ones, not the ones she'd used when she worked on the farm with her best friend in high school. Those were back in Missouri. But she was on her sixth blouse and still hadn't decided which one to wear. Finally, she settled for the first one she'd tried on.

"Where exactly is it we're going?" Ellie asked as she settled into the passenger seat of Jonathan's car. Could she slip her shoes off as she often did on long drives? Was two and half hours long enough to be a "long drive"? And did it take two and a half hours to get anywhere in Montevaro? But since she had her passport tucked into her purse, they were likely going to either Italy to the south or Mevendia to the north.

Jonathan just grinned. "You'll see. It's fun getting to surprise you, and I don't want to spoil it." For about forty minutes, they talked about all sorts of stuff ranging from Charlie and Addie's wedding to places they both loved back in Serenity Landing.

Ellie blinked as he pulled into the airport parking lot. "Are we flying somewhere?"

He drove around to a private area, swiping a card to get the gate to open. "Yep. Your private plane awaits."

"Private? Seriously?" Sure, she'd flown with Rick, but flying in a private jet? Would she ever get used to that?

Without the need to go through security or wait on time to board, they were in the air quickly.

Cocooned in the plush leather seat of the rental plane, Ellie asked again. "Will you at least tell me what country we're headed to?"

Jonathan smiled at her. "Ravenzario. They're a sister country to Montevaro and a guy I know from Serenity Landing runs a venue on one of the islands. They do a lot of weddings and fundraisers and things like that. He knew I was in the area and asked if I wanted to come. I think Queen Christiana will be there."

Great. More royalty to figure out. "Rick said something about the three countries having some kind of agreement dating back to the time of Charlemagne, but we haven't had a chance for him to go into the whole history of Montevaro. He promised to sometime soon, though."

"I'll let him tell you about it then."

As promised, the flight was short. Ellie spent most of it staring out the window at the landscape and then the sea below.

"There's a landing strip on the property so we'll just land there. I talked to Alexander earlier, and he said there was plenty of room. It's a lot easier than landing on one of the main islands and getting a cab and taking a ferry and hoping there's room inside so your hair doesn't get all messed up and doing it all backwards on the way home..." Jonathan rolled his eyes as his voice trailed off.

"Such a pain." She shook her head. "Private parking, avoid security, no long wait at the gate because of mechanical problems, plenty of leg room, and doing it all again on the way home."

He laughed out loud. "You have a point."

"So what exactly is this thing tonight?" Unless she was mistaken they had started descending.

"It's a barn dance and fundraiser. Alexander is an American whose family owns the property, and he runs it. He does a lot of work with charities around the world. I forget which one this is for tonight. It may just be a general foundation fundraiser and not for a specific group."

"And why a barn dance, exactly? Ravenzario doesn't seem to be a country that had cowboys."

"I have no idea. Maybe that movie last year was a lot more popular here than in the States."

What movie? When was the last time she'd even been to a movie theater? Was there some movie about line dancing the year before? Maybe she remembered that. Maybe. But she didn't want to show her ignorance so she just nodded. She'd look it up later.

"If you want to freshen up, you have about ten minutes before the seatbelt sign comes on."

Ellie looked around and grinned as she stood up. "I don't actually see a seatbelt sign." Jonathan's laughter followed her as she went into a much larger-than-normal airplane bathroom.

Chapter Thirteen

*T*wo visits to Ravenzario in just over a week. That had to be some sort of record for Richard. His plane landed on the small island off the main one as he bit back a groan. He didn't want to socialize. To dance. To smile and pretend that he wasn't already exhausted and missing his own pillow. Missing Ellie.

At least it wasn't a formal affair.

"How much longer before I need to deplane?" he asked Mark, one of Addie's regular team of bodyguards assigned to him for this trip. With the now-uneasy relationship, between the two countries and Steve and Dennis on a much-needed month long break, both his father and sister had insisted on sending the veteran team with him to Ravenzario.

"Half an hour, sir."

He gave a single nod and pulled his tablet out. Addie had emailed him an article to look at, talking about the changes to their travel relationship with Ravenzario. He skimmed through it. Nothing surprising, but one of the links at the bottom caught his eye.

Royal Almost-in-law Paints Town Red

A tap brought up the new story. A picture popped up. The first thing he noticed... Ellie. Her smile. Her sparkling eyes.

Her arm threaded through another man's.

Jonathan William Langley-Cranston the Fourth smiled down at the girl Richard wanted to marry. After staring longer than he should have, he slid the picture upward.

Ellie Brewer, cousin to Princess Adeline's fiancé Sir Charlie Brewer, has been seen out and about with Jonathan Cranston several times this week. As reported earlier, the couple had lunch at the palace with the princess and the recently-knighted Sir Charlie Brewer. Both couples were seen laughing their way through dinner at the princess's favorite bistro on Wednesday evening. Last night, Miss Brewer and Mr. Langley-Cranston attended a play at a local high school and picked up dessert before driving toward the home of the Marquis and Marchioness of Montago where Miss Brewer is staying.

Rick tossed the tablet onto the seat next to him. Had he imagined her response to his kiss on that balcony? The way she felt in his arms as they sort-of-danced at the ball? She'd promised him her first real dance, but had she meant it?

Had someone better come along?

Rick didn't know Jonathan well, but he seemed like a nice enough guy. Addie liked him. And he had a distinct advantage over Prince Richard. He had enough of the wealth and none of the royal restrictions. Addie and Ana both seemed to think he was plenty good looking. The tabloids certainly did.

Leaning back in his chair and stretching his legs out in front of him. The email from Christiana said the dress was casual but he doubted his hiking or camping clothes would fit the bill. The brown loafers, tan slacks, and dark blue button down shirt would have to work.

With his eyes closed, he could almost feel Ellie in his arms as they danced at the ball. What would she be doing tonight? Hanging out with Charlie and Lindsey? He was fairly certain

Addie had some kind of meeting with their father and some of the leaders in Parliament about the new restrictions on travel to Ravenzario. If he could, Richard was supposed to mention it to Christiana and get her feelings on the matter. Uncle Henry said he spoke on her behalf but until such a time as Christiana signed the edict, it didn't matter.

A cleared throat off to the side told him it was time to go. When he reached the bottom of the stairs, no one waited for him. Odd. Usually he was met by *someone,* but they *were* on the small island property belonging to the Bayfield family and not the main airport. Scanning around, he noticed a couple of other private jets and a walkway that seemed the most likely place to go. As he rounded the corner of the small building with a waiting area in it, the other buildings in the complex came into view as did a woman hurrying his direction.

She stopped a few feet away and bowed her head slightly. "Good evening, sir. I'm Diana, the queen's assistant. If you'd follow me, she's waiting for you."

Richard nodded back and followed her down the path, grateful for his long legs, because she was in a hurry. They reached the door to the building and she stopped, looking around anxiously as he neared.

"Is everything all right?" he asked.

She scanned the area again. "Please keep an eye on the queen, sir? Stay close to her tonight, even if you're both dancing with someone else. I've got a bad feeling about something, but I can't really explain it." Her furrowed brow told him one of two things: either she was really concerned or she was an excellent actress.

There was more the woman wasn't telling him, though he had no idea what it could be. "Of course." Before entering the building, he turned and motioned the security guards he'd borrowed from his sister's detail. "Tell Mark and Todd your concerns."

He walked into the room to see the queen seated in one of

the very formal looking chairs. She wore blue jeans, which shocked him. His mother would be scandalized when she saw the pictures. Standing next to her was Alexander, going over some sort of paperwork with her. The other man grinned when he saw Richard.

"Prince Richard!" Alexander bowed his head slightly. "I heard you'd arrived. There's a few things we need to go over." After talking through things like where they'd be sitting, Christiana was led away by her stylist for a last minute touch up. Alexander pulled Richard to the side and lowered his voice. "Listen, I know the queen grew up with you, and I know there are some hoping for a marriage between you and the queen to solidify the centuries old relationship between the two countries. I don't know how you feel about that, and right now, I really don't care, sir." The man stood toe to toe and eye to eye with him. "But tonight, if I'm not with her, you need to be. You need to be on your guard."

This guy was serious. "What's the threat?"

"We're not sure. It's a very long story I can't get into now, but there *is* a threat. The only one I know for sure you can trust besides me is Tony, the queen's head of security."

Richard nodded. "I understand. Make sure my security team is aware?"

"Of course." Alexander moved to discuss it with Mark and Todd who arrived while they were talking.

Richard walked to the window to wait for Christiana and the word it was time for their grand entrance.

To a hoedown.

With his hands clasped behind his back as he stared over the hayfield between the administration building where he waited and the barn where the fundraiser was held. What was going on in Ravenzario? Did Christiana have any idea? Both her assistant and Alexander made sure she didn't overhear the conversations. Where did the danger come from?

Todd and Mark flanked him a moment later. "There is no reason not to believe Alexander and Diana. We don't know much about Diana, but Alexander and Tony have been vetted by us for years."

Tony made sense. They worked with Tony regularly for security reasons. "Why have you looked at Alexander?"

"We looked again before tonight's appearance, but your father has always kept an eye on who got close to the queen. She's been to a number of events here and with the Bayfield family over the years. They check out clean."

"So what do we do?"

"Stay close to the queen at all times. If not you or Alexander, then one of us. There may be a few other people here that we know we can trust. We'll let you know when we get through the rest of the guest list. There were some last minute additions."

Richard nodded as he heard his name called. It was time.

Ellie sat next to Jonathan and waited for the queen to arrive. The barn looked about like she expected though many of the attendees seemed far less comfortable in their attire than she did when she was all dressed up. Straw bales with wool blankets or saddles on them rimmed the outer edge of the dance floor. One wall had clothes lines with long johns, plaid shirts, denim overalls, and socks clipped to them. A mechanical bull was set up in one corner.

She would *not* be trying that one.

Several other stations were set up around the perimeter of the room - bobbing for apples, face painting, and...was that a kissing booth? Who would be manning that? Before she could think any further, trumpets blared. All of the seats scraped back and everyone stood.

"Ladies and gentlemen, Her Majesty Queen Christiana of Ravanzario and her escort, His Royal Highness Prince Richard of Montevaro."

Ellie's heart dropped in her chest as there was a smattering of applause from around the room. She could only see the top of his head and couldn't see the queen at all. Was her hand in his elbow? Had he covered it with one of his own? Did he feel the same thrill in his stomach when he looked at Queen Christiana that Ellie felt when Rick looked at her? Jonathan's hand on her shoulder reminded her it was time to sit down.

"Did you know he was going to be here?" he asked her softly.

She shook her head. "No, but I haven't heard much from him since he left. I don't have access to much more than the bare bones of his schedule unless it overlaps with my family's. For the next few weeks all it says is 'out of country on business.'"

Servers began moving around the room with plates of barbecue ribs, baked beans, and coleslaw. She and Jonathan talked a bit with each other and with those sitting at the table with them while they ate.

As the meal wound down, Alexander Bayfield stood at the podium. "Ladies and gentlemen, thank you for joining us this evening to raise funds for the Bayfield Family Foundation. These funds will go to..."

Ellie tuned him out and wished she could see Rick from her seat. Was he whispering something in the queen's ear? Something that would make her try to hide a smile or laugh? They'd grown up together, at least sort of, according to what she'd gleaned from conversations around her. Many of the Ravenzarians seemed to like the idea of the two countries solidifying their relationship with a marriage of their queen and the prince.

Her stomach twisted at the thought of Rick - no, Richard - kissing the woman the way he'd kissed her on that balcony in

Greenland or more.

Jonathan's hand covered hers, squeezing it in sympathy. "Are you all right?" No one else would hear his whispered question.

Ellie took a deep breath to steady herself. "Yes. Even if there is something between them, I have no right to be upset. We had no real understanding about what we are to each other. If anything." And he was a pretty boy. Just like Glenn had been. Bitter experience wormed its way back into her mind. She would do well to remember they couldn't be trusted. "Is there a receiving line tonight?" Would she have to see them together? Smiling, sharing an amused glance at something a guest said.

"No, but the dancing will start soon."

Ellie picked at what remained of her dinner until the waiter removed it. Even the chocolate decadence that took its place couldn't tempt her out of her funk. The music picked up from barely noticeable in the background to loud enough to start feet tapping. The scraping of chair legs against the wood floor caught her attention. Everyone was turning to face the dance floor.

Prince Richard stood there facing a lovely young blonde. He held one of the queen's hands in his as they moved closer together. Rather than starting with a typical barn dance, a waltz began to play. She'd seen Rick in action before at the ball for her aunt, uncle, and cousin. He and the queen danced flawlessly. Everything about how he looked, how he held himself was so different than the Rick she'd first met or even the one who showed up after her fall. After her fall, he'd transformed from cocky to confident, his movements sure.

She sensed some of the same now, though he wasn't as relaxed as he'd seemed the night they sat against the tree. When the dance finished, the audience clapped politely, but before Jonathan could ask her to dance, a man asked to speak with him. As the dance floor filled up, Ellie watched, noting Richard continued to dance with the queen. About the time the next dance ended, Jonathan returned.

He smiled and bowed to her. "May I have this dance?"

She took his hand. "Of course." Prince Richard had asked her to save her first dance for him. But he was dancing with another woman and didn't even know she was there. After all, he hadn't vowed to save his next dance for her, and this wasn't a ball in Montevaro either.

Rick didn't want to dance with anyone but Christiana until whatever threat existed had been neutralized. Their conversation had flowed easily during dinner, both with each other and those around them. They didn't talk much during the dance, though it wasn't uncomfortable in the least. He smiled at other couples until something, or someone rather, caught his eye.

Jonathan?

His friend was smiling at the woman on his arm but Richard frowned. The brunette hair, the tilt of the head, set of the shoulders. It couldn't be. Could it?

"Who is that?" Christiana's voice sounded in his ear.

"Jonathan is a friend of my family's. He met Addie in the States and came to visit a few months ago. He's been a fixture ever since. I think my mother hopes he'll marry Ana."

"Do you know the girl?"

The other pair spun around and his suspicions were confirmed. "Ellie."

"Who is she? The one lost in the woods with you?"

"Yes. She's Charlie's cousin." And so much more.

Christiana squeezed his hand, bringing his attention back to her. "And who is she to you?"

How to describe his relationship with Ellie? He finally settled on, "My friend."

Christiana's eyes were serious as she stared at him. "And

more?"

He blew out his breath. "I hope so."

She gave him a soft smile. "You are in love with her?"

No sense in denying it. "I believe so, but we have had little time together. We have known each other less than a month, and I have been traveling half of that."

She moved a bit closer to him. "I believe I have found such a person, too."

Shock didn't begin to describe Rick's reaction. "You have? Then why are you with me tonight?"

"We have not been seen together in public yet. In fact, our relationship is secret for now. He values his privacy and knows that once everyone is aware we are dating, his privacy could well be gone forever. Until we know if this will work between us..."

Rick nodded. "I understand."

The song came to an end and Rick felt a tap on his shoulder. He turned to see Jonathan standing there.

"Would you care to trade partners, sir?" Rick hesitated until the other man spoke again, communicating more with his eyes and expression than his words. "Alexander said he thought you would enjoy a dance with Ellie."

Rick turned to see Ellie looking uncertain, but he took her in his arms and pulled her closer than he had Christiana. As they moved off, she stared at his shoulder. "You don't have to dance with me. I know you didn't expect to see me here."

"No, but I am very glad I did." He leaned over until he could whisper. "They're afraid there's a threat against Christiana and didn't want me to leave her with anyone but a very short list of people. Jonathan wasn't on that list, but his comment about Alexander told me he knows what's going on."

A look of concern crossed her face and stayed. "Is she going to be okay?"

"If we have anything to say about it." They turned around the floor. "What about you and Jonathan?" Rick wasn't sure he wanted to know the answer.

"He kept me company for one dance at the ball then Addie and Charlie introduced us again. He's a nice guy but that's it." She squeezed his upper arm where her hand rested. "He's kept me company."

"I am sorry I've been gone but glad you have had someone to keep you from being bored."

She ducked her head. "I would rather have you with me."

"I will be home in a few weeks, but in the meantime, I'm headed to the other side of the globe. My European business is concluded for the time being."

Their second real dance came to an end. The only time he'd be allowed to dance with her as many times as he wanted would be after their wedding. The one where he married Ellie.

But that time wasn't now. He stepped back and, after making certain Alexander was with the queen and Jonathan back with Ellie, he turned to dance with the woman standing next to him, waiting for her chance.

Two-and-a-half more weeks. Eighteen days before he'd return home for good, as long as his schedule didn't change again. Despite Ellie's statement that Jonathan was just a friend, would that much time be enough for her feelings to change?

Chapter Fourteen

M y dance card seems to be very limited tonight."
Jonathan took Queen Christiana's hand in his as the
next to last song of the night came on. "I'm afraid I
don't know much about that. Just that Alexander and Richard
told me I should ask you to dance again." He gave her his best
smile. He didn't know much, but he did know a bit more than he
said.

She looked over his shoulder. "Richard's card seems to be a
bit repetitive, as well."

Jonathan glanced over. Sure enough, Rick and Ellie were
dancing. Again. The second time? Third? More than anyone else
Rick had danced with except Christiana.

"Have we met before this evening?" Christiana tilted her head
to look at him.

"I don't believe so."

"You look familiar."

Jonathan grimaced. "My family is well-known in the States.
You may have met my uncle." He gave the name of a sitting
Senator from North Carolina.

The queen shook her head. "No. My uncle takes care of most of the meetings with foreign dignitaries. If your uncle visited Ravenzario on business, he likely would have met with Henry."

"Maybe you just happened to see me or one of my family in a tabloid or something."

She shook her head. "No. Did you date Addie?"

A grin spread across his face. "For a few weeks this spring. Just until everyone was convinced Charlie was a much better choice for her."

"That must be it." Her face took on a sad, faraway look. "She and I were very close when we were younger."

"You lived with them for a time?"

Christiana nodded. "After my parents and brother died, my uncle sent me to Montevaro so I would have parents while growing up. He didn't believe he could give me what I needed while still running the country on my behalf."

Jonathan did his best to keep his reaction under control. It seemed odd to him. A regent sending away his charge? Even to a friendly, sister country? Maybe it was perfectly normal. What did he know about ruling a country with such a young queen?

The song came to an end and Jonathan took a step back. "It has been my pleasure, Your Majesty. I hope to see you again before I return to the States after Adeline's coronation."

She gave a regal nod. "It would be my pleasure."

Alexander stepped in and thanked Jonathan for attending. Jonathan turned to find Rick smiling at, but backing away from, Ellie.

Jonathan moved to her side.

She didn't look up at him. "Can we go now?" Her voice sounded tired. Weary.

"Of course." He rested his hand on the middle of her back and guided her toward the door. It didn't take long to get to the plane and board. The pilots ran through their pre-flight checks while Ellie sat in one of the plush chairs and leaned her head back.

The lights remained dim and her eyes were closed but he thought he might have seen a tear sneak down her cheek.

"Are you okay?"

She shifted in her seat. "I'm tired."

"Hard seeing Rick with another woman even if you know there's nothing between them?"

"I don't know if that's the case. How could I?"

"The queen told me she has a boyfriend." She didn't look at him. "Besides, I happen to know the prince is quite smitten with a certain American about to be his cousin-in-law of sorts."

She didn't answer him and seemed to be asleep by the time the pilots were ready for take-off. Ellie slept the whole way back to Montevaro.

Christiana walked through the garden toward her cottage on the palace grounds. Footsteps pounded behind her, but she wasn't worried. No one made it onto the property without being properly vetted.

"Queen Christiana." Alexander puffed to a stop next to her. Odd. He was in such good shape. Being out of breath didn't seem to be the norm.

"Yes?"

"Security asked me to make sure you made it to your cottage safely."

She glanced at him but kept walking. Her feet were killing her despite the lack of heels. "Why would I not?"

"No reason. Just making sure."

"Your behavior has been very odd this evening, Alexander."

His voice was the picture of studied nonchalance. "It has?"

"Yes. It seemed to be at your urging that I offended half the people at the fundraiser, perhaps more."

"And how did you do that?"

"How many men do I normally dance with at such a function?"

He shrugged. "I have no idea."

"Maybe because you have never been to one before." The barb at his status was meant to sting a bit.

Instead of letting it get to him, he chuckled. "I haven't been to a Ravenzarian royal ball, but I've been to plenty of fancy shindigs."

"I rarely dance with the same man twice. Usually whoever escort's me gets the first and last dance. Tonight, I danced with Richard, you, that Jonathan fellow, and your brother. Who made that decision? I saw several other men, including members of Parliament, turned away."

She glanced his way in time to see a careless shrug. "I don't make security decisions. You know that. Your head of security barely trusts me."

Christiana knew that wasn't true. For some reason, Alexander had quickly wormed his way into her inner circle. She'd known him through his family for several years but suddenly he was everywhere.

They arrived at the rock cottage on the perimeter of the property. One wall of the building was also the exterior wall surrounding the grounds. The building held secrets only Christiana knew and it was her haven. A space where she could be truly alone instead of followed and hounded by people like she was the moment she stepped out of her little home.

"Good night, Alexander. Thank you for walking me back to my place." Really, she was ready for that privacy. To see if she had a new message from...No. She wouldn't even let herself think his name for fear someone would find out. Not until things were more defined.

Alexander said something, probably "good night" back, but Christiana ignored it, choosing instead to block the world out when the door closed behind her.

Something Rick said stuck in the back of her mind as she got ready for bed.

"I would have rather seen you last week instead of your uncle. Father wanted me to conduct business with the monarch, not the former regent."

"Uncle Henry still helps me, a lot. I have not been to university like Adeline or William have. I had to come home as soon as I turned eighteen and begin ruling myself. Your parents did a wonderful job trying to prepare me, but I'm not ready to run everything, so Uncle Henry helps."

Rick's eyes were compassionate when he spoke. "I understand that, truly. But don't you think dealing with Montevaro or Mevendia would be on the 'easy' list of things to do?"

Christiana had not replied. The truth was she hadn't known Rick would be in Ravenzario, much less be meeting with her uncle on matters of state.

And that bothered her.

The ding from her laptop brightened her mood and she quickly forgot to be puzzled about Rick and her uncle and Montevaro. She was falling in love and couldn't wait until she could tell the world.

"Happy late Fourth of July!"

Ellie looked up to see Jonathan trotting down the steps at the back of the March, a watermelon tucked between his arm and his waist like a football. With the ceremonies for her cousin, aunt, and uncle actually *on* July 4, they'd decided to get together a couple weeks later. "You didn't say you were coming today."

He stopped next to her and set the melon on the table. "I found the invitation after I got home last night. Couldn't pass it up. Are we playing baseball?"

Ellie shook her head as she arranged the hot dog buns. "I don't know that we have enough Americans for a baseball game, but maybe? I can't play anyway."

Jonathan lifted the arm with the cast on it. "You could use this as your bat. That could work."

"No."

"How many Americans are around here, anyway?"

Ellie picked up the watermelon and started up the stairs. She couldn't cut it up one-handed but maybe Wilma would help her. "Charlie, Lindsey, Charlie's parents, you, me. My parents are back home for a few days, so that's pretty much it."

"Six is enough for three-on-three basketball." Jonathan held the door open for her when they reached the top of the stairs.

"Good luck with that. Maybe you and Charlie can play some one-on-one."

Addie wouldn't be there. Ellie would miss her. She'd grown to like her cousin's fiancé, but her mind kept turning back to the night before. She'd done a line dance with a for-real prince. Talked with a queen, only for a minute, but how many people who grew up in Serenity Landing could say they'd had real conversations with not one but *two* monarchs?

And that she was considering dumping a prince for someone else?

Sure, she and Rick weren't in a real relationship, but he'd made it clear he was interested in something more. Sitting out the first dance at the Montevarian ball, making sure she wasn't left alone, and the "dance" out on the terrace...all of that meant something.

Unless she was very much mistaken, though, Jonathan - the American equivalent of royalty - could be interested in a relationship with her as well. He hadn't said anything, but he wouldn't be hanging out with her so much if he wasn't. Would he?

She didn't listen to Jonathan talking baseball while they made their way to the kitchen. There had to be a shorter way to get there than upstairs to the back entry then downstairs to the kitchen. Ellie didn't know what it was yet.

Wilma put the last of the hamburgers on a tray before washing her hands. "Watermelon? I haven't had that in years!" She put her hands on Jonathan's cheeks. "Aren't you sweet for bringing it? I wish I could carve this into something incredible. Have you *seen* the pictures on Pinterest?"

Jonathan laughed and kissed her cheek. "Let me help. I can't do much more than wedges, but they'll taste the same as something fancier."

"Good point, young man."

Ellie planted herself on a barstool. "Whose idea was the barbecue?"

Jonathan popped a grape in his mouth. "Your aunt's I think. Doesn't matter, though. It was a great idea."

Ellie agreed and watched as the other two worked together to cut the watermelon into manageable chunks, stealing grapes and small bites of watermelon as they did.

The afternoon went by quickly as Charlie and his dad grilled burgers, hot dogs, and bratwurst. Everyone sat at the gigantic, and likely very expensive, picnic table. It had come with the house, though Ellie was pretty sure it had been in storage and used to replace whatever had been there before. Laughter filled the gardens as they decided to forgo the baseball game and played games everyone could participate in. After the final round of charades, Ellie took the advice of her aunt and went to her room to rest for a while. She had mostly healed from the accident three weeks earlier, but she still found herself wearing out more quickly sometimes. An afternoon in the sun had drained her.

When she came back downstairs, Ellie found Jonathan and Charlie grilling steaks for dinner.

Charlie grinned at her. "About time you woke up, kiddo."

Ellie glared at him as she took a seat. "Don't call me that."

"Whatever." He turned back to the grill. "Feeling better?"

There was the Charlie she knew. Concerned about others.

"Much, thank you." Ellie opened a bottle of water and took a sip. The only thing this day was missing was Rick and Addie.

After darkness fell, Ellie sat on a blanket with Jonathan. Lindsey sat with them for a few minutes but didn't sit still long. Instead, the preteen spent her time bouncing between the blankets spread out on the lawn until the fireworks started.

"What are you doing not next week but the week after?"

Ellie turned to see Jonathan looking back at her. He leaned back on his elbows with his legs stretched out in front of him. "Nothing in particular," she told him. "Just hanging out and working on the proposal." She and Jonathan hadn't gone on that horseback tour yet. Until they did, she had to rely on Internet research.

"I'm headed back to the States for a few days. It's not for about a week and a half though. You wanna come?"

Ellie turned that idea over in her mind. "Sure. Why not?" It wasn't like she had anything keeping her in Montevaro at the moment. She usually went home a couple of times during the summer for parties or weddings but so far this year, she'd only been back for Easter and Dan's wedding. In fact... she pulled out her phone and checked Facebook. Yep. A friend from high school was getting married in two weeks. She'd already said she wouldn't be going, but Ellie sent a quick message to see if it would be okay for her to change her answer. Two minutes later, she had an enthusiastic *yes* in response - and an admonition to bring a date, too.

She tapped out a reply and didn't look at Jonathan as she asked her question. "Want to go to a wedding with me while we're there?" She explained the note she'd just gotten as she leaned back to watch the fireworks as they continued to light the night sky.

"Sure. I'll have to double check my schedule. I know my family has a few things going on, but I think it's okay." He leaned her direction. "If you wouldn't mind to return the favor a couple times, I'd appreciate it. My mom is trying to set me up with some debutante."

Ellie turned that over in her mind. "I'd be happy to, but, um..." How to put it without seeming cheap? "Depending on what kind of events we're talking about, I'm not sure I have enough nice clothes without wearing the same dress over and over."

"No problem. I have a sister about your size who will be there next week. She'll bring extras or take you shopping for something you can both use."

Would a Southern debutante really want to share clothes? She had no idea but she pasted on a smile and said, "Sounds great then." The only thing that would make it better was Rick instead of Jonathan, but Ellie couldn't do anything about that. Instead of dwelling on the prince whose business called him far away, she focused on the fireworks in the sky above her and sighed. Going home for a visit sounded like just the thing she needed.

A few days later, a breeze ruffled Ellie's hair as the horse in front of her shook his head. The big horse. The one bigger than any she'd been close to in her whole life. Not that she'd been close to many despite a few friends with farms growing up.

"You've never ridden a horse?" Jonathan just stared at her as she crossed her good arm over her cast.

"Not in a really long time. Is that bad?"

"It means today could be rough on you, especially tonight, but if you really want to see the trails this is the way to do it." He led the horse a step closer to her. "The stable manager says this is the gentlest horse they have, but that she's plenty strong enough to do what we want to do today."

This big ol' horse was a she? Ellie shook her head. So much for her preconceptions about female horses being smaller.

The trail head called to her. The hike would be too hard. Her ankle was only at about 75%. Not well enough to do this the way she'd want, especially not with her arm still in a cast.

"Fine. Let's go."

Jonathan stood next to the horse and cupped his hands together. "I'll give you a boost."

She put her boot in his hands, bounced as he counted to three, and pushed off the ground. With her weight on her good hand, she swung her leg over and found herself, for the first time, astride a horse.

So tall. So high up. She could see everything.

Jonathan showed her how to hold the reins and told her he'd be right there to help her. A minute later, she was watching his back as they started down the trail. The shifting, rocking feel of sitting on top of the large animal would take some getting used to, and she would be sore. Not all of her aunt and uncle's home had been renovated and updated but her suite had been. The large clawfoot tub would surely be calling her name by the time they returned.

The woods were peaceful, broken only by the sounds of the wind rustling through the trees and the horses hooves against the mostly dirt path. They rode along for a while before they came to a clearing.

Jonathan moved his horse off the path and came to a stop. "Just pull back against the reins," he told her as she came up beside him. Her horse stopped and shook her head just a bit. Ellie's insides churned but she didn't freak out.

"Look." She followed Jonathan's finger.

"The heavens declare the glory of God; the skies proclaim the work of his hands," she whispered.

"What's that?"

Ellie gave a small shake of her head. "When we stopped for the first night on the trip with Rick and his bodyguards, he went and stood at the outlook, raised his hands in the air and shouted that verse. He told me later he does it everywhere he goes."

Jonathan chuckled. "That doesn't surprise me."

"It's beautiful up here. I guess I can see why he does. It's true."

Jonathan seemed contemplative. "I came here with Addie once," he finally said.

"With Charlie?"

"No. It was right after she came back, and she and Charlie were convinced they had no future. I liked her even before I knew who she was and the queen kept pushing us toward each other. We agreed to start courting, she called it, even though I knew she loved your cousin." He nodded toward a tree. "I kissed her right over there. That's when I knew she'd never love me like she did Charlie, and I probably wouldn't ever love her that way either. We still dated a bit longer, both to keep her mom off her back and because if she couldn't have Charlie, she wanted to marry a friend."

"Would you have? If she and Charlie hadn't ended up together? Would you have married her knowing she loved Charlie, even if they could never be together?"

He thought that over for a long minute. "I don't know. Marry a woman I know loves someone else? I guess under the right circumstances, maybe? If I prayed about it and felt God telling me it's what I was supposed to do, but it wouldn't be an easy decision to make. Even if I loved her." He picked up the reins and clicked to his horse. "Let's keep going."

Chapter Fifteen

*J*onathan decided horseback riding would be too much for
Ellie as he planned the second day of exploring a few days
later. With the help of the butler at Lydia House, where he
was staying, he arranged a helicopter ride over much of the area
where she thought Rick would be interested in using for his
program.

The headsets helped with the discussion as he pointed out
things of interest. He'd learned a lot about the little country in
his time there. Unless he had been working with Addie on a
school project during the semester, he hadn't had much to
occupy his time. He'd done some business for his family in
Montevaro, worked on a wine deal with Mevendia, and visited
with and made an agreement with the Bayfield family in
Ravenzario. He'd tried to get a meeting with Queen Christiana,
but had been told she wasn't taking appointments and her uncle
refused to see him. He should have mentioned it to her at the
fundraiser, but it slipped his mind.

They stopped for lunch in a little town not too far from the
Mevendian border. Jonathan waited until they were done with

the meal to broach the subject of Richard.

"Would you like to go for a walk?" he asked as he held her chair. "Until the food settles a bit?"

"That sounds nice."

Jonathan didn't hurry her along but strolled along the quaint streets of the town. She stopped and looked in several shop windows but didn't go in.

"Have you heard from Richard?" he finally asked.

He could see her shake her head in the reflection. "Not really. I get a quick 'What's up?' type text once a couple of days, but no reply to my response."

"Did you ever define your relationship?"

Ellie snorted, making Jonathan grin. He liked it when a woman wasn't so intimidated by who he was that she couldn't be herself.

"I'll take that as a no?"

"No. He said we might talk after he gets back from his trip, whenever that is."

"I see." But he didn't. Not really. How could Rick let a girl like Ellie go? Why wouldn't he make sure she knew where she stood?

In two and a half weeks, Jonathan knew what an amazing person she was, and they hadn't lived through a major trauma together.

The rest of the day and the next passed without returning to the questions of love or marriage to anyone, but Jonathan made sure Ellie saw what she needed to of the countryside. Together, they poured over maps of the area with Ellie asking questions of him. He couldn't answer many of them, so he helped her find people who could.

And they worked to put together her plan. To find the trails, a building, a good location for the trail head. Calling for the best prices on equipment, both new and used. For the next week, until they left for Serenity Landing, every spare moment they put their time into making the plan the best they could.

Now if only Rick would appreciate it and let her help implement it, Jonathan knew Ellie would be ecstatic.

And if the prince would finally realize what he had in the woman, Jonathan could go back to knowing she was taken - and off-limits.

"Why are you here?"

Richard kept himself from raising an eyebrow, instead focusing on making himself look completely comfortable in his seat outside of Christiana's office. He shifted a bit and paid more attention to tweaking the lie of his suit coat than he did to Henry. "I was invited."

He didn't look up but could almost feel the man's eyes narrow. "By whom?"

Now he did, looking Henry straight in the eye. "The queen."

Henry didn't look pleased but changed the topic. "I presume you're leaving this evening?"

Now Richard grinned. "Nope. Christiana asked me to stay and attend a breakfast function with her. She offered me a room here in the palace." That was sure to bother the controlling man.

If he didn't know better, Richard would have thought that Henry's eye started to twitch. Why was he so opposed to someone staying at the palace? Was there still a threat to the queen?

But the way Alexander talked at the fundraiser, Henry didn't know about the threat - or at least hadn't been ruled out as a suspect. Richard decided it would be best not to say anything.

"That still doesn't answer the question of why are you *here?*" Henry crossed his arms and glared down at Richard. "In my office."

This time Richard knew he looked incredulous and didn't care. "Your office? I was under the impression it belonged to the monarch."

"It did. But when Christiana was young and I took over as regent, it became my office. When Christiana came of age, I kept it and she took another one. There are plenty to go around."

Which still didn't explain why Richard had been brought here by the staff when he asked to be shown to the monarch's office. Henry picked up the handset of the phone on the desk of the absent secretary. He spoke to whoever answered and barked instructions for someone to come get Rick and take him to the visitors' area.

Rick. Not Richard. As before, he normally preferred to be called Rick, but he'd certainly never given Henry reason to believe he could be so familiar. He almost wanted to call Christiana "Christy" just to see how the man reacted. Henry placed the phone back on the hook and crossed his arms, staring until the head of security arrived.

"Your Highness, my apologies for someone bringing you here instead of to the queen's offices." There was a noticeable lack of remorse in the man's tone.

"I don't believe we've ever met." Rick wanted to start a conversation with the man. See if Alexander's name came up.

"No, sir. We never have. Come with me." His tone didn't encourage any questions. Maybe when they got where they were going.

Tony didn't take him to the public waiting area but instead to a conference room in the security office.

Tony motioned to a chair. "Please have a seat, sir."

Richard took one of the chairs near one end. "What can I do for you?"

"This room is safe to talk in. I cannot guarantee anywhere

else is."

"Safe from whom?" Richard knew his father had Tony checked out thoroughly and had kept an eye on him for many years. But could he be sure he could trust this man - or if this man was part of the problem Alexander had told him about? Alexander *had* told him the head of security was trustworthy.

"I'm not at liberty to say, sir." Tony's shoulders slumped. "Alexander Bayfield speaks highly of you. I know you were told the queen was in danger at the fundraiser. We were able to prevent an attack that night. The suspects were caught and didn't realize the queen was the target. For all their other faults, they are not traitors to the crown."

"Small comfort."

"True, but they're talking. They don't want to add treason to their other crimes."

The whole thing piqued Rick's curiosity. "Who was behind it?"

"There are only a few of us I trust implicitly, including Alexander. We have our suspicions about who is the mastermind, but I need help from your father and the intelligence services of Montevaro. I don't know who I can trust here."

"Of course."

"I also don't trust the communications here, not even the supposedly secure communications. Will you take a communique back to him when you leave tomorrow? It must go only to your father or Princess Adeline."

"Of course."

"Meet me back here before you leave? And if you find you are unable to..." Tony reconsidered. "I will make sure it's on your plane before you leave. Is there someplace where it would be hidden from the crew?"

Rick thought for a moment. "I have an attaché case in the

plane's bedroom. It's brown and beat up. It's sentimental and no one ever touches it. It should be safe there."

"And a back-up location?"

He had to think for another moment before remembering a hidden nook. After a few more minutes of conversation, Tony led him to a small sitting room where Christiana perched on the edge of a chair.

Rick noticed Tony let him walk in alone. "Good evening, Your Majesty."

She stood and smiled. "Hello, Rick. How has your trip been?"

He kissed her cheek. "Long. Here. Mevendia. Other parts of Europe. I even hopped over to Asia for a while. And I'm going back there next, I believe."

"How long before you return to Montevaro?"

"I may make a quick stop tomorrow, but only for a very short time." He needed to figure out how to get that paperwork to his father as quickly as possible. "But otherwise I believe I have another week or week and a half." He shrugged. "They keep changing my schedule. It was only supposed to be two or three weeks when I left."

"I would imagine that is how it usually goes." She shrugged. "Uncle Henry goes on most of the overseas trips for me. I will be at Adeline's wedding, but likely not the coronation. I believe I have a scheduling conflict I cannot change."

Was there more to it? "Addie will be disappointed, but she will understand. Montevaro is not your country, and I don't think anyone expects you to be there." After the conversations he had had recently, Richard was not even sure she would be allowed to attend the wedding.

"Still, I would like to be. She is really the first of our generation in our three countries to have a coronation."

Richard didn't know what to say to that. Christiana had become queen when her parents died. She was five. To Richard's knowledge, she'd never had an official coronation, but then he'd only been six. Should she have had one when she turned eighteen? Something to ask his father about.

A man Rick didn't recognize entered the room and nodded to them. Christiana tugged on the hem of the jacket she wore. He noted that she looked like a young professional, wearing a woman's suit with a straight skirt that came to her knee, but there was something else he couldn't quite put his finger on. He'd have to ask Ana or Addie to pay her a visit.

Maybe one of his sisters could help the monarch who didn't seem to quite fit in her own skin.

Or her own palace.

The dinner was interminably long. They always were. Christiana plastered a smile on her face and pretended to be interested in the guest the dinner honored. She could not remember his name or why he was being honored. Her uncle had set it all up.

She managed to do more than just pick at her food, but barely. Years of living in Montevaro with Queen Alexandra meant she had learned to eat what was put in front of her, especially in public. As soon as the dinner was over, she'd retreat to her cottage and then he'd call. A small, very real, smile threatened to cross her face. She loved their late night conversations and stolen moments when he came to the palace on business.

And he had not even kissed her yet.

"I want to kiss you the first time at our wedding."

Christiana swallowed hard as his finger trailed down the side of her face, across her shoulder, and to her hand, lacing his fingers with hers. "Wedding?" she whispered, searching his dark eyes.

"I'm falling hard for you, Chris. I thought you knew that."

At his wounded look, she rushed to reassure him. "I know and I am falling hard for you." She lowered her gaze, unable to meet his eyes any longer. "I just wish we could spend more time together."

"I do, too, but you know how much I value my privacy. As soon as people find out about us, I'll never have any privacy again. Even if things didn't work out for some reason. Remember the British press and 'Waitie Katie'?"

She nodded, hating it, but knowing he was right.

He took a step back. "If you can't understand that, then I don't think there's any point in us seeing each other anymore."

"No!" Christiana reached for him, to bring him closer. "I understand. I really do. I-I-I love you."

He smiled down at her, pulling her into his arms. "I know you do, Chris. And I can't tell you how glad I am. I want to marry you someday. Soon."

She relaxed into him, wrapping her arms around his waist. "I hope that, too."

"We'll be engaged by this time next year, Chris. And we'll be married before Christmas."

Christiana looked back up at him, wishing he'd kiss her anyway. "That long?"

"Yes. We can't let anyone think that our relationship is the reason why my business is doing well. By this time next year, I'll have everything set up so we can be together."

Two days earlier, Christiana had not liked the idea of waiting and she still did not. She picked at the threads fraying on the sleeve of her suit jacket. Not very noticeable. Yet. Soon, she'd need to ask her uncle to have someone go shopping for her. He hated it when she spent money, but Christiana was certain she wasn't supposed to wear clothes that were starting to wear out. In hard economic times or times of war maybe, but this was neither.

"Everything all right?" Rick had leaned toward her, talking out of the side of his mouth so as not to draw attention to them.

She nodded. "I am fine." She did not want anyone to know more about her mystery man just yet. She also did not want anyone to know just how...not in control she sometimes felt. Queen of her country through a twist of fate killing her younger brother in the same accident that killed her parents, but so little control of anything in her life. From buying her own clothes at will or deciding policies for her country, she often felt like little more than a figurehead. Some monarchies worked that way - Queen Elizabeth had political clout but no political power - but not in Ravenzario. Her uncle still did much of the work for her until she felt better prepared. Perhaps when she turned twenty-five. He still sheltered her so much.

The dinner eventually ended without Christiana saying a single word to those gathered. Her uncle gave a speech, saying he spoke for her as well. As the crowd dispersed, Uncle Henry gave her a look. One she had come to know well. He wanted to talk.

And he wasn't happy.

Two hours later, Christiana sat in the chair in front of the desk in her uncle's office. She still wore the suit she'd worn to the dinner. Perched on the edge of the seat, she wondered what exactly she'd done wrong this time. Probably a host of things. No matter how hard she tried, or how she followed Queen Alexandra's guidelines, Uncle Henry found something lacking.

In many ways, it was almost humorous. Once he'd told her she had eaten too much of her meal. That she should have left at least a quarter of it sitting on the plate. To show she enjoyed it, but that she was not a pig. His words. The next time she did as he said but he berated her for not finishing and offending the hostess in the process.

For several years, she'd struggled with trying to be a bit more perfect, to try to meet his exacting standards for her as queen, but after the second comment, she'd decided to just do her best and not worry too much about his nit-picky remarks. Easier said than done.

But the fury on his face when he entered and moved behind the desk told her a different story this time.

"What were you thinking?" he bellowed.

She raised an eyebrow his direction, doing everything she could to maintain her posture and not cower in fear. "Pardon?"

"You invited a member of another royal family to stay at the palace. Do you know how taboo that is? Why do you think it's never happened before?"

"Princess Adeline used to stay with me from time to time."

"Long before she was old enough to have any influence on matters of state. Rick was here just recently on official business. It's not appropriate for him to stay here." Uncle Henry pushed back from the desk. "Will you tell him he needs to go somewhere else or will I?"

Christiana sucked a deep breath in and stood. "Neither. Prince Richard is my guest, and he is welcome to stay at the palace if I say so. I will tell Tony any order you give to have Rick removed is remanded by me."

Henry leaned forward and looked her in the eye, anger seething from his every pore. "I'll fire him."

Christiana shook her head as she stood. "The head of security cannot be fired by the regent. Only by the regent with the approval of both the prime minister and the monarch, if he or she is over sixteen, or the leader of the minority party if not." She felt her blood run cold. "And you are no longer the regent. Rick, and his entire family, have a place to stay with me whenever they'd like it. I am not pleased I was not informed of his last official visit, and I would like to see the notes from the meeting."

Henry's voice was low and controlled. "There were no notes. It was brief. He left. He needs to leave now."

"No."

He walked around the desk until he stood directly in front of her and Christiana had to look up to see him. "Do not challenge me, little girl. You will not win."

Her stomach quivered, but she had to do it. "Do not challenge *me*, Uncle Henry. *I* am the queen of Ravenzario. If you challenge me on this, I *will* see to it you are removed from the palace and banished from the country." She held his gaze for long seconds then turned, walking out of the office on her own terms.

But before she could leave all together, she heard him call after her.

"Just try me."

Shivers of fear shot through her as her gut clenched. Before tonight, if asked, she would have said she never thought he would try something.

Now she was not so sure.

Chapter Sixteen

Rick flopped onto the ornate bed in one of the rooms in the Ravenzarian palace. He turned his phone into a hot spot rather than using the palace's WiFi. After pulling up his secure connection to his sister, he began an online chat with her. Not completely guaranteed to be secure but as close as he could get.

Something weird is going on here, he typed. *It wouldn't surprise me to discover the palace is bugged.*

Addie's reply took longer than usual, a consequence of the secure connection. *So that is why you wanted an instant message conversation. Papa will be here in a minute.*

How's he doing?

He could almost hear Addie sigh. *Better than he was, but still not fully himself. I would recommend calling me after we are done and we can have an innocuous conversation. It might look odd if you do not check in.*

Rick confirmed that he would and they waited for his father to arrive in his office where Addie waited. His conversation with Tony replayed in his mind. What should he tell his father and Addie about it before he left Ravenzario? Better to make some arrangements this evening.

Father is here with me now, Addie told him.

I will be stopping in Montevaro tomorrow morning, just long enough to meet with one or both of you at the airport. Both would be better. I can't go into details even here.

The response was delayed longer than he would have expected, but eventually it came through. *At least one of us will be there. Let us know what time you will arrive.*

They talked for a few more minutes about the next stop on his trip. After they disconnected, he picked up his cell phone and called her, talking for a few minutes about not much of anything.

Once done, he kept his phone out and texted Ellie.

JUST CHECKING IN. I KNOW IT'S LATE, BUT IF YOU'RE UP, LET ME KNOW. I WANT TO HEAR FROM YOU AND I'LL BE UP FOR A BIT YET.

He didn't really expect a response. It was nearly midnight, after all. After waiting a few minutes and not getting one, Rick headed into the bathroom and took a hot shower. The water flowed over him as he continued to turn the events of the evening over and over in his mind. When he reached no conclusions of any kind, he turned off the water and finished getting ready for bed. He found a text from Ellie waiting for him, but it just said that she was going to sleep and would talk to him soon.

Knowing he would be unable to sleep for a while yet, Rick went to the window and looked over the moonlit Mediterranean Sea. Answers wouldn't come like this, he knew that, but he took the time to approach the only throne that truly counted. He didn't kneel or even close his eyes, but his heart whispered prayers for Christiana and her safety, for Ellie's continued healing and for a way to show her she really could trust him, for Charlie and Lindsey as they adjusted to life in the spotlight, for wisdom and strength for both his father and Addie with the changes coming their way soon.

As he decided it was time to draw the curtains, he saw movement in the gardens below. A figure stood in the center and made his or her way toward the outer wall. When the shadow moved beneath a lamppost, he realized it was Christiana and he frowned. What was she doing out so late at night, even on palace grounds? She reached a building attached to the outer wall and opened a door, light spilling out before it closed. That's when it hit him. The cottage she had stayed in when she returned home as a child. The one that scared her. She still lived there and not in the palace itself? It seemed odd to him and he made a mental note to discuss it with Addie. Maybe Christiana had chosen to remain in the only childhood home she'd ever really known in Ravenzario.

Or maybe the hair on the back of his neck stood on end for other reasons all together. The puzzle pieces continued to pile up. He hoped they would be able to assemble them into something that made sense before it was too late.

The next morning, Richard never left the Montevarian airport.

He managed to deplane, but only to a secure meeting room in the terminal.

"What was so important you made me come all the way over here?" Addie wasn't really mad, and he knew it. She turned her face slightly and he kissed her cheek in greeting.

"Christiana."

Concern immediately crossed her face. "You said things were odd last time you were there and hinted at it last night. Father has not been able to talk with her to discuss the changes in travel policies."

"I was able to talk with her somewhat, but not about that. Turns out she didn't even know I'd been in town." He sat in one of the uncomfortable airport chairs.

Addie sat in the next one. "That is odd."

He held out a beat up manila envelope with the words

"Information on MMR vaccine."

"Vaccine?" She started to open it, but he stopped her.

"Wait until you're with Father. I believe the MMR actually stands for the three countries. It was left on the plane by Tony, Christiana's head of security. Something big is going on, but he said everything pretty much is taped or recorded so he needs Father's help to protect Christiana."

She frowned. "I do not understand. Who is threatening her?"

He shrugged. "I have no idea. I only know that Alexander Bayfield is one of the few people Tony trusts."

"Alexander?"

"You know him?"

Addie shrugged. "We have met, but not much more than that." She tapped the envelope against her hand. "Very well. Father and I will do whatever we can to help her."

Richard stood. "I know. So does Tony. That's why he asked. I don't think Christiana has any clue though."

Addie started for the door then turned. "Are you not going to stay long enough to say hello to Ellie even?"

He shook his head. "No. I'm kind of hoping she doesn't know I stopped. I didn't really have time. I'm on my way..." He sighed. "Somewhere. Asia again I think. I'll be home for good soon, though. I'll call her later."

"She will not be happy when she finds out." Addie used her disapproving older sister voice. "I cannot believe you. If I was in town only for a few minutes, Charlie would be here waiting for me, and I would not leave until I had seen him."

Richard sighed. "I do not know what to tell you. But I have to go." He gave her another quick kiss on the cheek and walked quickly back to the plane.

Back to work.

"He was here?" Ellie stared at Addie. "And he didn't tell me?"

Guilt covered Addie's face. "I was not supposed to tell you he had been here. I am sorry I let it slip."

"Why didn't he tell me himself?"

"He was on the ground less than thirty minutes. There was some very sensitive information that needed to be hand delivered to me or my father. No one else. He handed it over and left."

"I see."

A phone call came in that Addie had to take. She shot Ellie an apologetic look, but Ellie waved her off and left the office.

Most of the palace was off-limits, but many of the hallways were not. She wandered through them, eventually finding herself in front of the Hall of Kings. Rick still hadn't told her the whole history of how Montevaro, Mevendia, and Ravenzario came to be sister countries. Would he ever or would there always be something, or someone, more important? Would her life, if they worked things out, always be controlled by something or someone from the outside? Would she ever be in charge of her own destiny?

Her relationship with Glenn, which started on a hike just like the one where she'd met Rick, had been one where he tried to control her every movement, tried to tell her who she could spend time with when they weren't together. She didn't want to live through that again.

All of these thoughts and more churned in her mind as she turned away.

After a friendly dinner the evening before, Jonathan walked her to the door and, for a second, looked like he wanted to kiss her. Instead, he'd settled for a brush of his lips to her forehead. Her dreams that night had been troubled with Jonathan and Rick fighting for top billing in her life.

In the end, though, she didn't see a future with Jonathan.

Not right now. Maybe someday if things didn't work out with Rick, and she had serious doubts they would. One more day and her cast would be off. Three and she'd be back in Serenity Landing and all of this would be a distant memory for a short time.

Three nights later, Jonathan drove down I-44 toward the Serenity Landing exit. "Where can I drop you off?"

Ellie didn't know how to answer that. She didn't have a room at her parents' house anymore. Something she hadn't considered when she accepted Jonathan's offer to visit. Once she moved, her parents had sold the house and moved into a one bedroom cabin on the lake. She'd stayed with Dan, Charlie, and Lindsey for the last couple of years, but Charlie and Lindsey lived in Montevaro now. Dan and CeCe were newlyweds and, while they would let her crash on their couch, she didn't want to ask.

She thought quickly and decided on the only place she could think of on such short notice. "The hotel between the library and the train tracks on Highway 174."

Jonathan glanced over at her. "A hotel? Not with your parents or your brother?"

She shook her head though she didn't elaborate. If she'd had to pay for the flight, she would have called Dan anyway, but since it turned out Jonathan was taking a private plane, she could swing a hotel for a couple of days.

"Tell you what, why don't you stay with me?"

Ellie looked at him, sure her eyes were wide with shock. "What?"

He chuckled. "Not like that. It's a huge house with a bunch of bedrooms. My sister will be here tomorrow morning to stay for a week or so. All totally above board." He held up three fingers. "Scout's honor."

She grinned at him. "Sounds good then. Thanks."

The rest of the drive to Jonathan's house passed in relative silence. They pulled up to a wrought iron gate where Jonathan punched in a code before it swung open. The house was shrouded in darkness as they pulled up the short driveway.

"It's just the two of us tonight," he explained. "The house has been closed since I left for Montevaro in the spring. It's ridiculously large for just me, but my mother insisted my father buy it when I decided to go to Serenity Landing University."

Crazy. Her entire, nearly unused, college fund might put half a down payment on half of the three-car garage. He pulled through the circular drive and parked in front of the main entrance. As much as Ellie wanted to explore the house, she needed sleep even more. As they started up the stairs, Jonathan pointed out the hallway that led to his room. A minute later, he flipped the light on in one of the upstairs bedrooms.

"And here's your home away from home for however long we're here." He pulled out his phone. "I'll text you some info you might need, like the wifi password. Do you have any plans tomorrow?"

Ellie shook her head. "Nope. I have nothing specific until the wedding this weekend. I'll probably make some lunch or dinner plans, depending on when you have stuff going on and you want me to go with you."

"I'll text you that information too." He grinned and moved out of her way. "Sleep well. I'll see you tomorrow. Sleep as late as you want, but I'll probably be gone by eight or so. I have a meeting my dad set up for me."

She said good night and shut the door behind her. In ten minutes, she was in bed and sound asleep.

Rick walked through the halls of the palace, wishing for the solitude of his private quarters. When he finally reached the family portion, he tugged his tie off and allowed his shoulders to slump. Three days before he needed to leave again. A national emergency had caused the king of the Sovereign Commonwealth of Athmetis to postpone their meeting. The royal family was related to his family, over a thousand years in the past, but it had never been a part of the Royal Commonwealth of Bellas Montagnes.

He walked into the apartment he sometimes shared with his twin sister and found her rinsing a cup out in the sink.

"Rick!" The excitement in her voice made him smile. "What are you doing here?"

"One of the towns in Athmetis had a major fire."

Ana frowned. "I have not heard anything about that. What does it have to do with you?"

"The king postponed our meeting until next month. The other vendors I was to meet with did the same. It's becoming something of a national tragedy. A number of the members of Parliament were there for a fundraiser. The last report I heard they knew of a few dead, a few hospitalized, and an unknown number still missing. They're wondering if it was an assassination attempt."

"And none of that was on the news."

"It wouldn't be. It's still the very early stages." In fact, his plane had changed directions over the Med when the word came in. "I'm just glad for the break so I can spend some time with Ellie."

Ana's silence surprised him. He would have thought she would be excited he could spend time with her new friend and their future brother-in-law's cousin. "What?" he finally asked.

"Ellie is not here."

"I didn't think she was. She's at the March isn't she?"

His sister turned back to the sink. "No. She went with Jonathan to the States for a week or so."

Rick's stomach dropped. With Jonathan? Because she wanted to spend time with the man, or because Rick hadn't been around, and she wanted to spend some time at home? He worked hard to keep his voice under control. "What are they doing in Serenity Landing?"

Ana shrugged. "Ellie mentioned a wedding and some event Jonathan asked her to go to. I don't have any more details than that. Danica might."

Right. Ellie's assistant when she stayed at the palace. "Or Charlie." Surely her cousin would know. Rick pulled his phone out and called his soon-to-be brother-in-law. Charlie had been invited to the same wedding and gave him the details, assuring him it wouldn't be an issue for him to just show up without an invitation. After hanging up the phone, Rick made a snap decision. He made one phone call to his assistant and in an hour he was back in the air, this time planning to sleep on his way to the States.

But turbulence over the Atlantic meant he didn't sleep as much as he'd wanted to. Instead of contacting Ellie once he was sure she would be up, he'd crashed, hard, until nearly noon. He tried her cell phone but there was no answer, and he decided not to leave a message.

Picking out a tie was the most difficult part of deciding what to wear. He'd only brought one suit with him for such a short trip. He likely wouldn't have brought that many if it hadn't been for the wedding.

He picked his tablet up off the bed and set a timer to let him know when he would need to get ready to leave. In the meantime, he needed to get some work done.

"Are you sure I don't need to wear a tux?" Jonathan asked as

Ellie entered the foyer.

She rolled her eyes as she put a small pack of Kleenex in her bag. "You'll probably be the only one in a suit. We're not that fancy around here." She spun as she reached the center. "This is as fancy as I get."

He took in her black skirt, fitted through her hips and flaring to the knees with a flowing maroon top. Lightweight, but still with long sleeves, like she'd worn for the last several days to cover the lack-of-cast on her arm. But maybe he was overdressed. "I've lived here for a while now, and I've never not worn at least a suit to a wedding. Usually I wear a tux."

Ellie laughed. "Yeah, well your friends are probably a little fancier than most of mine. I doubt even the groom will be wearing a tux."

Jonathan shook his head and met her near the door. "Should I change?"

"Nah. I think you'll be fine. It's not like it's in a barn." She winked at him. "I went to a wedding this spring that was."

"Seriously?" Was she telling him the truth? He knew Alexander Bayfield's family's facility in Ravenzario did some country weddings, but in an actual barn?

"Yep. North of town. This one's all normal at a church with a reception at the equestrian center."

Right. And it was so much more than an equestrian center - boasting not only 3500 stalls and a 40,000 seat arena, but a five star resort and spa. He extended his arm. "Shall we go then?"

She slipped her slender hand through his elbow. "Sure."

He held her door and walked around to the driver's side. As they pulled out of the drive, he asked more questions. "So who are these people?"

"I went to school with Ginger for about ten years. She met Troy in college. She and I double dated to prom my junior year, but more because our boyfriends were friends than because we were."

He turned onto another country highway. "Is that where you became friends?"

Ellie shook her head. "No. We really only connected on Facebook after high school. She likes to do day hikes, but not the survivalist kind of thing I do at work. We've gone on a few hikes and float trips with groups of friends. She takes fantastic pictures of the places she goes. Her parents have some money, though they're not in the 'Langley-Cranston' league. She's been some super cool places."

Jonathan kept his thoughts to himself. If Ellie and Rick worked things out, they'd go all sorts of cool places together. And if things didn't work out with Rick, Jonathan vowed he'd take her at least a few of them. Maybe send her to a few more.

"What're you thinking about?"

He glanced over at Ellie. "What?"

"You have something on your mind all of the sudden."

If it had been anyone else, he would have said the sidelong glances were attempts at flirtation. With Ellie, it was far more likely to be discomfort and fear of overstepping some imaginary boundary.

Jonathan shrugged. "Just hoping you get to go some pretty cool places, too. Put her pictures to shame." He could make it look like she'd won a drawing or something. She wouldn't just let him send her.

"It's not a competition."

Jonathan chuckled at the sound of her voice. She wanted to be at those cool places, too. He turned into the parking lot of Grace Community Chapel. When they made it into the sanctuary, they sat on the bride's side as the sound of a string quartet filled the room. A muted squeal caught his attention as a young woman hurried toward them from the other end of the row.

"Ellie!" she soft-squealed again as the two women hugged. "I haven't seen you in forever."

He couldn't hide his grin. It probably wouldn't be the last time it would happen before they left for the reception, much less before they headed back to the house later. Jonathan focused on the program someone handed him. He didn't expect to recognize any of the names, so it surprised him when he saw one who'd been in his undergrad classes with him.

The other girl left to talk to someone else, and Ellie looked at her program, telling him quietly who each person was. She knew everyone in the wedding and many people in the seats surrounding them.

The music changed and the door to the side of the sanctuary opened. The groom and two other men walked in. One seemed to be his best man and the other the preacher. Everyone twisted in their seats as the double doors at the back of the center aisle opened. Several sets of bridesmaids and groomsmen walked down the aisle. The sounds of "aw" came up from around the room as two little girls with incredibly serious looks on their faces dropped flower petals on the ground. Two little boys followed with a chalkboard sign saying "Here Comes Your Bride."

The music changed again and everyone rose. Jonathan urged Ellie to trade spots with him so she could stand on the aisle and see her friend better. A tap on his shoulder made him turn. Standing on the chair was a little girl, maybe four years old.

"I can't see," she whispered. Her mother tried to shush her but Jonathan found himself grinning.

"How about if I hold you?" He picked her up before she had a chance to answer.

The bride passed by and he turned more toward the front so she could still see. Ellie slid back to his other side as the bride reached the front. When the preacher said everyone could be seated the mom reached for her little girl, but Jonathan told her she could stay with him.

The wedding proceeded as most weddings do and after about half an hour, the happy couple shared their first kiss as a married couple. Everyone cheered as James Brown's *I Feel Good* played while they practically ran up the aisle. Once the rest of the recessional was over, Jonathan gave the girl back to her mom.

When their row was released to leave, Jonathan rested his hand on Ellie's lower back as they moved slowly up the aisle. Several of the bridesmaids and the bride squealed when they saw Ellie. Jonathan nodded and made appropriate comments about the wedding, shaking hands and exchanging greetings with the groomsman he knew and the groom. He gave the bride a kiss on the cheek and gave exploding knuckles to the little kids.

He reached the end of the line and turned to find Ellie across the foyer in a conversation with a man he didn't recognize. She didn't look happy but by the time he reached her side, the guy had stalked off.

"You all right?" he asked.

She took a deep breath and squared her shoulders. "I'm fine. He can't get to me. I won't let him."

"Who is he?"

"No one of consequence." She turned. "Let's get to the reception. There's no assigned seating and I want to get a good spot."

Jonathan didn't press her for more details, but promised himself he'd keep an eye out for the other man. He wouldn't let that guy bother Ellie again.

Chapter Seventeen

Rick wanted to swear. Even under his breath would be all right. He and the two-man security detail had left Addie's Serenity Landing home in plenty of time to make it to the wedding ceremony, but a snafu with the GPS had sent them to Grace Community *Church* in Strafford, a good forty miles from Serenity Landing. By the time the error was discovered, it was far too late to make to Grace Community *Chapel* in time for the ceremony.

Instead they drove to the Serenity Landing Equestrian Center, Resort, and Spa. By the time they arrived, those who had attended the ceremony were beginning to straggle in. Rick's security detail took up spots in the foyer and the ball room where they could keep an eye on things. The chances of being needed were slim to none - or less - but they would keep a look out anyway.

Rick unbuttoned and rebuttoned his suit coat as he looked around the room. No sign of Ellie yet. After a few minutes of trying to be inconspicuous, he saw a familiar face enter the room.

Jonathan.

And on his arm? Ellie.

Rick should have known.

He took a deep breath and walked toward them anyway. He knew when they saw him. An annoyed look crossed Jonathan's face, but Ellie's lit up.

"Rick!" She let go of Jonathan's arm and reached to hug him.

Rick pulled her to him, but didn't hold on nearly as long as he would have liked. When she stepped back, it was to stand by Jonathan.

Bowing slightly from the waist, Rick said something he didn't truly feel. "My apologies for interrupting your date. I was told you would be here, Ellie, but not that you would already have someone accompanying you."

She waved him off. "Jonathan agreed to come with me, so I wouldn't have to show up dateless. I'm attending a couple of events with him next week for the same reason." The three of them started walking toward the tables that weren't already reserved for family or members of the wedding party. "I thought you were still on your trip?"

"There was a national emergency in the Sovereign Commonwealth of Athmetis so the king and other leaders I was to have met with postponed our meetings. I will likely make a short trip next month instead."

She cocked a brow his way. "The who-what now?"

Right. She'd likely never heard of it. "The Sovereign Commonwealth of Athmetis is a small, island nation between Italy and Greece. We have common historical ties with them, though not the same kind of relationship with them as we do with Mevendia and Ravenzario."

Ellie rested her hand on his forearm. "I'm glad you came to visit us, but I'm sorry we won't get more time together."

Us. The word cut through Rick like a knife. "I planned to call, but I didn't want to wake you early this morning and then slept most of the day." The three of them reached a table near the dance floor.

They took seats and made small talk while everyone else filed in. They stood and cheered along with everyone else when the couple was introduced. When it was their turn to make their way to the buffet line, Rick found himself separated from Ellie and with Jonathan.

"I'm not really her date you know." Jonathan put some pasta onto his plate.

Rick looked over at him to see that Jonathan didn't return the glance. "Okay?" He wasn't quite sure what he was supposed to do with that information.

"She was bored in Montevaro, I was coming back to Serenity Landing. She asked if I wanted to join her here so she wouldn't be the only one without a 'plus one.' I have a couple things going on that my mother will try to use to set me up with someone so she's going with me. That's it."

Rick shrugged. "Ellie and I never defined our relationship. I have no real claim to her or her time."

"But everyone knows there's something between the two of you, and I don't want you to think I'm trying to get in between whatever it is."

He sighed and looked down the other side of the buffet table. Ellie spoke with a man and laughed, her eyes and face lighting up. "I'm not sure there is anything to get in between."

"If you say so."

The conversation died off as they finished making their way through the line. Jonathan was stopped by someone he knew. By the time Rick made it back to the table, Ellie was setting her plate down.

"Can I get you a drink?" she asked. "There's no alcohol, but there is an 'open bar' of sorts with lots of options."

Rick held her chair for her. "It would be my pleasure to get yours for you. What can I get for you?"

Ellie thought about it for a minute before naming a soft

drink. Jonathan reached the table as Rick started to walk off. He made himself ask the other man what he wanted and went to the bar to get two sodas and an ice tea.

He returned and passed the drinks out, taking his seat on the opposite side of Ellie from Jonathan. Friends of Ellie's had filled the other seats at the table. She had a way about her. For a woman who claimed to prefer the woods to a ballroom, she was much more comfortable here than she had been back in Montevaro. She talked with everyone, never making any of them feel as though they were getting slighted in favor of someone else.

It confirmed Rick's belief that Ellie was the one he wanted by his side when he had to do all the formal, socializing stuff he loathed. It was something he'd always strong believed. The best friendships, especially marriages, were made when two people complemented each other. One's weakness was often the other's strength. He could force himself to be the extrovert when he needed to, but he was infinitely more comfortable in a small setting. Having Ellie at his side would make it much easier.

Before he knew it, it was time for the dancing to start. The bride and groom had their first dance to "Just the Way You Look Tonight." The bride and her father danced to...

Rick didn't recognize the song though everyone else in the room laughed.

He looked over at Ellie. She had nearly doubled over with laughter.

"What?" he whispered.

Before she could answer, about half the crowd broke into a chant. The groom, with a grin on his face walked around the room waving his arms above his head in a "stop" type motion.

Peculiar.

More chanting. Some seemingly good-natured boos. Smiles on everyone's faces meant there were no hard feelings behind them.

But...What on earth?! He could hear Ellie chanting with the others. Jonathan joined the boos. He thought he heard something about some guy named Jay and birds, specifically hawks, among those who booed.

Wild cheers and good-natured jeering greeted the end of the song.

When the crowd settled down a bit, Rick turned to Ellie. "Pardon my European ignorance, but what on God's green earth was that?"

Ellie's eyes twinkled. "Her family has gone to Mizzou, the University of Missouri, for generations. His has gone to the University of Kansas." As though the conclusion should be obvious.

"So?"

"They've been rivals going back to the Civil War in the 1860s. It was one of the longest college rivalries before Mizzou joined the SEC. The teams haven't played each other in a few years. The song was the Mizzou fight song."

Right. Americans and their college football. "The SEC?" he asked. Her enthusiasm as she joined in singing the fight song meant he'd likely need to study up.

"Southeastern Conference. It's a different group of schools who play each other for championships and stuff." Ellie took a sip of her soda. "Around here, it's a pretty friendly rivalry, but it's been known to be rather bitter at times and in places."

"Of course." For all of his outdoors-loving, Rick had never followed a sports team passionately enough to play the fight song at his wedding. He took another drink of his soda as more people joined the laughing couple on the dance floor.

He wanted to ask Ellie to dance, but she had come with Jonathan. Asking her before her date did would not be the gentlemanly thing to do.

But when Jonathan excused himself to visit the men's room, Rick threw caution to the wind and turned to her. "Ellie, may I have this dance?"

Jonathan came back from the bathroom to find his date in the arms of another man.

Except he'd told the man it wasn't a date, and the prince hadn't hesitated to move in.

Jonathan pulled a chair out at an empty table in the back of the room and sank into it. He didn't let his eyes stay on the dancing couple. It would only torment him to see how happy Ellie looked. He liked Ellie, he really did, but he didn't have feelings for her, not even a bit of a crush.

Well, maybe a bit of a crush. An attraction. But nothing more.

How could he be mad or annoyed at her for dancing with the man she thought she could love?

A tap on his shoulder caused him to turn but he didn't see anyone when he looked up behind him so he glanced down. Standing there, with her bottom lip caught in her teeth, was the little girl from the church.

"Hi, mister."

He put aside his unreasonable annoyance over Ellie dancing with Rick. "Hello, young lady." He tilted his head and narrowed his eyes. "Is it past your bedtime?"

A grin spread across her chubby face. "Sh. Don't tell Mama." She leaned in closer. "She said tonight's special."

Jonathan chuckled. "I suppose it is a special night."

"Is it past your bedtime?" she asked, completely serious.

He whispered back. "I don't have a bedtime."

Her eyes widened. "Really?"

"Yep." He held out his hand. "I'm Jonathan."

She slid her tiny hand into his and shook it. "I'm Lorelai."

"Hello, Miss Lorelai." He stood up and bowed to her. "May I have the pleasure of this dance?"

She cocked her head at him. "Huh?"

He grinned. "Will you dance with me?"

The smile that crossed her face could be rivaled only by the sunshine. "Yes!"

He bent down far enough she could slide her hand into his elbow. "Then I get the first dance with the prettiest girl here."

"I'm not the prettiest. The bride is always the prettiest at the wedding."

Jonathan hid his smirk. "Then you are the second prettiest."

She beamed. "Thanks, Mr. Jonathan."

They reached the dance floor and she put her hands on her hips, staring up at him. "You're too tall."

Jonathan dropped to one knee so he was nearly eye-to-eye with the little girl. "Is this better?"

Lorelai gave a single, very serious, nod. "Yes."

He put one hand on her waist and helped her rest hers on his shoulder then took her other hand in his own. "This is one of my favorite songs."

She shrugged. "I dunno it."

He gave a fake gasp. "You don't know 'Fly Me to the Moon'?"

"You can't fly to the moon!" She giggled. "That's silly."

Jonathan gave her his best frown. "You can't? Can you dance in the stars?"

More giggles. "No, silly."

He pulled their clasped hands to his chest. "Say it ain't so, Lorelai!"

"Sorry, Mr. Jonathan."

He heaved a deep sigh. "I suppose I'll have to dance with a little girl pretty enough to be one of the stars then."

As she twirled around, her giggles turned into another very serious nod. "Mama said the other lady was your g'friend."

"She's not my girlfriend." He leaned closer as though to tell her a secret. "But you, Lorelai, are prettier than one of the stars."

"Lorelai." They both looked up at the sound of a stern voice. "I thought I told you not to bother the nice man."

Jonathan stood, keeping the little hand in his. "It's no bother, ma'am. I asked her to dance."

The woman seemed to hesitate a moment, then nodded. "Okay then."

"Mama, this is Mr. Jonathan!"

"I know who he is, sweetie, and he's here with another lady, remember?"

Of course she knew who he was. The grocery stores in Serenity Landing carried tabloids, after all. He'd been on the cover of every one of them, more than once, plus *People* and the rest of the more news-y ones. He smiled at Lorelai's mother. "We're just friends, and she's dancing anyway."

Gold flecks in the woman's eyes captivated him as he held her gaze. Finally, she nodded. "Okay, then."

Lorelai tugged on his hand and he looked down at her. "You should ask Mama to dance."

"Lorelai." Her mother's voice held a warning tone Jonathan recognized as universal.

He knelt down next to Lorelai and whispered something in her ear. She nodded and turned, skipping toward her table. Jonathan stood and bowed slightly to her mother. "May I have this dance?"

She eyed him cautiously. "Sure."

Jonathan kept a respectable distance between them, but the atmosphere wasn't uncomfortable. They didn't talk during the song and a half they danced, but Jonathan found himself oddly disappointed when Lorelai's mother took a step back.

Before he could ask for her name or say anything else, another woman intentionally put herself between the two of them.

"You're Jonathan Langley-Cranston IV, aren't you?"

Jonathan nodded, not really looking at the new woman but

watching Lorelai's mother walk off.

"Do you want to dance?"

Jonathan stifled a sigh and let the politeness long ingrained him by his grandmothers take over. He danced with that woman then three others before excusing himself back to the table. He stopped to get another drink at the bar and noticed Lorelai and her mother leaving.

He sat back down in his seat, turning down a couple of offers to dance. Before the next song started, the band announced they would be taking a break for the cutting of the cake and would be back soon. Ellie returned to her seat without Rick. A quick glance around showed the prince talking with a young woman as he walked their way.

"Having fun?" Jonathan asked Ellie.

She nodded and took a sip of her drink. "I am. I haven't seen a lot of these people in a few years."

"Are you glad Rick's here?" He kicked himself for even asking. Not like either answer would make him feel any better.

Before she could answer, the prince showed back up at the table, distracting her. Jonathan nursed his iced tea until he could find a reason to excuse himself and find somewhere to hide out until it was time to go home.

Chapter
Eighteen

After cake, Ellie stared at her reflection in the bathroom mirror. She still looked okay. Not great but not bad. Rick's appearance at the reception had thrown her for a loop. Jonathan, too. Even worse was Glenn's appearance at the wedding. She should have expected it, but somehow, seeing him in the foyer had caught her completely off-guard.

After a quick retouch of her makeup and lip gloss, she emerged to see her ex-boyfriend leaning against the wall and smirking her direction.

Oh! How she hated that smirk!

"Hello again, Eleanor."

And how he always used her full name. At first it had seemed sweet, but the longer they were together, the more it grated on her. "What do you want?"

He shrugged and took a couple of steps toward her. "To see how you're managing on your own. You've lost some of your abilities, or more likely never had them, what with getting lost in the middle of nowhere and all. Couldn't keep yourself safe, much less the member of *royalty* foolish enough to entrust you with his life."

Ellie took a deep breath and did her best to calm herself. He was trying to goad her, to make her feel less than what she knew herself to be. Competent. Good enough. All of those things he'd tried to tell her she couldn't be without his help and "guidance." Guidance that disguised a controlling, obsessive personality.

At first she'd appreciated his sense of style, the way he helped her pick clothes that would flatter her figure and be appropriate for the engagements he took her to. She'd spent more time in the Springfield area in the six months they'd dated than she had in all of the time since high school ended - combined.

It wasn't until Ellie missed a planned weekend in New York - with the separate hotel rooms she'd insisted on - that she began to really see his true colors. It wasn't her fault she'd eaten bad shrimp at an event he'd taken her to. She'd been sick for days afterward, and not just her. The local news had even done a story on it. At least a dozen people had ended up in the emergency room, and who knew how many people, like her, had toughed it out at home.

Glenn had called her almost obsessively while he was gone. He wanted to know who she was with, who she was talking to. When he returned, he stole her phone to look through her recent texts and calls. When he found nothing but a few messages from concerned friends and family, he wanted to know why she'd deleted them all.

All of the reasons why she wanted nothing to do with him flashed through her head in a matter of a second or two.

She went to move past him and back to the ballroom, but he blocked her way. "I'm not interested in a conversation, Glenn. Let me by."

His warm breath on the side of her face sent chills down her back. And not the good kind like when Rick stood this close to her. "You're only invited to the ball because of who you're related to, not because of who you are or what you're capable of.

Because we all know you're not capable of much of anything without a man who knows better helping you look good."

She closed her eyes, trying desperately to shut out the sight of him looming over her and breathed a prayer for strength. And safety. And an earthquake to open the ground in front of her and swallow Glenn whole.

"You've got a famous guy here with you and you know what?"

She didn't respond. Wouldn't give him the satisfaction.

"He's only here because your cousin is marrying the Crown Princess. You're a trophy to him. Nothing more. And as soon as the wedding's over, he'll drop you like a hot potato. He's using you to get close to the other princess. Once he knows her, you won't be worth anything to him."

Ellie hated the tears that welled up in her eyes, but she couldn't stop them, no matter how she tried.

Glenn was a liar. He'd never been anything but a liar. Deep down, she knew she could trust nothing of what he said, but what about when his words on confirmed her deepest, darkest fears?

"Ellie!" Rick's voice echoed through the foyer.

Glenn took a step back.

"There you are." Rick wrapped his arm around her shoulders. "I am so glad I found you." He turned to look at your ex-boyfriend. His voice cooled considerably. "Have we met?"

Glenn held out his hand. "I'm Glenn Shotzen." He tipped his head toward Ellie. "The one that got away."

Rick just stared at Glenn's hand. "I am Prince Richard Antonio David Nicklaus of Montevaro. I have never heard of you. Thank you for keeping my lovely friend company, but I have an urgent matter I need her help with."

With Rick's hand on her back steadying her, they went through a side entrance and into the gardens. "Are you all right, Ellie?"

"What was that about?" She wanted to take a step back, to launch into a tirade about how she could take care of herself, but instead she turned into his embrace.

"I heard what he said." He rested his cheek on the top of her head and she felt safe. "Nothing could be further from the truth. You are wonderful, amazingly competent, and any man should count his blessings to have you on his arm. I know Jonathan does. There is no possibility he sees you as a stepping stone to Ana. He enjoys your company because of who *you* are, not because of anything else."

"Thanks, Rick." Ellie stepped back and used the tips of her forefingers to wipe underneath her eyes. Was there mascara running down her face?

"There you are."

She turned to see the door shutting behind Jonathan. "Sorry I disappeared on you."

The cautious look on his face turned to concern as he neared. "What happened?"

"A run in with my ex-boyfriend." She gave him a small smile. "I know better than to listen to anything he has to say, but it's hard not to let him get to me."

Barely concealed anger crossed his face. "Whatever he said that made you cry is wrong."

"Exactly." Rick folded his arms over his chest and stood next to Jonathan, the look on his face mirroring the other man's. "You are far too good for him."

Jonathan tilted his head toward Rick. "What he said."

Ellie gave them both a small, but genuine, smile. "Thank you both." She wiped under her eyes again. "I am grateful for both of you. I think I would like to leave now, though." She'd already talked with everyone she knew. While she wouldn't be opposed to spending more time inside, she had no desire to run into Glenn again.

Rick took a step toward her. "Then I will say my goodbyes

here." He kissed her cheek. "I am glad I got to see you. Please be safe the rest of your time here, and I will see you when you return to Montevaro. I will make sure your purse and wrap get to Jonathan's vehicle in the next few moments."

"Thanks, Rick. I appreciate it."

He went back inside and Jonathan took a step closer. "Are you sure you're okay?"

"Yeah." Her grin widened. "But I wouldn't turn down some ice cream when we get back to the house." She shuddered as the cooler night air gave her a chill.

Jonathan laughed as he shrugged out of his suit coat and wrapped it around her shoulders. "That can be arranged." Rather than going back through the interior of the resort, they walked around the outside. As they turned the corner, she noticed Rick getting into the back seat of a sedan before it drove away. How did she feel about him knowing about Glenn? About what Glenn thought?

When she and Jonathan reached the valet stand, her purse and wrap waited for her. In a few minutes, they were on their way home and putting her past where it belonged. In the past.

Rick collapsed back on the bed in his apartment at the palace. After long weeks on the road, he would be home for the foreseeable future. He hated traveling on behalf of his family. He did it. He did his best while he did, but it just was not his forte. Adeline did a much better job, but with her impending promotion to queen more and more would fall on his and Ana's shoulders. His days of tromping around the globe at a moment's notice to hike and camp were over. Looking into university classes for a business degree should probably go on his to do list. Could he get one online? Actually taking seated classes was tedious and his changing role at the palace would impede his ability to attend regularly.

"Sir?"

Rick opened his eyes to see Todd, one of Addie's security team, standing there. Could he not even get a moment's peace in his own bedroom?

He sat up and ran a hand through his hair. "Yes?"

"I am sorry to bother you, sir, but Princess Adeline would like to see you tonight if at all possible."

"Let her know I will be there in a few minutes." The suit and tie was not his natural choice of attire. Everything that went along with his suit-and-tie job drained him. He needed a chance to just be Rick. He missed Ellie and wished he was going to see her instead.

With a deep sigh, he stood and headed for Addie's office. He spent half an hour going over plans for one of the charity fundraisers during coronation week and talking about some of the VIP guests scheduled to be at the wedding, official ball and coronation. A number of Europe's royal youth - from Great Britain, Norway, the Netherlands, Luxembourg, Lichtenstein, Athmetis, and others - would be in attendance for one or the other or both.

"I know you want to rest," Addie told him as they walked out of her office. "But I thought if we got this done tonight, you could sleep in some tomorrow as I have meetings all day and we would have to meet early."

"It is good to get it out of the way tonight then."

Addie stopped at the staircase where they would go their separate ways. "She has missed you, Rick."

His mind was too worn out to play pronoun games. "Who?"

"Ana." He caught the amusement in her voice.

"Ana does not miss me enough for it to warrant a mention." His twin sister loved him and missed him when he was gone, but not that much.

"Ellie. She has moved to stay with her aunt and uncle, but we have seen her several times. I talked with her for some time at dinner last night, and she has missed you. She knows you were here to drop off the paperwork and was quite hurt that you did not even attempt to see her, and you didn't mention it in Serenity Landing."

"I have missed her, too." Rick leaned one shoulder against the stone wall. "I wish I could have but taking the time to stop at all nearly made me late for my next meeting. Seeing her in Serenity Landing made me miss her all the more."

"I know." Addie's eyes twinkled at him. "Are we going to be cousins-in-law, brother?"

Would he ask Ellie to marry him? He knew *how* he would if they made it to that point, but would they? Finally, he settled on, "Perhaps."

"Are you being coy?"

"I do not know how to be coy, Addie." He tried to keep the exasperation out of his voice but failed miserably. "I am tired. I like Ellie, a lot. Are we going to fall in love and get married? I do not know, and it is a question for another time."

Addie stretched up and kissed him on the cheek. "I just want you to be happy."

"I know. And I know Father would like me to get married before his disease has progressed to the point he would prefer not to be seen in public."

The siblings rarely mentioned their father's Parkinson's disease outright to one another, though it always hovered over the discussions about the coronation.

Her face sad, Addie nodded her assent. "He would prefer to be done with official appearances sooner rather than later, I believe. The only ones I can think of besides the possible funeral of a friend or a member of Parliament, would be our weddings. I know he would love to walk Ana down the aisle but she has not even met anyone, yet. I know he fears he will not be able to. I thank God I met Charlie when I did. He and Mother wanted me to be married before the coronation, fearing it would impede my chances of finding a spouse."

"I like Charlie and I am glad you found him." Rick ran a weary hand down his face. "Right now, I am exhausted and want only to go get some sleep."

She nodded and gave him a quick hug before walking toward the staircase and running lightly up them. Rick went further down the hallway and into the apartment he shared with his twin sister for the time being. She had been gone when he arrived, but giggling coming from the living area told him that had changed.

"Rick?" she called. "Is that you?"

"Yes."

"Come here for a minute?"

Rick stopped and shoved his hands deep in the pockets of his pants. She would want to talk for hours. He had barely seen her when he was home last time. "I just came from a meeting with Addie but am exhausted. Can we talk tomorrow?"

"No," she insisted. "It will just take a minute."

"Fine." He pulled his tie off and wondered why he had not done so earlier. "What is it?" he asked as he walked through the door.

And then he stopped short. "Ellie?"

There on the couch, sat the woman who had invaded his thoughts more often than not while he was gone. Next to her sat his sister with a Cheshire cat-like grin. Whatever he had expected his sister to want to talk about, he had not expected to see Ellie.

Chapter

Nineteen

*E*llie couldn't believe how weary Rick looked. It had only been a few days since she'd seen him in Serenity Landing, but the weeks as a formal representative for his country's businesses had done more to wear him out than the days trekking around the woods. When he saw her, a smile crossed his face and his eyes didn't seem quite as tired.

"What are you doing here?" he asked, walking all the way into the room. "I thought you were living with your aunt and uncle."

"I have but I'm spending the night with your sister." She had spent quite a bit of time with both Jonathan and Ana working on her project and enjoyed every minute of it. "I didn't know you were getting back tonight, though."

Rick settled into the chair across from her. "We were supposed to arrive tomorrow, but our business was concluded. I asked if we could return rather than spend another night in a hotel."

Ellie nodded in sympathy. "I can understand that. I only sleep at my apartment about twice a week, my bed is old, and not very good, but even then I think I'd rather be home if I could."

"And that is my cue." Ana jumped up and walked to her brother's side. She gave him a quick kiss on the cheek. "I am glad you are home, bother."

Rick groaned. "Must you?"

Ana ruffled his hair as she walked toward the hallway leading to the bedrooms. "You will always be my big bother, Rick. Don't fight it."

Rick just shook his head, but once the door to Ana's room closed, he moved to sit on the couch next to Ellie. She wanted to scoot over next to him, to rest her head on his shoulder, but she didn't know what he would think about that. Especially after Serenity Landing.

Instead, she stayed where she was. "How was your trip?"

"Productive but long." He shifted on the couch so he was turned toward her, one long leg folded in front of him with the leg of his suit pants riding up.

What she saw between the hem of the pants and the dress shoes that would set her back at least a year's salary made her break out into laughter.

"What?"

Ellie pointed at the bright purple and green argyle socks. "I never would have pegged you for a crazy sock guy," she managed to say between gasps of laughter.

He grinned again and stuck his other leg out in front of him, pulling up that pant leg as he did. "They match."

Tears started rolling down her cheeks. "It's awesome. I love it. The only way it would be better is if they didn't match."

"Even I can't go that far." Rick started chuckling with her, laughing until Ana reemerged into the living room.

"What on earth are you two...?" Through her tears, Ellie saw Ana shake her head.

Ellie pointed at Rick's socks and tried to take a deep breath to stop the side-splitting laughter. Ana rolled her eyes and walked back to her room. After a couple more minutes, Rick reached for the hand no longer encumbered by the cast. "I am glad to be home."

"I'm glad I could make you laugh." She watched as he laced his fingers with hers, loving the feeling of them together. "You look less tired."

"I feel much more refreshed sitting here with you. Can I get you something to drink? Some water perhaps?" He started to stand.

Ellie squeezed his hand so he would stay. "I'm fine."

He pulled his phone out of his pocket and did something she couldn't see. Music began to play. "This is not quite what I had in mind for the first dance in Montevaro, but..." Rick stood and bowed slightly. "May I have this dance?"

One of her eyebrows shot up. "Really?"

"Yes."

"I don't know how to waltz." But she took his hand anyway and stood.

"Just follow my lead." She rested her still-weakened arm on his again and slid her hand in his. She could do this. Learn to dance.

But when she looked up into his eyes, he simply took her breath away.

All too soon the song on his phone came to an end and he had to move away from Ellie. Not that they were waltzing terribly close.

"Thank you for the dance, love." The endearment slipped out naturally. Did it mean he *loved* her? No, not yet, but he had never used it with anyone else.

"My pleasure." A flush spread into her cheeks as she moved to rest her good hand on his chest. She stood on her tiptoes and brushed her lips against his cheek. "Good night, Rick."

He watched as she walked down the hall and into the room next to Ana's. Walking into the kitchen to get a glass of water, Rick contemplated his options. His sister was next door to Ellie, with a door connecting the two rooms, and he was across the hall, but perhaps he should go stay in one of the other rooms. There were plenty to choose from. Surely Addie had a room ready for company.

A quick call to his other sister confirmed she did. Lindsey had stayed with her the night before. Going back to his room to get a change of clothes, he texted security so they would know where he would be in case anyone needed him.

It was not his own bed, but anything would be better than another night at a hotel or on the plane.

Sunlight woke him. He had forgotten to make certain the drapes were drawn before going to bed. Rick felt more refreshed than he had since before he left on the trip. More than he had in a long time, if he was truly honest. His phone buzzed. A text reminding him of a meeting in an hour. If he did not respond, they would be banging on the bedroom door in less than ten minutes.

A glance at the schedule did not tell him anything about Ellie's possible plans for the day. He would have someone find some time for him to meet with her, maybe take her to dinner in town. An electronic note to his assistant for reservations at Rick's favorite restaurant took care of that.

Now to ask her out. He texted Ana to find out where they were, but she did not respond. He showered quickly and dressed in a pair of slacks and a button down shirt, but no tie or coat were required for his appointments. He returned to his own apartment, knocking before entering - just in case. No answer, so he grabbed his laptop and soft-sided briefcase, slinging it across his body satchel-style. Maybe Ana and Ellie were in the breakfast room. Sure enough, by the time he reached the smaller dining room near the kitchen, he could hear laughter coming from his sister and Ellie.

"Good morning," he said to the room as he walked in. Ana, Ellie, Addie, and his mother. What a combination of estrogen. All of the women greeted him then went back to their conversations. He sat across from Ellie and next to Addie, flipping his napkin onto his lap before reaching to put some scrambled eggs on his plate.

Rick let the conversations flow around him, trying to pick up on clues about plans for the day. His mother left after just a few minutes, citing an early appointment.

"What time is the appointment with the wedding coordinator?" Ana asked Addie.

"Ten, followed by the dress designer. Hopefully, we will finalize the plans for both of our dresses today, including mine for the balls and galas and parties that week." Just the mention of it seemed to stress Addie out. "I wish Papa was not ill for many reasons, including more time between marrying Charlie and becoming queen of my own country."

"It is not just your country, sister." Rick put an arm around her shoulder.

Addie rested her head on his shoulder. "I know and I know I have many people working with me, but it is still quite the responsibility and a lot of stress on a new marriage."

Ana sighed. "Maybe I'll just elope when the time comes. This is overwhelming."

"It will not be nearly so stressful for your wedding, Ana," Rick admonished her. "No coronation to go with it. And, unless you marry an American, there will be far fewer people watching than will be watching a Crown Princess about to be promoted."

"Still."

"What was wrong with the first dress?" Ellie asked.

"Too much like Kate's. Kate's dress was lovely, but it is not quite what I want for myself and then there would be the paparazzi and entertainment shows and everyone else saying I just copied Kate in an effort to make mine more popular for copycats and the museum and..." Addie sighed. "I doubt Kate would mind, but it never ends."

Rick munched on a piece of bacon. Who knew so much went into picking a wedding dress?

"Wait." Ellie leaned forward on her elbows. "You know Kate? As in married to Prince William? The Duchess of Cambridge? *That* Kate?"

Somehow, Rick managed to contain his chuckle. "I did not take you for a royal watcher."

"I'm not, really, but my roommate made me watch the wedding." Ellie's shrug was a study in false nonchalance. "It was cool." It was more than cool. It made her wish - for a few minutes anyway - to be a princess. And the way the man across the table was looking at her...

"You are welcome to join us, Ellie." Addie took another sip of her water.

Ellie shook her head. "I promised my aunt and uncle I would be home this morning. My aunt wants to take me shopping."

They talked for a few more minutes before Addie and Ana left. Rick leaned forward on his forearms, staring into her eyes. "Do you have dinner plans this evening, Ellie?"

She thought for a minute then shook her head. "Nothing I can think of."

"Would you do me the honor of allowing me to take you to my favorite restaurant?"

Was he asking her out on a for-real date? "That would be lovely. What kind of restaurant is it?"

"Local cuisine. Nothing too out of your comfort zone I am sure." He smiled in the way that made her feel warm and safe all over. "*Tavola del Re* has the best food in Montevaro outside of the palace."

"I look forward to it."

His phone buzzed and he frowned as he checked it. "I am sorry, Ellie, but I do need to take this. Hopefully, one of these days, when I figure out this new role of mine, I will have more time. Once things settle down."

Ellie nodded and he answered his phone in rapid-fire Italian. Once she was alone in the room, she pushed back from the table. Could she find her way to the dock herself? And once to the other side, would her car - on loan from the royal garage - still be hers? Or would there be a paperwork snafu? When would she let herself believe that she had friends with money and authority who wanted to help take care of her?

Would the specter of Glenn hang over her for all eternity?

It took about half an hour all together, but she made it to the garage and Garrett, the same member of the Montevarian Royal Guard who had helped her that first night, gave her a set of keys. A different car, but still at her disposal. The drive to her aunt and uncle's new home gave her time to think, to get nervous about her date with the country's only prince.

What on earth would she wear?

Chapter Twenty

For once, Rick convinced his team to let him drive his own vehicle and they could follow in a second one. He knew how to drive, but he did not get to as often as he wanted. Some of that was his own fault. When hiking the Appalachian Trail, there was no need for a car.

He needed to get a new car of his own. A sports car. Convertible. Rolling to a stop at a light, Rick closed his eyes for a minute and imagined himself driving through the Alps, hugging the curves of the road, down shifting into a turn, Ellie by his side, her dark hair streaming behind her as she laughed with abandon as she had the night he returned. Busy royal life, wedding and coronation planning, all conspired to postpone the date for more days than he cared to think about.

The day dream came to an end all too soon, but the reality of his first official date with Ellie was just down the lane he turned onto. Emerging from the car, he buttoned his suit coat and trotted up the stairs. Before he could ring the bell, the door opened.

"Prince Richard, how lovely to see you again, sir."

Rick grinned. "So this is where you ran off to, Wilson." He gave his former valet a big hug despite the man's reticence to do so. "I wondered why I had not seen you around the palace."

"There was no place for me with my charge being gone so often." The man's smile and soft eyes belied his words. "Truly, your parents offered me the chance to come here, and I snatched it. My parents both worked for the last Marquis, you see. I spent part of my growing up years getting into trouble in the gardens."

"Why does that not surprise me?" Rick kept an arm around the older man's shoulders. "How do you like being back here?"

"The new Marquis and Marchioness are wonderful to work for, and the future Prince Consort is a fine man. Your sister could not have chosen more wisely."

"Good to know." He moved away from Wilson and looked around. "I am here to pick up Miss Brewer for dinner."

"I well know, sir. She should be down momentarily." Wilson led the way to a drawing room off the large foyer. "Mr. Brewer, His Royal Highness Prince Richard has arrived."

Ellie's father stood watching him and bowed slightly. "Good evening, Your Highness."

That was different. The woman's father being deferential to her date. "There is no need, sir. Rick is fine, as long as we are not in public, and then Richard will do most of the time."

"Very well, Rick." He held out his and Rick shook it. "Is this the part where I ask you what your intentions are toward my daughter?"

"Perhaps. To be honest, I have only dated a few times and their fathers were never around."

"I don't think either of us have thanked you and your friends for carrying her out of the woods."

Rick itched to shove his hands in his pockets, slump his shoulders, and scuff his shoe in the dirt like he had when he was little. Instead, he looked Ellie's father straight in the eye. "It is I who need to apologize to you. It was my thoughtlessness..."

"Are we really going through this *again*?"

He turned to see Ellie walking into the room.

So *that's* what they meant by little black dress.

Rick admitted it looked good on her. It wrapped around her somehow and tied on the side, flaring a bit as it flowed over her hips and down to her knees. Her legs looked even longer with the heels she wore. "Good evening, Ellie."

"Hello, Rick. I'm sick of going over and over the accident. You're sorry. Move on." She sounded exasperated. Not a good way to start a date.

"Then I will not mention it again." He turned back to her father. "It was good seeing you again, sir."

Wilson held a wrap and handed it to Rick who helped Ellie put it on. He leaned close to enough to whisper in her ear. "You look lovely this evening, Ellie."

"Thank you." She seemed to thaw just a bit.

He tucked her hand into his elbow as they descended the stairs to the car.

"Where are Steve and Dennis?" she asked as he opened her door.

"They're only with me twenty-four/seven when I'm on an adventure. They were off most of the time I was gone. Now that I'm home, they rotate hours with everyone else. They're with me for major events, and the rest of the schedule works around that." He nodded to the car behind them. "We have two new shadows tonight."

Shutting her door, he walked around, got in, and drove off with her hand in his.

Ellie felt all eyes on them as they walked through *Tavola del*

Re. White twinkling lights strung through potted plants lit the dim restaurant as the hostess led them to a secluded table in a corner.

"I take it you don't bring many girls here?" she whispered across the table.

"You are the first," he confirmed taking a sip of his water.

"Ever?"

Rick swirled the water around in his glass. "I believe so. Non-relative that is. I told you I have not dated much."

"I know, but I didn't know you meant not at all in Montevaro."

"No. I dated three women a time or two each while at university, but never anyone here in Montevaro." He picked up a piece of bread out of the basket and broke it into several pieces. "There was a girl, in high school, I thought highly of. She was pretty and popular. Many of my friends liked her as well. I planned to ask her to the Royal Family's Christmas Eve Ball." He popped a bit of bread in his mouth and chewed but didn't speak again.

"What happened?" she finally asked.

"I overheard her talking to one of her friends. She wanted me to ask her because I am Prince Richard. Not because of who I am, but because of who my parents are. She was under the misimpression that Montevaro still operated under the old laws of primogeniture, where the oldest son inherits the throne rather than the oldest child regardless of gender. That law was changed shortly before Adeline was born." The bitterness in his tone reached a new low. "She only wanted to date me because she thought she would one day be queen."

At some point, Ellie reached over and squeezed his hand. "Then it's her loss. I'm glad I got to know Rick long before I met Richard."

"Anyway, after that, I decided not to date anyone who knew I was really Prince Richard. That decision ruled out anyone living here in Montevaro. All three of us decided when we moved to university that we would keep our identities under wraps as long as we could. For Addie that lasted until my father's accident a few months ago. It lasted the whole year I attended, and no one in my travels knew it unless I was on official business. The only reason they did a few weeks ago is because we were lost and word got out."

"And then you didn't tell me..."

"I wanted to. I hoped to before you left for the hospital, but they rushed you off before I had a chance." He brushed his thumb across her knuckles. "I hope you can understand that."

"Yes."

"And to the best of my knowledge Ana still has not had her identity revealed at her university, though that may change with the publicity surrounding Addie and Charlie's wedding and Addie's coronation." He leaned back, and her hand felt empty as his slipped out of it. "That is why I have never brought a woman here before."

"Then I'm glad you brought me."

Ellie looked over the menu and remarked that she wasn't familiar with many of the entrees. A steak should be pretty safe though, right?

"Let me suggest something?" Rick asked.

She nodded, but before she could ask for his thoughts, the waitress arrived to take their orders. Without asking her, Rick ordered Ellie's dinner for her. Ellie tamped down her frustration, as Rick's mood seemed to have lightened some. They talked about his favorite places to ski and hike in the area. When dessert arrived, Ellie asked a question that had been bugging her.

"Something I don't understand. You're just south of Switzerland and surrounded by Italy on the other sides, but everyone speaks English. Why is that?"

Rick chuckled. "It's a long story going all the way back to the time of Charlemagne, the very early ninth century, not long after he became the first Holy Roman Emperor. The British Isles were fragmented and often attacked by Vikings, beginning about that same time. An emissary was sent to Charlemagne to..." He shrugged. "We are not certain what his purpose was, but he was an important man where he came from. He brought his family with him, including his daughter, Cynethryth, named for the wife of the King of Mercia in the British Isles. She *fascinated* the emperor."

Ellie leaned forward, drawn in by the explanation. "So then what?"

He sipped his water. "Exactly how it happened is a story to tell you when I have time to show you the Hall of Kings. Short version is that Charlemagne gave the areas that are now Montevaro, Mevendia, and Ravenzario to the emissary because of Cynethryth."

"Didn't the people already here speak... what? Italian? Latin?"

"Most of those originally here likely spoke Italian, but once the emissary took over as ruler of this area, the English of that time period became the official language. We have a few idiosyncrasies from British or American English, but not enough to be concerned with." Rick wiped his mouth with a napkin. "Would you like to return to the palace with me, and I can walk you through some of the artifacts and paintings?"

She swirled a bit of chocolate sauce on her plate. "Not tonight." His bright smile faded a touch. "I would love the tour, but it has been a long day, and I would like to hear it all when we have lots of time so I can ask all sorts of questions."

"That sounds like an excellent idea. I will talk with my assistant and we will find a time when I can block out several hours for you."

Something about the way he said it made her uneasy. His

phone hadn't buzzed since he picked her up, but it was the first time it hadn't in all the time they'd spent together since walking out of the woods. And now, his assistant would have to carve out time for them to spend together? What happened to the guy who flew off to the middle of nowhere Missouri to learn about starting his own company? Who had arranged the tours of Greenland and Iceland on a moment's notice?

She nodded but didn't say anything. He stood and came around the table to hold her chair. The people in the restaurant had changed, but still, every eye remained on the two of them as they left.

"Did you pay the bill?" Ellie stopped dead in her tracks as they emerged into the night.

"It is put on my family's tab." The valet handed Rick the keys and held the door open for Ellie to slide in.

The drive back to her aunt and uncle's home was even quieter than the ride to the restaurant. Something had shifted, though Ellie couldn't quite put her finger on what. When they arrived, Rick helped her out, walked her to the door and said good night. He kissed her cheek and waited for her to go inside.

She watched through the window next to the door as Rick walked down the stairs. He stood next to the car, shoulders slumped, then motioned to someone in the other vehicle. The man on the passenger side exited and held the door for Rick as he climbed into the back seat. The man then drove off.

"How was your date?" Charlie walked up next to her. "Spying?"

"Yeah."

"What happened?"

How could she explain it? "It went all right."

"What is it, small fry?" His arm went around her shoulder, and he steered her towards one of the couches in the foyer. "If anyone might be able to understand it's me, you know."

She leaned against him. "I just don't know if I can handle the whole royal thing. I like Rick. I really do. But I'm not sure if I like His Royal Highness Prince Richard. If - and this is a huge if - things were to go the distance, would I always feel like he penciled me and any kids in at the end of the day? Had his assistant remind him that he had a wife in labor?"

"It's a lot to take in, kiddo." That she didn't object to the nickname said more about her tumultuous emotions than anything else did. "I do know the last few weeks and the weeks coming up are abnormally busy. Rick is taking over more of the family business. There was already quite a bit scheduled for this summer. Addie had planned to go on most of them, but with everything else going on, the responsibilities got handed to Rick. It should slow down after the coronation."

"Still. I don't know."

"It's something only you can answer. For me and Lindsey, we love Addie enough to put up with the hectic schedule and know that there are some days we may not see her much, if at all. It won't be easy, but with God's help we'll find a way to make it work. Even when Addie takes back over after things settle down, she may not be able to travel as much at times. Like when she's pregnant or with a newborn. Then Rick or I will have to travel on her behalf. The question is do you love Rick enough to put up with Prince Richard's schedule sometimes."

"I don't know, Charlie. I just don't know."

Chapter Twenty-One

Y ou're on the news." Ana walked into the living room sipping what was likely her second cup of coffee.

Richard looked up from his tablet. "What?"

"There are pictures of you and Ellie at dinner last night."

He brought up the Montevaro Times in his internet browser. It was not the top headline, but close enough. *Has Prince Richard Found His Princess?* "Do they not have anything better to write about?" he muttered as he clicked on it. Someone had taken pictures from the restaurant with a cell phone most likely. Not the first picture of the two of them, it certainly was the most date-like. It was not terribly blurry, but it was not a very good picture either. Yet, there was no disguising that this was a very serious date. They both leaned over the table toward each other, and he held Ellie's hand in his. He skimmed the article, which correctly identified Ellie as the soon-to-be Prince Consort's cousin and the woman who had been stuck in the woods with Rick in the States.

It should not surprise him, but somehow, it still did. "Was there anything besides just this short speculation?"

"Not really." Ana sat down across from him. "The rest of us want to know. Is Ellie your princess?"

"We have gone on one date, and they have us married off?"

"You haven't gone on even one date with anyone else in Montevaro. Ever. Of course, speculation will be running rampant."

"I am not even the heir," he groused. "Why is it such a big deal?"

"The same reason it will be a big deal when I find a man to marry. We're part of the royal family of Montevaro. That's why." He watched her sip from her coffee cup. "It's part of life."

"You will not be so blasé about it when it is you being splashed in the papers. Mark my words, Ana."

"What man is going to ask me out? Between Papa being king, Charlie who loves me and will be Prince Consort before long, and you, my dear brother, any man who might want to get to know me better will be scared off."

She had a point. But the bigger problem was what Ellie would think of the article. He should have mentioned the possibility to her, but he did not have time to contact her at the moment. He flipped back to the notes he was making for the gala meeting. "I will talk to Ellie as soon as I can. This meeting cannot wait. Adeline's schedule is packed today."

"At least you don't have dress fittings."

Richard laughed. "True. I do need to get my uniform updated though. I have not worn it in about two years." He stood and ruffled Ana's still-mussed hair. "See you later, kid."

The meeting with Addie lasted far longer than anticipated, but Ellie would be arriving with Charlie and Lindsey for the wedding planning meeting immediately afterward. He had an hour instead of the two he had planned on and hoped Ellie would be available to have lunch with him. As the meeting broke up, he sent her a quick text telling her to meet him at his apartment. She replied almost immediately, saying there was something she wanted to talk to him about.

He met her in the hall outside the apartment he shared with Ana, leaning to give her a kiss on the cheek. "Do you mind if we have sandwiches here?"

She shook her head. "No. In fact, I'd rather not have anyone else around while we talk."

"I am sorry about the news this morning." He opened the door for her and saw someone he knew dusting the mantle.

"Prince Richard!" The woman was about twenty years older than Rick himself, but she had been working for the family since before Rick was born. She pulled him into a big hug. "You need to come home more often. And when you're here, you need to see me more."

He chuckled. "Of course. Good morning, Yvonne. Have you met Ellie Brewer? She is the cousin of Adeline's fiancé."

Yvonne nodded at Ellie who smiled. "No, we have not met. It is a pleasure, Miss Brewer." She turned back to Rick. "I did see the papers this morning, though."

"I think everyone did. We will be having lunch in the kitchen."

"I will leave and come back later." She patted his cheek. "I am glad you are home."

"You do not need to leave. I know you have a schedule to keep. Just save the kitchen for last?"

"Of course."

He gestured for Ellie to go in front of him to the kitchen. Ana's coffee cup and cereal bowl still sat in the sink. Rick pulled out some cold cuts, cheese, and sweet bread rolls. They made sandwiches while talking quietly about the upcoming wedding. Once they were both seated, Rick said a quick word of prayer, then looked over at Ellie. "What did you want to talk about?"

Here went nothing.

His text telling her to meet him rather than asking her rankled, but this wasn't the time to bring it up. If it happened regularly? Well, that would be different, but for now, even with the ordering dinner thing, she'd let it go. Ellie laid the tablet they'd let her use on the table. "I spent some time while you were gone talking with Ana and driving around. I did some hiking as soon as my ankle would let me, not as much as I wanted, but enough, I think. Jonathan even took me on horseback and helicopter rides."

"Enough for what?"

"To come up with some preliminary plans for your hiking and camping attraction." She held her breath as she slid the tablet to him.

He read and scrolled as she watched, too nervous to force food into her stomach. "Where did you get the price point data?"

"I based it off other similar programs, including ours in Missouri."

"And the trails you picked?"

"They're not used nearly as much during the summer. In the winter, they're used for cross-country skiing, but according to Ana, not very many people hike them when the snow's melted. One thing I don't really have any experience with is planning around a big winter. In Missouri, we work around the weather we're given, but rarely do we have big snow or snow and cold snaps that last more than a couple weeks at the most."

"And equipment costs?"

"There are two sets of figures there. One if you buy everything new. Another if you buy quality used products. You will most likely need to build a building. There isn't one around that would suit the purposes. You could have your main headquarters in town, but you'll likely want a building on site."

"Hm." He continued to eat as he read through the material, but he didn't say much of anything.

Ellie made herself nibble on the chips she'd found. Would he just say something?

"There is some good stuff here."

Some? She cocked an eyebrow at him, but he didn't notice.

He finished his sandwich and washed it down with some water. "Can you email this to me?"

"Sure."

Rick leaned back in his chair and smiled at her. "I would really prefer to talk about something else for now. Would you like to go look through the Hall of Kings? I can tell you more about our history."

"Do you have time?" If recent history was any indication, he'd be running to another appointment before long.

Frowning, he glanced at his watch. "We will have about thirty minutes by the time we walk over there."

She nodded and pushed back from the table.

"Were you not hungry?" he asked as he carried her plate to the counter.

"Not really." Her stomach was still churning, and he didn't seem to look too closely at the proposal she'd put together.

As they walked through the palace, Rick pointed out some of the various tapestries and carpets. There were a few they weren't allowed to walk on and they were roped off. She was glad she'd worn comfortable loafers rather than heels.

"And here we are." Rick pushed the doors open, leading her into a large room full of paintings and portraits. He led her to the far end and pointed to an obviously fragile painting of a battle. "Remember the emissary from the British isles? He named this area *Bellas Montagnes*." She nodded. "This is a few years later when they had to repel one of Charlemagne's sons. He was king of Italy at the time and wanted this area for his own. Charlemagne was furious. Charlemagne had fallen hard for Cynethryth, but when she turned up pregnant, her father was beyond angry. Charlemagne wanted to marry her, but for reasons lost to history was unable to. Instead, Charlemagne gave the large areas of land to her father."

Ellie spent more time staring at him than at the painting. "What happened to the baby?"

"Well, Cynethryth married one of her father's knights almost immediately and gave birth to a baby girl, named Marcellina. They went on to have three boys before she died in childbirth along with her second daughter."

Rick moved to another painting. This one was more of a map with boundaries outlined and a ship sailing away from the western coast of Montevaro. "By this time, of course, Charlemagne had died. His daughter with Cynethryth was the family secret. Everyone knew but though evidence shows Charlemagne was fond of even his illegitimate children, he had no contact with Marcellina."

Ellie had to know. "Why?"

"No one knows. Legend has it, he was so in love with Cynethryth that he abided by her wishes that her knight-husband raise Marcellina and be her father in every sense. Her father, who had ruled the whole area, died a few days before Cynethryth. After she died, her husband ruled the whole area. Eventually, Marcellina was given in marriage to the king of a small island country in the Mediterranean. Today, it's known as the Sovereign Commonwealth of Athmetis. The sons each took over a portion of the land. They always cooperated with each other. There were a few skirmishes between Mevendia and Montavaro but nothing of any real consequence. Daughters were married to eldest sons from the two other countries for a couple of centuries, keeping the ties strong. In 1000 A.D., they officially solidified the relationships and codified the *Royal Commonwealth of Bellas Montagnes*. And that, in about ten minutes, is the much-condensed ancient history of the Commonwealth."

"The long version must take years to tell."

His laughter echoed throughout the chamber.

She wandered around the room, stopping in front of a portrait. "That's an impressive crown this king is wearing."

"That is King Willem the Second. Those jewels are some of the ones your aunt and uncle found in the tunnels." The king looked something like Rick. Not surprising, she supposed, since he was one of Rick's ancestors.

Ellie's head snapped around to look at him. "Really? That crown?"

"Yes. Along with the scepter and several rings. There were multiple tiaras and other crowns as well. Millions of dollars worth of jewels, but priceless as Montevarian heirlooms. That is why my father decided to offer the March to whoever found them. King Antonio wanted that one for the new Mevendian History Museum, but we sent some other pieces instead."

She looked at a few more paintings though none quite captured her attention. Rick answered a couple of questions, but also tapped on his phone as she continued to wander the room. In fact, except for when he told the story, he was preoccupied the whole time they were together.

"It is about that time." Ellie looked up as Rick's quiet voice echoed through the room. "I am sorry, but no one is allowed in this room without an escort."

"Of course."

A minute later, she was handed off to a member of the security force. By then Rick had a phone call he just *had* to take. However, she thought their time together today might go, this wasn't it. But if was an indication of what life around Rick was like, she didn't want any part of it.

Which made it all the harder to say no two days later when Jonathan shocked her.

"I'm taking you out to dinner. Tonight."

Ellie looked up from where she was putting the finishing touches on the revised - again - proposal she still hadn't emailed Rick. "Pardon?"

Jonathan flipped the chair around and straddled it backwards. "I'm taking you to dinner. You've been working hard - we both have - and I think it's time we had a little fun."

She laughed. "You're right. It is. I need a night out." Without thinking about Rick. "Where are we headed?"

"Nope. Not telling. You'll have to be surprised."

"Okay then. How dressy are we talking?" She wrinkled her nose. "I don't need heels do I?"

His chuckle reassured her. "No. Probably not blue jeans but no little black dress either."

"Got it." Good because the last time she wore it... No! She wouldn't go there. Instead, Ellie rubbed her hands together in glee. "What time do I need to be ready?"

Jonathan looked at the time on his phone. "An hour and a half? We've got a bit of a drive."

Half an hour later, Ellie had managed to shower and wash her hair. With a towel still wrapped around her head, she pulled on a pair of casual khaki pants. When paired with a sweater set, it would be nice enough. The pale pink sleeveless top knocked the towel loose but by the time it was on, she felt much better. The task of getting her hair done? Yeah. She needed help with that. Her arm still didn't cooperate.

Giving up, she called Wilma, daughter of the butler, who would be happy to help. Ten minutes before Jonathan was supposed to arrive, Ellie tossed the long-sleeve sweater over her arm. She didn't need it right now, but the nights were sometimes cool enough she needed something more.

Much to the dismay of Wilson, Ellie answered the door herself. As she expected, Jonathan looked a bit nicer than she did. "Would you like to come in?"

He held out a single calla lily. "For you."

The gesture shocked Ellie. Did he think there was something more to their relationship than there was? Surely not. "Thank you." She glanced down at herself. "Is this okay?"

His smile warmed her just a bit. "You look great. It's perfect for where we're going."

Like a gentleman, he held her car door, and in minutes, they were driving toward... somewhere. He still wouldn't tell her where.

After a few minutes, Ellie dug into her purse. "I'm glad I brought these." The sunglasses would help, given their westerly direction. Of course, over half the country was to the west of the March.

"I'm glad you did. I should have mentioned we'd be driving into the sun."

She flipped down the visor of what had to be a palace-issued vehicle. "How much longer will you be in Montevaro?"

He shrugged as he switched lanes. "I'm not sure. Probably until the coronation, but I may need to return to Serenity Landing before then. The semester starts soon."

"I thought you got your degree."

"'*You need a degree in international relations* and *private sector relations. So you can run a multi-national corporation* or *be an ambassador.*'" He let out a sigh. "Sorry. Channeling my grandmother."

"Which one?" Not like it mattered.

But the question made him smile. "Both, actually. And my mother. And my father. A couple uncles. An aunt or two. Plus most of my cousins. Because if I do it, they might not have to."

Ellie leaned her head back against the seat. "What about you? What do *you* want to be when you grow up?"

Jonathan rested his elbow against the window, with his head resting on his fist. "You know, I'm not sure. For a while, I thought I might want to run a security firm, providing protective details for those who need them, but I'm not sure." He glanced over at her. "What about you?"

"What I am doing. But with more financial security."

"I'm glad you've found your passion." He switched hands on

the steering wheel and put his right hand on her arm. "Not everyone does and very few so early in life."

Silence filled the car until Ellie began to suspect where they were headed. She twisted in her seat, delight filling her. "Are we going to the shore?"

Jonathan's eyes twinkled. "Yep. Right along the Mediterranean. There's a little mom and pop place Garrett at the motor pool told me about a while ago that I've wanted to try out. I looked them up online, and they don't seem to be fancy, so we should be okay."

He slowed down as they neared the coastline. "Most of the population in this area lives within a couple of miles of the Mediterranean. It's one of the most densely populated parts of Montevaro."

"You are quite the tour guide."

"Ana brought me down here one day when she had some business to attend to and she knew I was bored. Addie and I did a ribbon cutting on an emergency shelter for kids not too far from here this spring."

Thoughts ran through Ellie's head until finally they had to come out. "I still have a hard time wrapping my mind around all of it."

"All of what?"

"Charlie. Addie. Rick. Ana. Spending the night at the palace occasionally. Being on a first name, non-title basis with *royalty*, even if I didn't know where the country was three months ago."

Jonathan checked over his shoulder before taking the off-ramp. "It's a bit surreal for me, too. And I've met several presidents over the years, along with several other members of royalty, including Queen Elizabeth and Prince Philip. Never much more than a handshake on a rope line or picture at a meet-and-greet, but still. I never imagined myself here either."

Before long, he had found a place to park and helped her wrap her sweater back around her shoulders when it fell off. It surprised her when he took hold of her hand, though with the crowd, it was probably for the best.

He had to lean close to her to be heard. "I hope there's not some festival or something going on that I didn't know about."

Ellie shrugged rather than shout to be heard. Jonathan led her through a narrow walkway between two old brick buildings. If she didn't trust him, she'd start to wonder what his intentions were. Two turns later, they walked into a small courtyard, filled but not overflowing with people.

Jonathan spoke in rapid-fire Italian to the woman behind the hostess stand.

"Ah yes!" she replied in heavily-accented English. "You call earlier and I give you my last table, vacated by someone who..." She tsk'd. "...had his heart broken by his lady. She is no lady! But you..." She looked at Ellie. "You are a lady! I have seen pictures of you with Prince Richard, no?"

Heat rose in her cheeks, but she realized Jonathan no longer held her hand. "Yes. I am a friend of Prince Richard's."

"From America! You are relative to the new Marquis and Marchioness and the Sir Charlemagne who will marry Princess Adeline, yes?" The whole time she talked, they had been walking toward the other side of the small restaurant. The woman led them back outside and up a set of wrought iron stairs to a patio on the roof. "The best seats for the lady who will be part of our royal family and her friend."

Jonathan held her chair as the lady set the menus down. Ellie smiled at both of them. "Thank you."

"I am Maria. My family come here from Italy when my mother, God rest her soul, died and left Papa to raise us. My papa, he from Montevaro. I was twenty-one, but I came with him to help with my siblings." She crossed her arms across her ample middle. "Now, you let Maria decide what to bring you. I bring you something special."

Jonathan shared an amused look with Ellie and thanked

Maria.

The woman's eyes narrowed. "You. I know you, too. You date the princess. Keep her from Sir Charlie, her true love."

"Oh, no!" Jonathan shook his head. "Princess Adeline and I were friends. That's all. We did date a few times, but that was when she thought, for many reasons, she and Charlie couldn't be together."

Ellie couldn't be sure if Maria believed him, but she finally gave a nod. "Very well. I bring you both something special."

Chapter
Twenty-Two

T hen they were alone at a small metal table. The kind with the holes in it, found at eateries worldwide, apparently. The only table on the roof and overlooking the waves crashing against the narrow beach.

Jonathan thought Ellie was trying, and failing, to hold in a giggle. Finally, she said, "I think Maria likes you, Jonathan."

He gave her an incredulous look. "I think I'm lucky to get out of here intact. That look she gave me? Man, I'm glad I got on her good side!" Turn on the old Langley-Cranston charm. Didn't work every time but often enough. "What do you think Maria's going to bring us?"

Ellie looked out over the water. "I don't know. Everything inside looked fabulous though."

It dawned on him how this table, alone on the roof, sun setting over the Mediterranean Sea, could look to her. "I promise I asked for a table. Not a table on the roof with the sunset." It wasn't a date. He hadn't meant for it to be a date.

But it sure seemed an awful lot like a date.

The breeze blew in, bringing with it the smell of salt and...

sunscreen? There weren't many people on the beach and the day had been too cool for most to sunbathe, but that's what Jonathan thought he smelled.

Or maybe it was coconut from the lotion Ellie was spreading on her still-withered hand.

"How's your physical therapy going?"

"It's a bear to deal with, but I'll survive."

"Your first broken bone?"

She actually laughed. "Not even close. I got into more accidents than Dan and Charlie combined. Broken bones, dislocated shoulder, black eyes. No fights, but falling out of trees or wrestling with the boys."

Jonathan never would have pictured her as a tomboy. Someone, he doubted it was her, had pulled her hair into some sort of knot at the base of her neck. Wisps of chestnut hair blew in the breeze, and he reached out to move one behind her ear. "I can't see it," he told her. "You don't strike me as the type."

In seconds, her cheeks matched her sweater. "Well, I was. I still am to an extent, but I've learned to embrace my feminine side, too."

Oh, Jonathan was well aware of her feminine side. Too aware given her up-in-the-air relationship with the prince. Still the coconut-y scent wafted his way and drew him closer. He leaned in toward her. No kiss planned, but suddenly he wondered what it would be like.

"I bring you dinner." The voice called up the stairs before the footsteps started. "You will like." When she reached the table, Maria set two platters of seafood and pasta in front of them. "This is not on the menu. This is my meal I make for my grandchildren tonight. They will have macaroni and cheese. I tell them the American cousin of Sir Charlemagne is here, and they insist."

Ellie's eyes went wide. "This looks *amazing*, Maria. I don't know how to thank you."

"I feed you tonight. You like it, you bring that handsome Prince Richard sometime when he returns from his trip. He should stay home. Be with you. Quit climbing those mountains."

Jonathan didn't know what to think as Ellie shook her head. "Oh, no. The prince and I are friends. Nothing more. I like him, but he's practically family."

Music started to play in the distance and Jonathan didn't like the gleam in Maria's eye. "Well, then. You and the man who kept my Princess Adeline from her Sir Charlemagne should eat. Go to the festival. The music will do you good." She covered her heart with her hand. "It is good for the soul."

More footsteps sounded on the stairs and a young man appeared holding a bottle of wine and two glasses. Great. It would be a good vintage, too.

"Mario, he pour your wine and you take whatever is left with you. My gift."

The young man poured the wine and set it on the table, leaving before he said a word. Maria muttered something in Italian. Jonathan didn't quite catch it as she hurried after her grandson.

Ellie picked up the glass. "To a lovely evening."

He took his silverware out of his napkin and laid the cloth on his lap. "Sorry, Ellie. But I don't drink."

She blinked. "Not even on special occasions?"

"No. I'm a recovering alcoholic. I've been sober way too long to risk it." He picked at one of the noodles with his fork. "I probably could have an occasional drink with dinner or something. I'm not the same person I was then. Not even close, but I don't want to take the chance that I could spiral back into that life. But, please, go ahead." Rarely did it bother him that he didn't drink, but times like this, when it would be nice to have a glass of wine, sometimes he wished he could.

The wheels were turning in her head as she took first a couple of bites and then a sip of her wine. "I remember hearing all sorts of stuff about your brother, but I don't think I ever heard anything about you being in trouble."

One of the downsides of being in the public eye all the time. "My parents and I managed to keep it out of the news. They didn't know how bad it was, anyway. They still don't know about my stint in rehab." He swallowed a sip of water. "No one does. Not even Addie. I told her a bit about my wild high school days when we were dating, but not much."

What possessed him to tell Ellie about it, he'd never know, but he had.

Ellie sipped on her glass of wine, only finishing about half of it.

"Do you not like it?" he asked, nodding at the wine.

"It's good." She gave him a half smile. "But it doesn't seem right when you're not having any."

He'd have to make sure to get her a bottle soon. She deserved to enjoy it without worrying about him. Jonathan wiped his mouth with his napkin and laid it on his nearly-empty plate. "Let's go see what that party's all about."

Ellie nodded, and he held her chair while she stood. "That sounds like fun."

Jonathan held her hand.

Ellie didn't know how she felt about that. It made sense, and it wasn't like their fingers were linked together. In the large crowd, it would have been very easy to lose each other, and Ellie *did not* want to be in a strange city by herself.

But it still felt... odd. The whole dinner had been a bit uncomfortable with the romantic setting and the wine. Knowing

Jonathan was a long-since recovering alcoholic made her uncomfortable drinking her wine in front of him. Delicious or not, she'd only had about half a glass.

The music in the distance was loud enough to hear, but not enough to make out the lyrics. She was pretty sure they weren't in English. The crowd noise made it difficult to talk, but she didn't know what she'd say to Jonathan if they *could* talk.

Eventually, they made it through the crowd to the other side of the musicians. Once away from the plaza where the festival - she still didn't know what kind of festival - was being held, the crowd thinned considerably.

But he didn't let go of her hand.

A minute later, they were away from the crowds all together. They kept walking, past the sand covered sidewalk and onto the beach itself. Ellie finally stopped him.

"Hold on." She pulled on his hand until he stopped. "I can't walk on sand in these shoes." Using Jonathan for balance, she pulled off one pump and then the other. With them dangling from two fingers on her weak hand, she smiled. "Much better."

Jonathan chuckled. "I didn't plan a walk on the beach. Honest."

Ellie just smiled back at him but kept hold of his hand to help in the soft sand. "I like the beach."

As they walked along, the music receded to the background. Before long, they reached a bench sitting on a concrete slab in the middle of the sand.

Jonathan let go of her hand to brush the sand off then sat down. She sat next to him, close, but not touching.

"It's beautiful out here." The comment didn't require a response and Ellie didn't feel compelled to give one, though she agreed.

The sunset had given way to the moon reflecting off the water. The silvery path along the waves seemed to lead directly in front of them.

"Do you ever wonder what it would be like to be up there, on the moon, looking down at the earth, like the Apollo guys did?"

She considered that for a moment. "I have. I think it would be cool, but I'm not sure I'd be up for the long days of weightless flight or sitting on tons and tons of explosives to get there."

"What if someday it were as safe as airplane travel?"

"Then maybe. I do think seeing earth rise would be way cool."

"I would imagine so." Wheels were turning in his head. After a few minutes, he spoke again. "Do you think that's how God see us? Just that little ball of blue and green and brown hanging in the middle of the black expanse of space? More like one of those people with marionettes. Or do you think He's closer than that?"

A serious question required a serious answer, and Ellie thought it over, formulating her answer before responding. "I think He's much closer. More like a parent than a distant ruler. He's there when we need Him, but He lets us learn to walk on our own two feet. He supports us and guides us, but ultimately, we make our own decisions. Hopefully, as we get older in our faith, we stumble less and less and make more decisions that would make Him proud. I really don't think He's a puppeteer just maneuvering us around for His amusement."

Jonathan reached down and picked up a seashell turning it over and over in his hand. "I've come to realize over the last few months that there are a lot of things I don't understand about God, about the Bible, and I want to. I know I'm not the Christian man I need to be. It's part of why Addie and I wouldn't have worked out, even if she and Charlie hadn't found a way to be together."

Ellie didn't know what to say to that, so she didn't say anything. They just sat there, breathing in the salt air.

Jonathan leaned toward her and pointed into the sky. "Make a wish."

A shooting star streaked across the inky darkness and Ellie closed her eyes. More a prayer than a wish but the sentiment remained.

"Want to tell me what you wished?"

Ellie shook her head. "No. Because then it won't come true."

Jonathan smirked her direction as he stood, holding out his hand to help her. "That's an old superstition."

With a laugh, Ellie took his hand with her good one, and he pulled her up. "And wishing on a shooting star is, what? Scientifically proven fact?"

Without letting go, Jonathan started walking further down the beach, away from the music and noise of the festival. He'd thought it would be fun, but as they'd found themselves surrounded by the crowd, he just felt overwhelmed. Almost claustrophobic.

They walked a bit longer, eventually stopped by a field of rocks leading to a cliff face. He turned and looked over the water then back the way they came. They'd come much further than he realized. The music had now receded so far he could barely hear it. "I'm sorry. It'll be quite the walk back." He looked around. "And doesn't look like there's anywhere you could wait while I get the car and pick you up."

"I'll be fine."

She shivered even with the sweater on and he wished for a coat to give her. Instead, he put an arm around her shoulders. "Better?" he asked, rubbing his hand up and down her arm.

"A little bit." They just stood there, staring over the ocean.

"Thanks for letting me walk and think." Something he'd

needed but not gotten. His life wasn't in shambles by any stretch of the imagination, but it wasn't just his grandmothers getting antsy about his love life. He didn't look at every girl who crossed his path as a potential love match, but he'd wondered about a few.

Like the soon-to-be queen of Montevaro.

And what about the nearly-queen's soon-to-be cousin-in-law?

He'd spent a lot of time with Ellie the last few weeks. There was definitely something between her and Prince Richard, but Jonathan wasn't convinced they were in love. Or even that Ellie wanted to be. She hadn't told him much about the run-in with her ex-boyfriend, but he knew she feared a relationship with royalty would be the same way.

Jonathan could compete with royalty on just about any scale. Money. Prestige. No crown or title, but a genealogical relationship to two U.S. Presidents, extremely distant relationship with both Queen Elizabeth and Prince Philip as well as Prince Albert of Monaco and King Willem-Alexander of the Netherlands, five U.S. Senators, and about a million prominent lawyers, including a distant cousin being eyed for the Supreme Court. There were also horse thieves and wife stealers, but he supposed every family had their share of bad eggs. Surely there were a few in the Montevarian monarchy's past.

He might win in terms of geography. After all, he lived in Serenity Landing for the moment.

Was he competing with Rick? Did he even have a shot with Ellie?

More importantly, did he *want* a shot with her?

To take the chance?

Jonathan decided to find out. One way to know for sure.

He moved in front of her, tipped her chin with a finger on his free hand.

And kissed her.

Chapter
Twenty-Three

Rick was frustrated with his ever-changing schedule. The longer it had been since he first left, the less he knew about where he was going and when. He hadn't been home nearly long enough, but at least this was a short trip with their cousins to the north.

Prince Malachi Van Rensselaer, younger brother of Prince William, second child of King Antonio and Queen Alicia, was the member of the royal family hosting this luncheon. A year younger than Rick, the two had been friendly since childhood. Much more so than Rick and William, who was several years older. The Crown Prince was good to work with, but not so much to pal around with.

"What's this I hear about you and Christiana?" Malachi elbowed Rick as they stood in the anteroom. "Wedding bells?"

"Your sister and Christiana's late brother are more likely to end up together than Christiana and I." Rick tugged on the shirt sleeve where it stuck out from under his suit coat.

"That betrothal is technically still in force, you know. Wedding is set for the week after she turns eighteen."

"You're the first of our three countries to change the rules of primogeniture but you still have arranged marriages for the royal family?" Rick shook his head. "Especially when the groom died a long time ago."

Malachi sighed. "The last few generations the couple has decided they want to get married, and then arrangements are made. I'd imagine that's how it'll be for all three of us. At least once the terms of my sister's arrangement are completed when the wedding doesn't happen."

"She should have been queen of Ravenzario one day," Rick mused. "They still follow the old primogeniture laws, right?"

"Yes. Christiana's younger brother would have been king if not for the accident. Adeline is the first in Montevaro under the new laws in your country. We'll all get there eventually. I'm hopeful that William will be able to do away with the arranged marriages for his children."

"Your father won't?"

"He hasn't shown any inclination that way."

"And you're not worried about being forced into one?"

Malachi grinned. "Father promised he wouldn't, and he's never been one to go back on a promise."

"Good." Rick knew it had to be about time for the luncheon to start but before they entered the room, a young woman joined them.

Malachi introduced them. "Lizbeth Bence, His Royal Highness Prince Richard of Montevaro. Richard, Miss Lizbeth Bence, a friend of mine and co-chair on a number of charity projects recently."

Miss Bence bobbed in a quick curtsy. "I'm so glad you could join us, Your Highness."

Before Rick could respond, an aide entered. It was time.

The luncheon was everything he expected and nothing more. In fact, in some ways it was less. Miss Bence insisted on sitting next to him, instead of Malachi, and keeping up a running commentary on everything from the significance of the color of the trim on the plates to which individuals in the room were important and why.

The longer he sat there, the more uncomfortable Rick became. Not because he was already crazy in love with Ellie, though there were definitely feelings there, but because Miss Bence seemed to want the position of his wife. Her hand lingered a bit too long on his arm. Or her eyelashes fluttered just a bit much. Or the mentions of ex-boyfriend this or other ex-boyfriend that and how she and Mal were just friends, despite tabloid tales to the contrary.

And she called his friend "Mal." Something Rick *knew* he hated.

The whole thing made him terribly uncomfortable, and he couldn't wait to leave.

Unfortunately, he was expected to be unfailingly polite for an extended period of time. The luncheon ended but just beginning was a tour of the new Mevendia History Museum. Because of the close ties between the two countries, Rick's father had been one of the financial supporters of the ancient wing of the museum.

Besides, the distance was short enough that many Montevarians would make the drive, and the museum would be part of their trip to Mevendia. It was common for residents of all three sister countries to travel freely. Rick frowned but quickly changed his expression to one of interest in what the tour guide was saying, though he wasn't really listening.

No one would be traveling to Ravenzario anytime soon. He'd not had a chance to talk to Christiana. Despite their time together, he'd been kept in the dark on whatever the security forces were doing, and he prayed for her safety daily.

Some of the ancient artifacts were ones found in the tunnel that led under the lake and into the Montevarian palace. Most were still being analyzed and preserved and documented, but when King Antonio asked if it would be possible for the grand opening, Rick's father and Adeline had done their best to comply. A few were already on display. More would be added as time went on.

Miss Bence continued to walk a little too close. To be a little too friendly. Rick longed to be able to just tell her off or walk away. But training took over and, when she stumbled over a line painted on the floor, he caught her.

Three days later, Rick couldn't take any more. Aside from the quick trip north, he'd officially been back two weeks. The wedding was in eight days. And Rick had not spoken to Ellie since the Hall of Kings. They had been at the same official functions several times but were seated as far apart as his mother could manage it. He had called a couple of times and texted when he got her voice mail. She'd texted back, but it seemed he was being pulled in sixty-seven different directions at once. Helping plan the coronation. Helping his father with his physical therapy. Helping plan the after party for the wedding. Planning a fundraiser gala in honor of Adeline's ascension to the throne.

He desperately needed some time away. Some time in the forest. Just him and God. Without his bodyguards if he could figure out a way to slip free of them. Dennis and Steve would be back on Rick-babysitting-duty full-time before the wedding. He would never be able to get away then. They knew him too well.

Without telling anyone what he was doing, he packed a backpack with everything he would need for a few days though he did not plan to be gone nearly that long. Rick bluffed his way onto the transport to the garrison by saying he just needed to talk to someone in the motor pool. That was accurate. At the motor pool, he wished for his new car, but it wouldn't be delivered for a few days. Black on black with enough horsepower to give his security team nightmares, the Ferrari was everything Rick dreamed of. But instead, he took one of the family sedans and spent nearly an hour driving to the family's country house. By the time he arrived, his phone was buzzing with calls from home. His schedule had been cleared so it could not be that. Had he missed something important? More likely just wondering where he was.

Rick parked the car in plain view, left a note on the dash saying he would be back in the morning and took off toward the trail. There were two trails he could take, and he chose the more difficult. He would not go all the way to the peak, but to his favorite overlook. If they really needed to find him, they could. Dennis and Steve would know exactly where he had gone.

Nearly three hours later, he reached the rocky outcropping. Far below was the country house and in the very far distance, he could just make out the shimmer off Montevaro Lake. First, he set up camp, ate a protein bar then pulled out his Bible.

"All right, God. It has been too long since it's been just You and me, but for the next twenty-four hours, I'm all Yours."

"Hello?" Ellie tucked the phone against her shoulder.

"Ellie, it is Adeline. Have you talked to Rick?" Addie's voice sounded stressed.

"No." Not since the tour of the Hall of Kings, except in passing or from a distance. "Why?"

"No one has heard from him since yesterday."

Ellie reached for her shoes. "I don't know what I can do but I'm on my way."

"No. Wait there. He may come to see you. We think he went for a hike near the country house, but we are not certain. His camp was where we expected it to be, but we have not found him yet."

"If I see or hear from him, I'll let you know."

"Thank you."

After hanging up and setting the phone to the side, Ellie rested her head in her hands. "Jesus, keep him safe," she whispered. Over and over, until finally she stood.

One thing her aunt and uncle's home had was plenty of room to pace. And pace she did. Up and down stairs. Through rooms she'd never been in. Up to the third floor where the old servant's quarters still needed a lot of work. She poked through them wondering if she might find anything interesting.

But through it all the refrain repeated in her head. *Jesus, keep him safe.*

Three hours after she first started her wanderings, she paced back into the foyer. She heard a car pull up and went straight to the door. It was probably just Charlie but maybe he had some news.

Instead, she saw Rick getting out of the passenger side of an old pick-up truck.

"Rick?" she called.

He waved and turned back to the driver. "Thank you, sir."

The man said something back but Ellie couldn't hear what it was. Rick shut the door and turned to her.

"Where have you been? Everyone's worried sick." Or so she'd been told. She hadn't heard a peep since Addie's call.

He held out a hand. "Walk with me?"

She walked down the stairs but didn't take his hand. He set his backpack against the bottom step and led the way toward the gardens.

"I needed some time with God." No preamble, no anything. Just jumped right into it. "The last month and a half have been the most hectic of my life, and my quiet time with God was getting shorter and shorter. I tried waking up earlier, but my nights were getting pushed later and later with meetings and all sorts of other things, and I just needed some time. Me. God. The mountains."

"Did you find what you were looking for?" She stopped at

the entrance to the garden maze and wrapped her arms around herself.

"I think so. I felt like God promised this busy time was a season, and it would end soon. That He created me the way He did for a reason, and He had known from the time He formed me in my mother's womb that I would prefer the outdoors. He knew that being cooped up inside in meetings, in airplanes, in board rooms would slowly destroy me. I have responsibilities and obligations because of who I am, and I have to honor those, but generally they are fewer and farther between than these past weeks have been."

Ellie stared at the mountains beyond the garden. "Why are you telling me this? And why didn't you go back to the other house to get home?"

"Remember I told you we had a home on the other side of the mountain?"

She nodded.

"I slid down the side of a ridge. It wasn't terribly high, but I tweaked my ankle. Not nearly as bad as you did, but enough to make the climb back up too difficult. It was much easier to reach the road. I planned to walk back to the house once I did, but as I emerged from the woods, a car drove by and stopped. This gentleman asked if I needed a ride. He would have taken me anywhere once he realized who I was, but the drive was much further around than the hike would have been, and I could not ask him to go so far out of his way. This was much closer to his planned route than our country home."

"Why didn't you call?"

"My battery is dead."

Made sense. "But that doesn't explain why you're telling me all this."

He took her hand. The touch sent thrills through her. "Because out of all the people around me, I thought you would understand better than anyone. Better than Steve and Dennis, though they have been my traveling companions for years." With his other hand, he brushed her hair back. "And because out of all people, it is you I hope understands this is a season and not my life. Unless, God forbid, something were to happen to Adeline before she has an heir or before the heir is old enough to take the throne, it will never be my life."

Rick watched the emotions play across her face. Could she understand?

"But why are you telling me?" she whispered again.

"Is it not obvious?" He cradled her face in his hand. "This is not my life, and I hope you can understand that. Give me a chance. In the last weeks, I have missed you more than I thought possible." He took a half-step closer. "I believe I am falling in love with you. If there is any chance you feel the same about me, I need you to understand."

Did she know she held his heart in her hands? She seemed to be searching for something in his eyes. In his face. In his soul.

Whatever she was about to say, it was interrupted by the trilling of her phone. She pulled it out of her pocket, looked at it, and held it out to him. "It's your sister."

He took it and swiped across the screen. "Hello, Adeline."

"Richard? Where are you?"

"I am at the Montago March."

"How did you get..." She stopped mid-sentence and he could hear her take a deep breath. "Never mind. I need you home. Now."

Something in her voice propelled him toward the house. Surely Ellie could take him or there was another vehicle he could borrow. "What is it, Addie?"

"Just get home. Please."

"I am on my way." He turned back to Ellie, who agreed to go with him. They walked to the stairs, where he picked up his backpack. The car keys were inside the house, but Ellie grabbed them. Trotting down the stairs, she tossed the keys his direction. Less than five minutes after the call from Addie started, they were speeding down the road toward the palace.

What could have Addie so upset? Surely not just his hike. The boat was waiting for them when they arrived, and they were whisked to the palace. As soon as he stepped onto the dock on the other side, Lucas was there, rushing him through a maze of hallways. When he realized they were headed toward the medical wing, his blood ran cold.

Rick stopped in his tracks, staring at his assistant. "What is wrong? With who?"

"Sir, just come with me."

He turned around looking for Ellie, but realized they had gotten separated. Their talk remained unfinished but if something was wrong, if a member of his family was in danger, he needed Ellie with him. "Where is Ellie?"

Lucas shook his head. "I'm not sure, sir."

"Will you find her for me?"

"I'll take care of it." He nodded toward the door to the medical wing. "Go on in. I'll bring her as soon as I can."

Rick walked through the door to find Addie, Ana, and their mother sitting in the waiting area. "What is it? Is it Father?" Ana ran to him and flung her arms around his shoulders. This was the kind of greeting he had hoped for, but not received, from Ellie.

His mother answered the question. "Your father is fine. He slipped and fell down some stairs, and we were concerned for a few minutes. He will have a few bruises but otherwise is just fine."

Rick felt a weight lift off his shoulders, but he still wondered where Ellie had gone. He kept his arm around his little sister.

Addie filled him in a little more. "They are running tests right now. That is why we are out here."

"If you don't need me, I'd like to take off for a little bit. I want to see Father when we can, but I was in the middle of something when the call came, and I need to see it through."

"You were with Ellie?" Ana looked up at him, and he could see the pain the rift in his relationship with her friend was causing her.

"It is a long story, but yes, and I would like to finish my conversation with her." He squeezed Ana's shoulder and let his arm fall. "I will be back in a little while."

He started to leave but no sooner than he was outside the door to the medical complex than his mother caught up with him. "Richard?" She put her hand on his arm to stop him.

"What do you want, Mother?" His voice sounded tired, resigned even to himself.

"What is it you want with this girl? Is she a wild oat of some sort?"

"Mother, what goes on between Ellie and me is between Ellie and me. I am not the heir to the throne. Parliament has no say in who I date, who I marry."

"I am your mother. Do I have no say in this?" She looked up at him with tear-filled eyes.

"So let me get this straight. Charlie is good enough for Adeline, the Crown Princess, but his cousin is not good enough for me? Really, Mother? Did you learn *nothing* from the incident with Count Bladvile? Where *Charlie* protected her?" Rick shook her hand off his arm. "I do not know if things will work out for Ellie and myself, but it is not your decision to make."

His phone rang as he turned around to walk off. "Yes?"

"Ellie is outside the Hall of Kings waiting for you, sir."

"Thank you." He had not run inside the palace since he was a little boy, but he was sorely tempted. Instead, he walked quickly, slowing in time to catch his breath before he reached her side.

He smiled as he rounded the corner and saw her. "There you are."

Her brows pulled together in concern. "Here I am. Is everything okay? No one told me anything." She clasped her hands together but kept her distance as she looked up at him.

"My father fell but he is going to be fine." Rick rested his hand on her lower back and ushered her into the Hall of Kings. "I suppose they will have to change the name of this room. Montevaro has never had a ruling queen except for a few years, kind of, about four hundred years ago when the king died and his heir was not yet of age. His mother ran things until he turned twenty-one." He came to a stop in front of her painting. "Queen Mother Esther the First. She was quite the force of nature."

Ellie's head tipped sideways as she studied the painting. "She's pretty, in a stern, no nonsense sort of way."

"She is the only woman in here until Adeline's formal coronation portrait is added." He took her hand in his and started to walk. "This has always been one of my favorite rooms. The sense of history here fascinates me. But I did want to talk about them. I told you some of what happened between me and God since yesterday, but I also need to apologize to you."

Rick stopped and turned to face her. "You worked quite hard on that proposal, and I did not even reply to the email to let you know I received it. I wish I could tell you I have had time to look through it all, but I have not. All I can do is promise to look through it in a month or so after things calm down. What I did see looked excellent."

"Thank you, Rick. I can't tell you how much I appreciate that." She reached up, as though to touch his cheek but stopped herself. "We should go check on your father."

"There's something else we need to talk about first."

She tipped her head in that way he was coming to love. "What's that?"

"Us."

Chapter
Twenty-Four

*U*s? Rick wanted to talk about "us"?

Ellie's stomach clenched. Those words were never good. She took a deep, shuddering breath and blew it out slowly. "Okay. Us. What about us?" A difficult topic when she didn't know how she felt about all of it.

"I need to apologize to you again, for how I have treated you. I promise it was never my intention to shut you out or make you feel like I had to squeeze you in, and that was the only time we would have together." He gave a half-shrug. "Unfortunately, that's how the last few weeks have been, but I should have found a way to spend some time with you. Even if it was just a few minutes by phone before bed or while driving or between meetings, I should have made time for you."

Her traitorous eyes fluttered closed as he trailed his fingers down the side of her face, along her neck and shoulder, then down her arm until he took her other hand in his. "How's it feeling without the cast?"

"Much better, but my arm still isn't back to normal, not even close." And the warm tingles spreading through that arm had nothing to do with trying to with getting it back in shape and everything to do with the man standing in front of her.

"What I want to do is promise you that I will never do that again. If you agree to see what this is between us, I will promise you that. I cannot promise my life will not get that busy again from time to time." The intense look on his face told Ellie he meant every word. "I *can* promise I will do everything in my power to make sure I carve at least a few minutes out of my day to spend with you. Just you. Not just a few minutes while waiting for the phone to ring or for the next meeting, but time for *us*."

Ellie hesitated, turning it over in her head before finally answering. "I don't know. I know your life can get busy. I understand that, but if you promise me we'll make time for each other, then yes, I'd like to spend time with you. I can't be in a relationship where I'm just one more thing on the to-do list every day." She deepened her voice and laced it with sarcasm. "'Oh, don't forget to pencil a few minutes in for a phone call with Ellie.'"

"I cannot promise there will never be days like that, but I want them to be few and far between." He cupped his hand around the back of her neck. "Can you believe that?"

"I want to. I think I can." Her words were breathless. Despite her uncertainty, he was going to kiss her. She reached up and touched his chin. "You're scruffy."

The crooked grin spread across his face. "I have not shaved since yesterday morning."

"I kind of like it."

The grin came closer, but before his lips covered hers a knock reverberated through the hall.

Rick groaned and rested his forehead on hers. "I told them we were not to be disturbed so we could talk."

Another knock echoed off the stone walls.

"Come," Rick called loudly before lowering his voice. "I am sorry, Ellie."

She nodded, but the sense of unease started to nibble at her insides again.

Rick's assistant cleared his throat. "Your father is asking for you, sir."

"I will be right there." He brushed a kiss across her forehead before leading her out of the room. "I have no idea how long this will take, but I will talk to you later?"

Ellie could sense his question held more than the words alone and nodded. The next few days would be busy, and she would be lucky to see him at all outside of wedding rehearsals and the like. A sense of foreboding hung over her, like a rain cloud over the donkey from the children's stories.

Whispered prayers she didn't quite understand flew from her heart and winged their way heavenward. She watched him walk away, talking to his assistant as he went. Did she really understand what she might be getting herself into?

Christiana stared at the memo in utter disbelief. She was not attending Addie's wedding? Since when? Who had changed her schedule? She picked up the phone to call Tony and ask what he knew about it, but decided to walk to the security office instead. When she arrived, Tony waited outside the conference room. He pushed the door open and held it for her.

"How can I help you today, Your Majesty?" he asked before the door swung closed behind him.

She held out the memo. "What is this?"

Tony took it from her and skimmed the contents. "It says you decided not to attended Princess Adeline's wedding due to security concerns."

"What security concerns?"

He set the paper down on the table. "I have no idea, ma'am. There are no threats as far as my office is aware. I would have spoken with you about it, not sent a memo around."

"Then who sent the memo?" Christiana stared at him. "I certainly did not."

"I don't know. I'll send out a retraction memo momentarily and see what I can find out." Christiana waited while he read the memo again before he looked up. "It will be at least this afternoon before I can give you an update. Shall we meet back here at four-thirty?"

"I will check my calendar and let you know if there is an issue." Christiana knew she had nothing scheduled for that afternoon. She rarely did. And Tony would know it, too, but it gave her the illusion of control over her own life.

She went back to the small office in the back corner of the administration section of the main floor. In ten minutes, her email dinged with a retraction of the earlier memo. Rather than dwelling on it, she went back to work looking through information she'd been given about a charity she considered donating to. Her door flew open and banged against the wall.

Christiana hand clutched her stomach at the intrusion. "What is the meaning of this?"

Her uncle glared down at her. "No. What is the meaning of this?" He slapped a piece of paper on her desk.

She skimmed the short paragraph. "I am going to Addie's wedding. Is there a problem with that?"

"Your safety cannot be guaranteed, Christy."

Oh, how she hated that name! "Tony said he has heard nothing of any threats and saw no reason I should not attend."

"You talked to him instead of me?" Uncle Henry bellowed.

"He *is* in charge of my safety and security."

"And *I* am in charge of your public image."

Christiana took a deep breath and did something she had only done once before. Stood up to her uncle. "I fail to see how attending the wedding of my distant cousin, with the family that helped raise me, in our sister country, will hurt my image."

"You have always trusted me You should trust me now. The recent changes to travel rules mean the general public cannot travel as freely between Ravenzario and Montevaro as they could before. They will resent you doing so."

"There are new travel restrictions?" Christiana tilted her head. "What new travel restrictions?"

Uncle Henry waved a hand to dismiss her question. "You would have to ask your *cousins* about that. Regardless, I do not think it is a good idea."

"*Regardless*," she repeated, "I am going to the wedding."

Uncle Henry put both hands on her desk and leaned toward her. "Do not cross me, Christy. This will not look good, and the people will turn on you."

Her insides quivered but Christiana schooled her features like Queen Alexandra had taught her. "I appreciate your guidance in this matter, Uncle Henry, but you have been telling me for years it was time for me to make some decisions on my own. I am grateful for your assistance as we handle the transition in a deliberate manner, but this decision? This is one I am making on my own. Unless Tony finds a real threat to me, there is no reason for me to stay away. I will not."

Uncle Henry straightened up and straightened his suit coat. "We'll see." He turned on his heel and walked out.

Christiana slumped back into her seat. She had stood up to her uncle and lived to tell about it. Why was it so hard for her to do? She had been queen for many years and had no need for a regent since she turned eighteen. Why did she not feel confident enough to take the reins herself? At least Uncle Henry had not simply dropped the whole thing into her lap the day after her birthday. She would have been overwhelmed and proven correct his fear that she was not yet completely prepared to rule her country.

She spent the rest of the day working diligently with the never ending paperwork that crossed her desk. A few minutes after four, she went back to the security offices to check in with Tony.

He was waiting for her when she entered and held the door to the conference room. "I trust your day has been productive, Your Majesty."

Christiana shrugged. Helping charities was a noble job and shuffling paperwork had to be done sometime, and sometimes it had to be done by her, but she often wished she could do more things that *mattered*. "It has been just fine. Have you figured it out?"

After only the slightest hesitation, he shook his head. "I have some leads, but no. I have not determined exactly where the memo came from."

Something in his voice told her Tony knew more than he was saying, but she decided not to press him at the moment. If he knew anything for certain, he would have told her. Suspicions were not enough to worry her with at this point, right?

"You will notify me as soon as you know more?"

"Yes, ma'am. I've been making security arrangements for the trip. Will you have an escort traveling with you?"

Christiana shook her head, hiding her disappointment. The love of her life still was not ready to be seen in public together and lose the privacy he loved. "No. I believe arrangements have been made for Jonathan Langley-Cranston to accompany me to the wedding itself. I have chosen not to attend the ball afterward and will return home once the festivities are over." She did not want to stay to see the couples dancing and know that she could not dance with the one who meant the most to her.

Tony inclined his head toward her. "I will make certain the pilots, your security team, and the Montevarian security personnel are aware of your plans."

Christiana thanked him and decided she was done for the day. Walking through the palace and out into the gardens, she turned the conversations with Tony and Uncle Henry over in her mind. Could Uncle Henry be the one behind the memo? It would make sense given his reaction to the second memo. But why would he not just say something to her? Why would he be mad, rather than rational, and lay out his reasons for her to stay home?

She shook her head as she neared her little cottage. The one bedroom home had been a guest cottage prior to her seventh birthday. Whenever she returned home after turning seven, she stayed in this little home. Alone. For many years, it had scared her. She would huddle in her tiny single bed and fear every creak and groan was a monster coming to get her. She confided in Rick once, and he managed to show her a different way to look at things. He had convinced her and his sisters to spend the night in a guest cottage at their home in the mountains. The same creaks and groans came, but rather than hearing monsters, Rick made up stories about woodland creatures and elves who worked through the night, like the ones who helped the cobbler in the children's story.

After that, she never feared the noises again. She wondered, though, if now she might have more tangible monsters to deal with.

Three days later, her stomach continued to quiver, but she would not swerve from the path she decided on. With her head held high, and her uncle's eyes boring holes into her back, she left for Montevaro.

"Who are you taking to the wedding?" The disembodied voice of Jonathan's younger sister came through his phone.

"Queen Christiana."

Her exclamation came through loud and clear. "You're taking the queen? Seriously?"

"As a favor to Addie. The queen has a boyfriend, but they're keeping it quiet for now and a wedding between a woman who will be queen in a few days and an American? They'd be all over the Internet."

He undid his bow tie and started over. Stupid thing didn't want to cooperate.

"Still. A date with a queen! Grandmother will be over the moon!"

"I've also dated Addie and Ellie in the last few months. Sort of. Not really. But the press thought so. Walking in with Christiana won't even register on the gossip scale with the wedding and everything else."

"Maybe not." A thinking sound kept her from talking for a moment. "Grandmama will have you two married off before you know it, though. What did happen with you and Ellie?"

A good question. The kiss had been very nice. Not overly so. Not the first kiss he'd remember on his deathbed, but a nice kiss. There was some chemistry between them, but in the end it boiled down to two things.

He wasn't Rick.

And Jonathan didn't love her.

"We were just having fun together. I helped her with a business proposal. We spent some time together while Rick was out of town. That's it."

"Grandmama will be disappointed you're not marrying royalty or at least a relative of royalty."

"Well, I could introduce you to Princes William and Malachi from Mevendia. Neither of them are attached to anyone at the moment. You can marry the royalty."

His sister laughed. "Thanks, but no thanks. I've already got my eye on a guy. Grandmama will *love* him."

Jonathan chuckled as he tweaked the retied bow tie. "What's he do for a living?"

"He's an electrician."

"They make pretty good money."

"I know that. You know that. He knows that. And he's very good at what he does. But Grandmama and Grandmother will flip out, and you know it."

"Oh yeah. I think you should elope then announce it, and you're pregnant all at the same time."

She snickered. "Giving my grandmothers a stroke sounds like my idea of a good day."

He laughed again, glancing at the clock. "Good point. Besides, Christiana isn't going to the ball this evening anyway. She's headed back to Ravenzario. Anastasia and I are going to several balls and stuff this week. She needs an escort, and I don't have a girlfriend."

"So you could still end up part of the Montevarian royal family?"

Jonathan slid his keys in his pocket and picked up the phone, turning the speaker off. He tucked the phone between his ear and shoulder. "I'm pretty sure there's someone she has her eye on. I'm not sure why she's not going with him, but Addie asked me to be Ana's escort, too. You don't say no when the about-to-be queen asks for this kind of favor."

"No, you don't." She seemed to be struggling with what to say next. "Have you heard from Philip?"

Jonathan sighed. "Only once this summer."

"He's in rough shape."

"I can imagine so. I won't give him any money, though. You shouldn't either."

"I haven't. I won't." He could hear the tears in her voice. "I'm scared for him."

"Me, too."

He heard her suck in a deep breath. "I'm praying for him."

Jonathan heard a discreet knock at the door. "I am, too, but I gotta go, kiddo. Love you."

"Love you, too, old man."

He shook his head as the line disconnected. Time to watch his ex-girlfriend get married.

Chapter
Twenty-Five

*C*hristiana slipped her hand into Jonathan's elbow. Despite her bravado in front of her uncle, despite wanting to be here to support her friend, the text she received reminded her that she had given up time with the one man she wanted to be with more than anything. She wanted to be home, stealing those precious few moments with the love of her life. Or perhaps planning her own wedding. He promised it would not be much more than a year before they started their lives together. But he still was not ready to be seen in public with her. She hated it, but she understood.

And so Jonathan would escort her to the wedding. She would not be staying for the ball. Christiana could not make herself without a real date.

She let Jonathan lead her to a pew near the front of the chapel and took a seat a few rows back on the bride's side. Jonathan took the seat next to her.

"Are you all right?" he whispered.

She nodded. "I am fine." It was not the whole truth. Not even close. Not only did she miss the man in her life, but her uncle had been acting even more odd after their confrontation. So had Tony. She had a feeling something big was about to happen, but she had no idea what it could be. The whispers of a security threat had made their way to her ears, but nothing more than rumors and innuendo she was not even supposed to know about.

The crowd seemed to hush, and she turned to look backwards. Just enough to glance, not enough to gawk. The king and queen of Montevaro walked down the aisle. Christiana fought tears as King Jedidiah walked slowly. Was there more to the story than just his ski accident? That had been nearly six months earlier. The man had been more of a father to her than any other since the death of her own family.

The queen took her seat in the front row and the king disappeared out the side before the music changed. This time, everyone turned in their seats, watching Charlie lead a procession down aisle. Behind him was another man she thought to be his cousin and bringing up the rear was Rick in his royal uniform. She was not disappointed there would be no marriage between Rick and herself.

The music changed again and everyone stood. Soon it would be Christiana's turn, but now it was time for Adeline to marry her Prince Charming.

Rick stood at the front of the church in his royal uniform - a cross between a tuxedo and a military uniform but reserved for the royal family. He stood with Charlie and Dan, Charlie's cousin, waiting for Addie to enter. Sara, a little girl with cancer who befriended Addie several months earlier, served as the flower girl. When she reached the front, Lindsey walked down the aisle followed by Ana. He should probably be watching his twin sister, but he had a hard time tearing his eyes away from

Ellie.

She sat in the front row, reserved for family of the groom. Even if he had not been in the wedding party, he would not have been able to sit by her. Customarily, the wedding party only consisted of one attendant on either side, but Addie wanted to include Lindsey in the ceremony and he added balance.

When Ellie stood, along with everyone else, and Rick forced himself to look away from her and toward the doors in the back. The Montevarian Wedding March started as the doors opened.

As Addie came into view, hand tucked securely in his father's elbow, Rick admitted his sister had grown into a beautiful woman. Charlie's sharp intake of breath told Rick his about-to-be brother-in-law felt the same way. He made himself focus on the wedding, though he had no responsibilities except not to stare at anyone but the happy couple. Addie and Charlie said their vows, went through the American tradition of the unity candle before exchanging rings and taking communion. But as a children's choir sang *Ave Maria*, his mind began to wander. The wedding would be over about ten. There would be the traditional first kiss on the balcony on the third floor in front of the cathedral. Pictures were scheduled to last an hour followed by a luncheon with the families and the Council.

But then...then there were about six hours before the next function. Addie and Charlie would tour the countryside in the official motorcade. The ball did not start until seven but he would have to be back at the palace by six to do the men's get-ready-for-the-ball-and-get-a-bite-to-eat thing while the women did the same thing somewhere else.

Just as he began to formulate a plan, the song ended, and he made himself focus on the rest of the ceremony. A few minutes later, he offered Lindsey his arm and escorted her up the aisle behind Ana and Mark. Outside, they went into a side room where Charlie held Addie's radiant face between his hands.

"I know no one would know, Charlie, but the first kiss is on the balcony in a little while." Rick watched Addie take Charlie's hands in hers. "I would not feel right about it."

Charlie kissed her forehead. "Fine." Rick didn't think he was supposed to hear Charlie's whisper. "But I can't wait until I can kiss my wife whenever I want."

Rick chuckled and pulled Addie away from her new husband into a hug. "Congratulations, Adeline."

"Thank you, Richard."

He released her, and she moved to talk to someone else. Rick smacked Charlie on the arm. "Welcome to the family, Prince Charlemagne."

Charlie groaned. "Must you?"

"I do not think it will be official until the coronation. Until then you are just Mr. Adeline Montevaro."

They laughed and turned to talk to the others streaming into the room. Ellie was the last family member in. As soon as she greeted Addie and Charlie, Rick was at her side. Things had been weird again since the day in the Hall of Kings.

He leaned close to her ear. "You look lovely today."

A blush spread across her cheeks. "Thank you. You look quite handsome in that get-up."

"Thank you." He lowered his voice even more. "Do you have plans once the luncheon is over?"

She shook her head. "Not until it's time for the get ready for the ball stuff later."

"Would you like to go on an adventure with me?" He made quite sure she knew it was a request.

Her face lit with cautious optimism. "An adventure?"

"Drive up to the mountains and go through part of the tunnel your aunt and uncle discovered. The treasure has been removed from the secret room, but I am told the room itself is spectacular."

"Have you been down there?"

Rick shook his head. "No, but I have seen a few pictures and your uncle told me some."

"Let's go." She started to walk off, but Rick stopped her with a hand on her arm.

"We cannot go yet. We have the first kiss in a few minutes, followed by pictures and a luncheon. Meet me at the garrison half an hour after the luncheon ends. I will have to dodge Steve and Dennis unless we want them to go with us." She could take the official boat, and he would commandeer one of the smaller ones reserved for small groups in a hurry. "Wear something you can hike in."

The wedding coordinator informed them it was time to go to the balcony. Rick kept his hand on Ellie's back as they walked up the steps. Addie and Charlie went first, followed by the king and queen, then the rest in no particular order. He probably should have gone to stand by Ana, but he did not want to leave Ellie's side. There would be talk and pictures all over the news by later in the day, more speculation that he had found his princess, but Rick did not care.

He also knew Addie had made certain they would ride together in the same car with Dan, his wife CeCe, and Ana. As he suspected, when they sat in the Rolls Royce, Ana deftly maneuvered things until he and Ellie sat in the smaller seat, facing backwards as they rode through the cheering crowds. The pictures seemed to take much longer than the hour promised, but by one, Rick convinced one of the guards that he simply needed to check something at the garrison, and he did not need Steve and Dennis with him.

Ellie waited for him at the dock. She had looked beautiful that morning in a nice dress, but here, in jeans and a long sleeved T-shirt with hiking boots on her feet and a bright yellow jacket in her hand, he thought she had never looked more amazing.

As much as he wanted to stay, to kiss her hello, he knew they needed to get moving before his bodyguards caught up to him. Instead of walking to the desk at the motor pool, he pulled a key out of his pocket and dangled it in front of Ellie. "How about a ride in my new car? I have not even had a chance to take it out yet."

"You got a car?" Her eyes lit up again.

He walked to the sleek black Ferrari with the convertible top already down. Pulling the passenger door open, he bowed dramatically. "Milady, your carriage awaits."

Laughing, she climbed in and moments later, they were on the open road, wind blowing in their hair as they sped to the mountains.

The ride into the Alps in the low-slung sports car was everything Ellie would have dreamed. Riding next to a prince just added to the adventure. "How much farther?" she called over the rushing wind.

"Not much." He turned the car off onto a dirt road and slowed down considerably, so the dirt wouldn't fly into the car and get all over the seats, she imagined. A minute later, they came to a stop in a ghost town.

Ellie counted six buildings in various states of decay. Four appeared to be houses while the other two must have been businesses of some kind.

"We don't know much about this town. In fact, everyone had forgotten it was here until your aunt and uncle found it." Rick opened her door and helped her out of the car. "But even then, the entrance to the tunnel was well-disguised. I hope I can find it."

It turned out to be easier to find than either of them expected. The entrance had been covered by a new steel building with a door that could only be opened with a code on the keypad.

"Do you know the code?" She was surprisingly disappointed.

Having put her doubts behind her for the time being, she wanted to get on with the adventure.

Rick winked at her. "Of course." He punched it in, and she heard the locks click. Pulling it open, he motioned for her to precede him inside.

She set her backpack on the ground and pulled two headlamps out of it. "I didn't think you'd be able to grab anything without anyone getting suspicious."

He pulled a small LED flashlight out of his pocket. "This is all I could get, but from what I hear it would be enough."

Lights inside the small building highlighted the well in the middle.

"It's not really a well," Rick told her before she could ask. "It's a disguised entrance to the tunnel."

Ellie turned on her headlamp and shined it into the hole. Sure enough old, but sturdy-looking handholds were embedded into the stonework. "So we climb down?"

"Yes. Do you have any rope? I have some in the car if you do not."

She pulled a coil out of the backpack and looked around. "We tether to each other?"

"Yes." He wrapped the rope around his waist and tied it off before coming to stand directly in front of her. His nearness caused her breath to catch in her throat. As he reached around her to tie the rope to her waist, she wanted nothing more than to pull his head to hers and kiss him again. To see if the chemistry was real or the product of a lonely, overactive imagination.

But she didn't. The last few days had been too reminiscent of the weeks before. She knew it was because of the wedding and preparations for the coronation, but it still weighed on her.

As she looked back up into his eyes, she knew he was thinking much the same thing she did.

"There you go." His voice had taken on a deep, husky tone. "Do you want to go first?"

"I better. I don't fully trust my arm yet." It was stronger, but not nearly back to normal.

Rick's hands were warm on her waist as he steadied her on the climb over the top of the well. She stayed with her strong hand as much as she could. When she made it about ten feet down, Rick started after her. The climb wouldn't have been terribly taxing if her arm wasn't trembling already. About halfway down she started to wonder if she was going to make it.

"How are you doing?" Rick called from above her.

"My arm's weaker than I thought, but I'll be okay." Through grit and grim determination alone, but she would.

And she almost did. About six feet from the bottom, the foothold was a bit wet and Ellie slipped. With a cry, she tried to hold on, but her weak hand couldn't. She wasn't dangling but Rick had stopped, helping hold her weight.

"Stay there." He scrambled down until he was right above her. "Can you get down?"

"Yeah. Just be careful on this next one. It's wet." This time, she made it past the hold in question and to the bottom, with Rick always one step behind her. If she fell and took him with her, they wouldn't fall far.

The ground under her feet never felt so good. Rick jumped down next to her a second after she landed.

"Let me see your arm."

"There's nothing you can do." And she didn't really want to show him. Still shriveled and white from the time in the cast, she would have to wear long gloves over it at the ball. Even then she hoped no one would notice the disparity.

But he took her hand and pushed her sleeve up anyway, before frowning at the sight of her arm. "You've lost quite a bit of muscle mass. Why didn't you tell me it would be too much? We shouldn't have made that climb."

"You're probably right, but we're here now, so let's go." She turned to look around. "It doesn't look like much from here."

Rick let go of her arm and with that movement, the tingles left. She wasn't sure she liked him having that effect on her.

Rick didn't say anything but started down the tunnel. She followed only when the rope tugged at her waist.

He had no idea what went on inside the head of a woman. What was she thinking climbing down with her arm that atrophied? And how had he not realized it was still so weak?

As much as he wanted to stay mad at her, the tunnel distracted him. Every few feet, the family crest had been etched into the stone. At ten foot intervals, holders for torches lined the walls, though the torches were long gone. They continued in silence, but Rick could tell from the way Ellie's light moved, she was looking around like he was.

"What are these for?" Her voice echoed in the enclosed space.

He turned to see her standing in one of the alcoves. "We believe they stored supplies in them. Off to the side so they would not be in the way if the family needed to escape from the island quickly, but enough they would be able to survive either in the tunnel or they could pack it out."

"Very smart." She ran her good hand over the wall. "Whoever dug this out did an incredible job. It's been here for centuries and hasn't crumbled."

"They did good work. It took decades to finish completely, though they completed a narrow tunnel much faster." A few steps later, they came to the chamber he longed to see.

Taking a deep breath, he walked through the opening. His headlamp did not light enough and he took the flashlight out of his pocket. Using his thumb to turn it on, he stepped further across the threshold.

The walls were filled with once-vibrant colors faded through the ravages of time. Pedestals and tables stood in lines throughout the large chamber. Places where the crown jewels and other Montevarian treasures had lain for centuries. He rested a hand on the largest pedestal. The king's crown had rested here and the one next to it held the queen's. Adeline would wear it only for pictures later in the week. It was too old and delicate for regular wear. Replicas had already been commissioned but would not be ready for the coronation.

"This is incredible." Ellie's whispered words reached him with no problem.

He turned to see what she was looking at. Her neck craned so her light illuminated the ceiling. The paintings continued there. History surrounded him and filled him.

"Who is this?" Ellie pointed her light at a painting on the wall.

"I am not sure." He turned around and studied the paintings more carefully. Moving closer to the door, he started at the right side. "I believe the paintings tell the story of Montevaro up to the point this chamber was sealed off the last time. These three here?" He pointed at two men on horses and a woman in a carriage of some kind. "They are the emissary, his knight, and Cynethryth." Taking another step to the right, he saw ships leaving for Athmetis. An avalanche. A castle on an island. Invasion by an army. Repelled invasion. And so on. He did not know how long he spent telling Ellie the history he had learned from his parents and teachers growing up, but it had to be close to an hour.

"What's this?" Ellie bent down to pick something up. Her light shone off the gold coin in her hand.

"They must have dropped it when they cleaned it out." Rick moved behind her and looked over her shoulder. The face on the coin was visible, but worn. "I believe that is Queen Mother Esther the First, but I can't be sure."

"We should take it back with us. Is there anything else left in here?"

He did not want to look for more treasure. Rick would much rather spin her around, take her in his arms, and kiss her soundly. Before he could, she moved away. Ellie didn't make it far before the rope tugged at his waist. He turned and his light hit the rope.

"We have a problem." Maybe.

"What?" She did not turn around.

"The rope frayed. Most likely when you slipped." He picked the offending section up and studied it. "It is not all the way through, not even close but I don't think we should count on it to climb out."

"So what do we do? Just climb out anyway? Retie the rope? It's doubled so one shouldn't make that much difference should it?" He knew she knew the answer as well as he did.

"If there was no other way, yes."

"What other way is there?"

"We walk to the palace."

Chapter Twenty-Six

*H*er jaw dropped. Ellie stared at him in disbelief. "Are you nuts? It's miles from here and goes *under a lake*. A *lake*! I know they've said it's safe and all, but really?"

Rick cocked an eyebrow at her. "It is quite safe. Engineers have been over it, cleared out the blockages, reinforced a few places that seemed slightly less safe, though that was more precautionary than anything, and assured us that it is fine. Unless you plan to set off explosives, the only danger is sore feet."

She rubbed her hand along her weak arm. It couldn't be trusted to support her in case of a slip. The rope would help, but the climb down the wall had been enough for her to realize the trip back would be much harder.

"Fine. We walk to the palace." She hitched her backpack up a bit higher. "Let's get going then. It'll take a lot longer to get back that way and I don't want to be late to get ready for the ball." She headed for the entrance. "Maybe we can come back some other time and bring a floodlight so we can see it all better at once."

"Perhaps."

Something in his tone annoyed her. Why? She didn't know, but she *did not* want to be late for the ball. Seriously. How often did a girl - even one much more comfortable in the outdoors than in a ball gown - get a chance to go to a ball after a royal wedding?

She'd seen the young European royalty at the wedding. Several would spend the night at the palace as it was a secure location. She didn't want to spend hours talking with them but an introduction would be nice. How many other chances would she have to meet the Duke and Duchess of Cambridge? She didn't think any of them would be around for the coronation. Addie wasn't going to be *their* queen, after all. So tonight was her only chance.

The walk through the tunnel was as quiet as the trip into the mountains had been. Their boots made a thumping sound that echoed through the stone, but little was said.

"How far is it exactly?" she asked after they'd walked about a quarter mile.

His voice drifted back to her. "I'm not certain, but it will take us a while."

They reached a set of stairs. Each step was narrower than she was used to, and they slowed their speed accordingly. The downward slope of the tunnel increased the further they went, though never so steep she worried about slipping or sliding. Another set of stairs, another long stretch of walking.

Every step annoyed her.

She'd forgotten both her phone and her watch when she rushed to change in the room assigned to her. Who knew what time it was or how long this stupid trek would take. "Any idea where we are?"

Rick stopped at the top of the next short staircase and looked at markings on the wall. "These numbers are getting smaller. They are at regular intervals. The chamber with the treasure had the number one hundred next to it. We are to seventy."

"So we're almost a third of the way?"

"It would seem that way. The numbers started at the chamber not the well entrance. It is possible they end before we get to the steps that lead to the garden in the palace." He sat on the top step. "Why don't we take a short break? Did you happen to pack any food or water in your bag?"

She slipped her strong arm out of the strap and swung it around. "You really didn't plan this outing very well at all, did you? If you had, you would have stashed a backpack in your car."

"To be honest? I planned it during the wedding."

"*During* the wedding?" She sat on the top step and pulled a bottle of water out. He took it without so much as a "thank you." He'd probably want a protein bar, too. She handed one over before ripping the wrapper on one of her own.

"My mind wandered during the children singing."

"For your bride's sake, I hope you won't be so distracted during your own wedding." She took another bite and wondered who that bride would be. Jealousy surged through her. The last few days, few weeks, had shown her what life with a prince would be like, and she didn't think she wanted any part of it.

Her internal war raged on, more fierce than those depicted on the walls of the ancient room.

But the more she was around *Rick* and not *Richard* the more she thought she might want a life with *him*. Without the trappings. Except he couldn't escape who he was. Who he was born to be. Where did that leave her? Them?

"I promise. I'll be very attentive to my bride when I marry her." She looked over to see he'd leaned against the wall and shifted his body so he could watch her. "Besides, I'm not the Crown Prince. My wedding will likely not have nearly so much pomp and circumstance around it."

Good to know. "Good answer." She turned her head down the stairs, the light disappearing into the darkness. Popping the last bit of protein bar in her mouth, she packed her things back up. "Ready?"

Before she could stand, Rick leaned toward her and rested a hand on her arm. "Have I offended you somehow, Ellie?"

"What?"

"I thought we were better. That we were going to see what happens between us. And I have done my best to make time for you the last few days. I know I didn't see you at all yesterday but I called. Twice. Both times you texted back to say you were busy and would talk to me later, but you didn't call me. We texted several times last night, though. I know you know this week is unusual with the wedding and coronation, but don't I get credit for trying?"

Ellie fiddled with the zipper on her backpack. "I don't know, Rick. I'm not sure I want this life. Any of it. And if I don't, if I don't think I am willing to live with this sort of schedule sometimes, then why would we even start? Why end up hurting both of us?"

It was too late, but he didn't need to know that. Her feelings were already too wrapped up in Rick.

"I know this week will be tough as will next week when Addie and Charlie get away for a few more days, though they will not go far, but after that... Give me a chance to prove to you what my life is really like? Let me court you. Stay in Montevaro and help me set up the excursion business."

The idea of helping him set it all up was an intriguing one after all the work she'd done on the proposal he still hadn't really looked at. And being courted by a prince certainly sounded like it could be fun, but at what cost? Jonathan, though officially just a friend, could offer many of the same trappings of wealth and had let it be known he'd be open to seeing if there was something more between them.

Her heart was torn between protecting itself and the dream that dangled just out of reach. Or was it?

Rick took a sip of the water she'd given him. "What is it that's really bothering you, Ellie?"

She stared at the zipper on her backpack and didn't answer.

He pushed a bit harder. "What is it that I've done? Besides the busy schedule which we've talked about *ad nauseum*?"

"It's the dresses," she blurted out.

Whatever he expected, that wasn't it. "What?"

"You picked out dresses for me. Gave them to me to wear, and I didn't feel like I really had any option but to wear them. You ordered dinner for me when we went out. You didn't even ask what I liked or didn't like or if I was allergic to anything."

He didn't know how to respond.

"And I'm not allergic to anything that I know of, but that's not the point. You don't know that I loathe seafood. I have since a nasty bout of food poisoning ended my relationship with Glenn. He did those things. Picked my clothes, did things without asking, wanted to know who I was with and who I was talking to and to run pretty much every aspect of my life. He dumped me after he went out of town, and I stayed home because of bad shrimp. A few days later, he came home, expecting me to beg him to take me back." She wiped the tears from her cheeks. "It wasn't the first time it happened."

Rick moved his backpack out of the way and slid closer to Ellie. He wrapped an arm around her shoulders and pulled her to his side. "Ellie…"

She moved away from him. "No. I need space." Pushing up from the stairs, she moved a few feet away. "I *know* you're not him, Rick. I get that. But some of the behaviors are too similar for me to ignore completely."

His heart ached, knowing he'd caused her to feel as something less than what she was. "I wish you would have said something sooner."

"I know. I should have. But all of this, everything, is so completely overwhelming. I go from my everyday humdrum life, to lost in the woods with a broken arm and busted up ankle, to a palace in just a few days. My head was spinning. And you have good taste. I *liked* the dresses you picked, but I liked the things he picked, too."

He stood and took a step her direction, but stopped when she glared at him. "I'm sorry, Ellie. I never wanted you to feel that way. I was trying to do a nice thing. That's all."

"I know."

"Your brother said you were stressed about the ball for your aunt and uncle and were worried about what you would wear. I made a few calls, looked at a few pictures, and had the one I thought you would like best sent over."

"I *know!*" She nearly exploded. "I *know* you're not him. I *know* you were just trying to be nice and take care of me, but that's what I thought about him, too."

A soft answer turns away wrath. The verse wasn't entirely applicable. Ellie wasn't wrathful, but something inside told him this was the way to go. "Oh, Ellie. I'm so sorry. I don't want to bring back those bad memories for you. I don't want you to be anything but the wonderful person you already are. But I do want to take care of you, to love you, to make your life easier, because I *can.* I have the access to the means to make your life easier. That's all."

Ellie turned back to him, arms still wrapped around herself. "I know," she whispered. "I know you're not the same. If the same thing happened in the cave with him, I know the outcome would have been very different. I would have laid down at the bottom of that cliff until someone finally got around to finding us. Because he wouldn't have helped me up. He wouldn't have gone for help. He would have taken care of himself, walked himself back out, and then probably given them the wrong directions on how to find me. Anything to make sure he didn't come off looking badly."

He took a chance and took another small step toward her. "I can't believe that." Her glare returned. "I mean, I believe you. I believe that's what would have happened, but I can't believe he would actually leave you there, exposed to the elements and make it that much harder for them to find you."

"You didn't do that. Yes, Dennis and Steve helped, but you were right there, making sure I stayed calm and going above and beyond to take care of me."

He started to protest, but she held up her hand.

"And none of this 'it was my fault' nonsense. It was. We all know that. Your intention was never to push the limit to see how far we could go without getting hurt and you never, ever would have done it if you knew what the result would be. You took responsibility for your actions. You hiked out carrying me. He never would have taken responsibility or helped anyone if it wouldn't somehow benefit him."

He took another step and rested his hands on her shoulders. "I didn't know, Ellie. I don't want to control you. I don't want to run your life. I want to take care of you."

She leaned into him, her forehead coming to rest on his chest.

He wrapped his arms around her and held her tight. "Will you let me? Will you help me? If I start acting too much like him, if I start doing things that seem too controlling, even if that's not my intention, will you tell me?"

They stood there for several minutes before she nodded against him. "I will."

She looked up and he wanted to kiss her, but he didn't, for two reasons. Because as much as he wanted to, it didn't seem like the right time. And because if they stayed in this spot too much longer, they would be late getting back to the palace.

And that's when it hit him. He planned to take her with him to the ball. He even had a surprise planned. One he hoped she would love. But had he ever actually asked her to be his date?

Did she assume they were attending together? Even if she did, that wasn't acceptable behavior on his part. Especially not after what she'd just told him.

Only one way to find out. He had to ask.

Chapter Twenty-Seven

Ellie found herself relaxing into his embrace. She'd known all along that Rick was nothing like Glenn, but that tiny bit of fear continued to assault her. Glenn never would have apologized - not and actually meant it. There was a sincerity in Rick's voice, in his eyes, that never existed with her ex-boyfriend. Her hands slid around his waist and the tension released from her shoulders.

After several minutes, he moved back and took her good hand, leading her back to the bottom of the staircase. When she was on the second step he turned her so she looked straight into her eyes. "Have I officially asked you allow me to escort you to the ball this evening?"

She'd wondered about that. He'd said a few things that presumed he would escort her, had picked out her dress, but never actually asked. Ellie shook her head. "No, you never asked."

Rick took both of her hands in his and stepped back. When he bowed, she struggled to hold back a smirk. "Milady, may I have the honor of escorting you to the Crown Princess's

Wedding Ball this evening?"

"Yes, you may." She let go of his hands and walked down the rest of the stairs. "As long as we get back in time."

He stopped her and pressed a kiss against her forehead. "Thank you for giving me a chance, Ellie."

The tender moment lasted a few seconds and then she shook herself out of it. Giving him a fake glare, she picked up her backpack. "If I'm late for this ball, I may change my mind."

He grinned. "Then we better get moving."

After another ten minutes of walking downward, the tunnel leveled off. "I would imagine we are under the lake." Rick stopped and took a sip of his water. "We should be back in time to get ready."

"You better hope so." Her muttered words didn't seem to have any effect on him as he trudged onward. "When will they notice we're missing?"

"They will have already noticed I am. When they noticed I was, they likely looked for you and discovered you are also nowhere to be found."

"And where will they start looking? Do they have any idea where we might be?"

"I set up an email to send at four-thirty. If we made it back to the car, I would have used my phone to cancel it. They should have gotten it by now." He pulled his phone out of his pocket and turned it back on. "There is no reception down here so I could not call if I wanted to."

"Will they come searching?"

"Perhaps. I told them where we were going and when I expected we would be back. I said five-thirty, though I really thought we would be back long before then."

They trudged along for at least another half an hour when Rick spoke again. "I would think we would be getting close. Perhaps even under the palace."

They turned the corner and Rick stopped dead in his tracks.

Ellie ran into his back, smushing her nose. "What is it?" She peeked around him to see what he saw.

Two tunnels.

Rick stared at the tunnels. No one had said anything to him about more than one tunnel, but he knew it had been thoroughly studied so someone had to know about it. Perhaps the other tunnel let to secret passages in the palace, ones he knew existed but no one knew how to find.

"Which one?" Ellie didn't sound afraid but annoyed instead.

"I have no idea. I didn't know it branched off." He took a few steps down the right hand branch and shone the flashlight around. There were no markings he could see except another number counting down. They had made it to number five. Backtracking, he took a few steps down the other corridor. This one also had a five, but this one had a royal crest above it. "We should go this way." He explained his reasoning, and she agreed.

A few minutes later, they came upon a tightly set circular staircase made of stone.

Ellie stood in the middle and looked up. "I can't see the top but I don't guess we have a choice."

"No, we don't. Up we go."

He lost count of how many stairs after about fifty, but they kept on climbing. When they finally reached the top, he was out of breath and Ellie had to be weary. She sat on the top stair and he sank down next to her. She held out another bottle of water which he took gratefully. "Thank you."

"You're welcome." There was a crack in her voice and a hitch in her breath.

"What is it, Ellie?"

She looked up and he saw a tear streak down her face. "I just hope no one told Addie and Charlie we're missing somewhere.

They shouldn't have their wedding day messed up because we did something stupid."

"If I had to guess, I would imagine no one has told them."

"I hope not."

He reached out and brushed the tear away with his fingers. "We should get moving again then."

They stood and a moment later were in front of another choice of passages.

"Now where?"

Rick shrugged and picked one. Ten minutes of twists, turns, stairs and narrow passages later, they reached the end.

"They told me how to open the wall into the garden." He went to the end of the wall and felt around. "I don't think this is it, but hopefully it will work. As long as we exit in the palace we will be fine." He ran his fingertips over the rough-hewn wall until he found the indentations. He pressed his palm into the rock and it rewarded him by creaking open.

"Where is this?" Ellie whispered as she followed him into the room.

"The old chapel." Stained glass windows covered three of the walls, depicting scenes from the Bible. "I have not been in here in years."

Ellie ran her hand over the back of one of the pews and walked down the center aisle. "What is it used for these days?"

"Not much. The occasional wedding or funeral or a place to pray, but not often. Addie and Charlie would have come here last night to pray and get a blessing from my father, but it is a very private ceremony. Not even other family members are allowed and only for the Crown Prince or Princess. She will also receive a blessing here this week from my father and from a priest. The morning of the coronation, I believe. It is also private. Just the three of them." A shaft of light came through one of the windows, landing on Ellie, giving her a bit of a halo as she reached the steps to the podium.

This was it.

He knew in that moment.

One day, he would marry this woman.

And he would marry her in this chapel.

Just as he'd known where he'd propose, he knew.

A small ceremony with family and a few friends. Ellie walking down the aisle in a beautiful white dress on her father's arm. Promising to love, honor and cherish her for the rest of their lives.

Kissing her.

"What?"

Her voice interrupted his daydream and he looked up to see her watching him. "Pardon me." He slipped back into his more formal persona. "I was lost in thought. Shall we go find everyone else?"

She walked back up the aisle and toward the door. "I've gotten to know my way around the palace pretty well, but I have no idea where we are."

"I will show you."

A few minutes later, a stormy looking Steve and Dennis met them in the hall outside his and Ana's apartment. Ellie was only a few minutes late getting to her girls' thing, and he had fifteen minutes before the men were getting ready. They did not take as long to get ready as women.

"Do not start with me," he warned them. "We ran into a bit of trouble, but walked out under the lake and into the old chapel."

"There's an exit in the old chapel?" Dennis's expression said he had not known this.

"Yes. I do not know how to open it from this side, but I could get you there from the other end."

"We will discuss it later, sir, with the head of security. He's furious."

Rick sighed. "Do Addie and Charlie know?"

Steve shook his head. "No, only a few members of the security team."

"Good."

He went into his apartment, found what he was looking for and headed for another part of the palace to meet Charlie, Dan, their fathers, his father, and the other men who were a part of the royal wedding party.

Ellie stared in the mirror for another minute. Rick had impeccable taste, she'd give him that. She needed to move, she knew that. Addie would be waiting on her if she didn't - and Charlie and Addie would be in the ballroom before anyone else entered and do a small receiving line with their parents, but everyone else would be introduced by some kind of announcer as they entered. As the oldest sibling, Rick would be last and she would be with him - unless she didn't hurry. Then they might start without her.

"Miss Brewer, it's time." Danica tried not to look annoyed, but she still did.

"I know."

"You look lovely. Prince Richard will be hard pressed not to drop to one knee and propose this evening."

"Goodness, I hope not." Despite their conversation in the tunnel, she wasn't ready for that, and she didn't think Rick was either.

She followed Danica to the ballroom. A number of couples waited in line, including Ana and Jonathan. She was sure the queen was behind that match. And...she squinted and tried not to stare. Was that Will and Kate talking to them? Had they brought the new baby with them? Was the new baby, now four months old, somewhere in the palace with a nanny? Were the royals in attendance introduced in some sort of order of importance? If so, it made sense they would be last before members of the Montevaro royal family. None of the members of the royal families in the *Royal Commonwealth of Bellas Montagnes* had stayed for the ball, citing unavoidable business to attend to.

"Ellie." Someone hissed her name.

Looking around she saw Rick standing behind a potted tree. He motioned at her. When she got close, he reached for her, pulling her into the shadows with him. She stumbled into him, hands resting against the red sash across his chest. His black tuxedo jacket boasted tails this evening with a white tie. The sash met at his right hip with the family crest in bright blue holding the two sides together. From his left hip, dangled a sword with a fancy grip on it and a scabbard that would make Captain Jack Sparrow jealous.

"Do you know how to use that thing?" She pointed to the sword.

"I do." His full, drool-worthy grin, complete with dimples appeared and melted her insides. "All good princes learn fencing and sword fighting at some point, though I pray I never have to actually use it."

"I pray the same."

He smiled down at her, his eyes tender. "You look incredible, Miss Brewer."

She ducked her head so he wouldn't see the blush. "Thank you, Prince Richard. You don't look half bad yourself." In truth, he looked much better than that. He looked better than the prettiest pretty boy ever, and she marveled that God had somehow brought them together.

"There's something I wanted to give you before we go in."

Her stomach dropped. Surely Danica hadn't been right. He wouldn't propose, would he?

Rick reached into his pocket and pulled out a necklace. He draped it over his other hand to show her the locket. The silver was studded with jewels forming the family crest.

"Rick, I don't know..." It was too much.

"This is a family heirloom, passed down for the last two hundred years." He ran his thumb over the heart.

Two hundred years? What would her family say? His family? "It's too much."

"It's not a proposal or a formal engagement or anything of that nature. But it does mean you are very special to me and that we are together and serious. It will be in the papers, and the speculation will explode after the wedding. But I'm fine with that if you are." He smiled at her, melting her heart.

"Yes."

"Now, just because my mother will ask me if I mentioned this to you, this stays in the palace. It is yours to wear whenever you choose as long as we are together, but it remains the property of the family." He brushed his fingers down her neck. "If my mother asks, I can be honest with her, though I know it wouldn't be an issue even if we were to end our relationship. She is a stickler for those sorts of things."

"Of course." That his mother would expect him to tell her that annoyed her, but she had a feeling the queen would never approve of anyone she didn't choose for her children. She'd accepted Charlie reluctantly at best.

Ellie turned around as Rick undid the clasp. He reached around in front of her and settled it in the hollow of her neck as he reclasped it. His lips were warm as he kissed her shoulder while the necklace slid into place.

"Is this why Danica mysteriously couldn't find the pearls my mother brought for me to wear?" She twisted her head to look up at him through tear-filled eyes.

"I would imagine so." His arm remained around her waist as he guided her toward the much diminished line of people getting ready to enter. "Would you like to meet the Duke and Duchess before going in?"

Oh my.

Rick laughed at a comment Prince William made. They had always gotten on well, though they were several years apart and William would someday be king while Rick never would. William's younger brother had been unable to attend due to a charity event he'd committed to long before the wedding date was set. He could tell Ellie was apprehensive about meeting them, but the Duchess immediately put her at ease, and they chatted like old friends until it was their turn.

Ana and Jonathan were introduced next. Rick tucked Ellie's hand into his elbow and squeezed it gently. "You will do just fine. You look lovely, truly. No one will notice your arm." He knew she wore the elbow length gloves to cover up her weak arm. Her navy blue dress was as high quality and beautiful as any at the ball, with the possible exception of Adeline's.

The doormen nodded at him, and he urged Ellie forward.

The announcer called loudly. "Ladies and Gentlemen, His Royal Highness Prince Richard Jedidiah David Nicklaus of Montevaro escorting Miss Ellie Brewer of The United States of America."

The doors opened, and they entered to a smattering of applause from around the room. Their turn through the receiving line went quickly until he reached his mother.

"What did you do?" she hissed. "Giving her that locket?"

"Do not question me on this, Mother. I had Father's blessing, and Adeline's as well. If you gave her half a chance, you would love Ellie. You will say nothing to her, understand?" Rick had never used that tone with his mother before, but he would not stand there and allow his mother to make Ellie feel unwelcome or undesired because of his gift.

"Very well. We will discuss this more later."

He glanced to the side to see Ellie still talking with Charlie's daughter, who might as well be her niece, and she had not noticed any of his mother's comments. His mother greeted Ellie coolly but politely. As Ellie moved off, he offered his arm once again, noting the whispers around the room from members of Montevarian high society.

The announcer made his next one. "Ladies and Gentlemen, Members of the Montevarian Parliament, Honored Guests, Her Royal Highness Princess Anastasia, His Royal Highness Prince Richard, Her Majesty Queen Alexandra, and His Majesty King Jedidiah. Please welcome Crown Princess Adeline and her new husband, Sir Charlemagne Brewer to the floor for their first dance."

Adeline had changed into a white ball gown. Charlie had obviously taken lessons, and they waltzed beautifully around the floor together. As the song ended, the king and Charlie's mother walked onto the floor.

"Will you do me the honor of the next dance? The first one at the wedding ball." Rick reminded her, bowing slightly at the waist.

"Isn't it for Charlie with your mother and Addie with my uncle?"

"Yes, but the other members of the royal family can join if they want. My father will dance with your aunt."

"Then yes. It would be my honor."

A minute later, her hand was snug in his as he twirled her around the dance floor. He tried to keep from smiling as she concentrated. She had not been dancing like this nearly as long as he had.

"You are doing wonderfully."

"Thanks, but if I keep talking I'll trip and fall."

He chuckled, his sword slapping against his thigh. "Very well." All too soon the song wound down. Before he handed her off to her next partner, he ushered her onto the same balcony he had the last time they had danced.

"What are we doing out here?"

Rick shrugged. "Feeling a bit nostalgic perhaps." He stopped at the stone rail and turned to face her. "Ellie, I know we have some problems we will need to work through. Namely my schedule and the fact that palace life can be quite stifling at times."

"Yes, we do need to spend some time figuring out how we will work around all of that."

"I am grateful you are giving me another chance." He reached out and took one of her brunette curls between his fingers and rubbed the silky hair between them. "I am falling in love with you, Eleanor Rosaline Brewer."

Her eyes narrowed. "Who told you?"

Rick stifled the chuckle that threatened to escape. "I have my sources." The enormity of the moment demanded a serious demeanor, and he felt it sweep over him. "But, no matter what your name, I'm falling in love with you. I don't think I could stop myself if I wanted to."

She swallowed and took a tiny step closer to him. "I'm falling in love with you, too, Rick. In fact, I think I'm already there."

"Can you also love Prince Richard and all that entails?" His fingers trailed down her neck, her arm and when he reached her hand he squeezed it lightly. With both hands on her hips he drew her closer to him, praying she gave the answer he longed to hear.

"Yes. I think I am already falling in love with Prince Richard as well." Her arms slid around his waist.

"No one has ever affected me quite like you." He pressed a kiss to her forehead. "No one has affected me *anything* like you."

Rick lowered his face to hers and covered her lips with his own, pulling her closer in his arms. She responded by sliding her hands up his back, holding him tight.

A swirl of emotions filled him. His heart overflowed with the unfamiliar, but amazing, rush of feelings.

So this is what love feels like.

Long before he wanted to, he moved away, coming back for one more quick brush of the lips before tucking her into his chest. Rick rested his chin on her head, glad her hair was piled on the back of her head rather than the top so he could.

"We're not stealing Charlie and Addie's thunder are we?" Ellie pulled back a bit and looked up at him. "With the locket and everything on their big day?"

"No. I mentioned to Addie I wanted to give it to you, and she gave her blessing for me to give it to you today."

"Why doesn't Addie get it? If it's a family heirloom and all."

"Traditionally, the oldest son gives it to his bride. I know I haven't proposed, and I don't plan to just yet, but I wanted you to have it. To date, that has always been the future queen, since Addie will be the first daughter to ascend to the throne. She offered it to me several years ago when it came up in conversation, and she reminded me of it earlier this week. I thought about it but hadn't wanted to bring it up in the middle of everything else." He brushed a kiss against her forehead. "We should go back inside."

Before she backed away, Ellie stood on her tiptoes and brushed a kiss against his cheek. "The day we met, I asked God why He was giving me a pretty boy for a camper, but I am so glad He did."

"Me, too."

With his arm around the woman he loved, Prince Richard returned to the ballroom. He had run from his responsibilities long enough. He had allowed others to set his priorities for weeks. Though he knew it would occasionally be unavoidable, he intended to never let it happen again. And someday soon, he would ask the woman at his side to be his princess for the rest of her life.

Epilogue

Four Weeks Later

"Where are we going?" Ellie stretched out on the couch in the plane.

Rick grinned at her. "I'm not telling." He tipped his head toward Steve and Dennis. "They're not telling. The pilots won't tell. You'll have to wait until we get there."

"How much longer?"

"You sound like a little kid on her first road trip."

She sighed and closed her eyes. "Fine. I'm taking a nap. Wake me when we land."

So much had happened since they met, even since the wedding. She and Rick were making preparations to open Montevaro's Adventures in the spring. The larger concept encompassing two of the three countries in the Commonwealth would come in stages over the next several years. They would start with two minimalist camping trips a week - one just an overnight and one three nights. For now, they would be the guides, though at least two bodyguards would be on each trip as well.

He'd been right, she admitted. Once the coronation furor died down, his life had also calmed down considerably. She'd been living with her aunt and uncle, but she saw Rick nearly every day, either visiting the palace or out on a date or working somewhere else. When he had to be out of town, they video chatted for at least a few minutes every night. He'd promised he would make her a priority and he had. She loved him a little more every day.

Ellie was the reason behind this trip. They had returned to Allegiance to pack up her apartment and make her move to Montevaro permanent. Upon leaving, they had flown to New York City, where he took her to a Broadway show and to the top of the Empire State Building. They'd taken a day trip to Niagara Falls, gone to the base of the Falls and gotten soaked, before returning to the city for another day of site seeing. Rick had arranged a trip to the top of the Freedom Tower and semi-private tour of the 9/11 Museum. Always properly chaperoned, of course.

The plane took off in the wee hours of the morning without a word about where they were going. Rick told her to have warm clothes handy so she told him to keep the air turned down on the plane and she'd be fine with her jeans and sweatshirt.

When she peeked out from nearly closed lids, she saw the three men plotting furiously. What on earth? He was up to something, but dragging Steve and Dennis into it? That seemed odd.

Giving a mental shrug, she settled in to sleep. They'd been out late for another Broadway show, up early to get on the plane, and it didn't take much for her to doze off. Vaguely, she noted someone covering her with a blanket and kissing her forehead. She hoped it was Rick.

She drifted off until a soft kiss, right on the lips, woke her.

Blinking, she saw Rick's smiling face in front of her. She smiled as he kissed her again.

"Good morning, sleepyhead." He brushed the hair back off her forehead in a move she loved.

"Is it still morning where we are?"

His eyebrows pulled together. "Um... I don't know. But we will be landing soon so the pilots asked for you to put a seatbelt on."

Sitting up, she yawned and stretched. Rather than moving to one of the captain's chairs, she sat in the middle of the couch and buckled in there. Rick laughed and sat next to her. As soon as he buckled, he put his arm around her and pulled her close. Resting her head on his shoulder, she felt safe. Secure.

Then she looked around.

"You pulled all the shades so I can't see where we are?"

She felt as much as heard his chuckle. "Yes, love. And before we depart the plane, you will need a blindfold and earplugs."

"You're going all out for this, aren't you?"

"Absolutely."

She tried to figure out where they might be going. He'd promised to take her to the Ice Hotel in Norway sometime, but it was too early in the year for that. Maybe to Canada? The flight was too long. Antarctica was out. As were the Himalayas.

His words were warm in her ear. "Give it up. You won't figure it out."

Her first thought had actually been Iceland or Greenland, but just a week earlier, he'd promised to take her there after they were married - whenever that was - and share one of those igloos with her. Rick had even insinuated he might take her there for their honeymoon.

The sounds of the plane changed and the wheels thunked onto the ground. As they rolled to a stop, Rick stood and pulled a long, white scarf out of a cubbyhole. He stood in front of her, his eyes asking if she trusted him. Ellie nodded, knowing it was true. Just months earlier, she wouldn't have trusted him to take care of her cactus while she was on vacation, but now she trusted him with her life.

He handed her one wax earplug. She fit it in. Before she

could place the second one, she felt him lean over.

"I love you," he whispered. He took the second ear plug from her and started to put it in. She helped him finish. He leaned in again and she thought he was going to see if she could hear anything, but instead he kissed her. Then he said something. "Can you hear me?"

She nodded.

"Good. I will walk backward and lead you. When I squeeze your hands, that means stop. If I lower them, there's a step down. If I raise them, there's a step up. When we get to a car, I'll put your hand on the door and help you in."

She nodded again. "I trust you." Her voice echoed in her head as Rick tugged on her hands.

Getting to the door of the plane was easy enough. Getting down a bit more tricky. Climbing in and out of the car wasn't too bad. The next set of stairs puzzled her, but when Rick told her it was time to sit down, she realized she was in some sort of boat or aircraft. He helped her buckle in. The vibrations and lifting sensation told her they had boarded a helicopter.

Rick's arm went around her again, though there was a chair arm between them this time. The trip didn't last terribly long, not compared to the earlier flight. When they landed, he helped her stand up, get back off the helicopter, and onto solid ground.

When Rick swept her into his arms, she squealed and grabbed at his shoulders until he had a good grasp on her. Ellie felt his laughter as she relaxed against his chest.

"I will set you down now."

Wherever they were, he'd been right. The cold pierced her leather gloves and blue jeans. He ran his fingers up both sides of her neck and took the earplugs out. She didn't hear a thing except some nature noises she couldn't quite place.

"Do you know where we are?" Rick wrapped his arms around her and pulled her back to his chest.

"No." Her mind ran a million miles a minute as she tried to

figure it out.

"Close your eyes. I'll take the blindfold off, but it might be a bit bright."

"Okay."

The knot loosened at the back of her head. The scarf slipped down around her neck as Rick covered her eyes with his hands.

"I want you to get the full effect, love. I will move my hands back, but so your eyes are still shaded until you adjust."

He did just that and a minute later, she nodded. "I'm ready."

"Close them again until I move my hands." His arms settled back around her waist. "Open your eyes, Ellie."

Her eyes fluttered open. She couldn't contain her gasp. They stood on a glacier, close enough to see the ocean beyond. "Rick, this is amazing." Farther out, icebergs floated away from the mother ice she and Rick stood on. A humpback whale breached falling back into the ocean with a giant splash.

Rick moved to her side, taking her hand and handing her a pair of binoculars. Where had he pulled those from? He pointed to the other side.

Ellie squealed, just a bit, as several Orcas breached in unisons. "This is incredible." She squeezed his hand. "Thank you. How long can we stay?" She continued to scan with the glasses.

He let go of her hand and stepped back. She thought he was going to wrap his arms around her again, but he didn't. When he still hadn't a minute later, she lowered the binoculars, and turned around to see where he'd gone.

Her jaw dropped when she saw him, down on one knee, in his royal uniform, complete with sword. One part of her mind wondered when he'd put it on and noted his coat nearby, realizing it must have been on underneath.

The rest of her mind scrambled to understand the meaning. Dressed up. One knee. And in his hand, he held a velvet box. Rick opened the box to reveal a sparkling diamond and emerald engagement ring. "Eleanor Rosaline Brewer, I love you more than life itself. I cannot remember a time when you were not in my life, in my heart. Will you spend your life with me? Be my princess and the mother of my children?" He took a deep breath. "Will you marry me?"

Tears flooded her eyes and streamed down her cheeks. "Yes. Yes, I'll marry you."

Rick pulled the ring out of the box. She pulled off her glove and held out her hand for him to slip it on her finger. He stood, pulling her into his arms. "I do love you, Ellie. More than anything."

"I love you, too, Rick."

He kissed her, holding her to him for long minutes, telling her without words how he felt. When he released her, he grinned. The biggest grin she'd ever seen on his face. Rick took a step back and threw his hands in the air, letting out a caveman yell. "Woohoo! She said yes!"

Ellie covered her face with her hands, laughing at his child-like enthusiasm. Rick picked her up by the waist and swung her in a circle as she held onto his shoulders, laughing like there was no tomorrow. When he set her down, he kissed her again.

"We can stay as long as we'd like, more or less, love."

She turned in his arms to look at the view once again before glancing at the helicopter. Steve and Dennis both stood there, cameras in hand. "Uh, Rick? What are they doing?"

He chuckled behind her. "Trent and your brother insisted they get a video and photographic record of you saying yes to marrying a pretty boy."

Ellie laughed, twisting her neck to look up at him and accept another kiss.

She'd said yes to a pretty boy, and she wouldn't have it any other way.

Dear Reader,

Thank you for joining Prince Richard and Ellie in *Along Came a Prince*! I appreciate you and hope you enjoyed it! This is the second book in The Montevaro Monarchy series - and book 3, *More Than a Princess*, is out now! Following the acknowledgments, you will find a preview of Princess Ana's story as well as chapter 1 of *Finding Mr. Write*, book 1 in the CANDID Romance series!

I see a meme floating around Facebook from time to time that tells readers what they can do to help their favorite authors. Buying their next book or giving a copy away is kind of a no-brainer, but the biggest thing you can do is write a review. If you enjoyed *Along Came a Prince* would you consider doing just that? You can do so by going to the Amazon page and scrolling down until you get to the button that asks if you'd like to write a review of your own.

I would LOVE to hear from you! My email address is carolmoncadobooks@gmail.com. You can find my website and blog at www.carolmoncado.com. I blog most Sundays and about once more each month at www.InspyRomance.com. And, of course, there's Facebook and my Facebook profile, Author Carol Moncado. If you recently liked my Facebook *page* (Carol Moncado Books)...I hope you'll "follow" the profile as well. Facebook recently changed the rules again which means very few people (often 1-5% of "likes") will see anything I post there. Following the profile will show you my book updates, updates about books from authors I love, funny cat (or dog or dinosaur!) memes, inspirational quotes, and all sorts of fun stuff!! I hope to see you there soon!

Thanks again! I hope to see you soon!

Until next time,
Carol

Acknowledgments

They say writing is a solitary endeavor and it absolutely can be. Sitting in front of the computer for hours on end, talking to imaginary people.

And having them talk back ;).

But the reality is no one walks alone. Since I began this writing journey five and a half years ago, I can't begin to name all of those who've helped me along the way. From my husband, Matt, who has always, *always* believed in me and my best friend, Penny, who has brainstormed and critiqued and made me stop using passive voice more times than I can count. Others like Becki, Allen, Tina, Bobbie, Candice, the fitting room attendant at my local Wal-Mart, and so many others who encouraged, cheered, and cried with me. My mother-in-love, Andrea, who has prayed over us for years. All of the rest of my family and in-loves who never once looked at me like I was nuts for wanting to be a writer, including Gloria, my avid-reader sister, who has watched my kids countless times so I could work. Jan Christiansen (my "other mother") has always believed in me and Stacy Christiansen Spangler who has been my dearest friend for longer than I can remember.

Then there's my writer friends. My NovelSistas, Jessica Keller Koschnitzky and Kristy Cambron, both sisters of my heart. They're part of my BritCrit gals. Joanna Politano (who has talked me down off more virtual ledges than anyone), Jen Cvelvar (the best case of misidentification *ever*), and Stacey Zink (who never, ever fails to have a fabulous encouraging word) are BritCritters, too. We do a lot more living than we do critting, and I wouldn't have it any other way. All five of them are beyond gifted as writers and I thank God they're in my life. There's my MozArks ACFW peeps who laugh with me, critique, and encourage to no end. And Melanie Dickerson. What would I do without you?

Then there's the Seekers, the AlleyCats, the InspyRomance

crew, the CIA, my TSG peeps (you know who you are!), and all of the others who've helped me along on this journey.

I could go on for days about beloved mentors like Janice Thompson who has poured her time and energy into this newbie, going above and beyond for me. People like one of my spiciest friends, Pepper Basham, who inspires me daily, or Julie Lessman, who has prayed me to this point. People like Jeane Wynn (*the* top publicist in the business) and Kathleen Y'Barbo (one of the top authors) who take me along on late night Wal-Mart runs and kidnap me to Chili's so I'm writing on a full stomach. All of these and so many more are not only mentors, but *friends* - I am beyond blessed! And, of course, there's Tamela Hancock Murray, agent extraordinaire, who believed in me enough to want to be my agent.

Along Came a Prince, the first draft, was finished (at about half this length) two years ago. The transformation into a full "trade length" novel has been a long, painful process. It's been added to and rearranged (the sticky notes on my plotting calendar lost their sticky!) and tweaked and cried over in frustration to get where it is now. Only through God's grace did I not throw in the towel! Super special thanks go to everyone who helped it get to this point - I know I could never name all of you! And especially to Ginger V. who has read at least 5 different iterations, and Ginger Solomon (have you read her books?!), Jerenda F., and Emily N. who helped proofread.

I said I could go on for days and I could keep going. On and on. I know I've forgotten many people and I hate that. But you, dear reader, would quickly get bored.

So THANK YOU to all of those who have helped me along the way. I couldn't have done this without you and you have my eternal gratitude.

And, of course, last but never, *ever*, least, to Jesus Christ, without whom none of this would be possible - or worth it.

More Than
A Princess

AVAILABLE NOW!

"Anastasia Salome Keziah, Princess of Montevaro and her escort, Jonathan William Langley-Cranston the Fourth of the United States."

Ana tucked her hand inside Jonathan's elbow, knowing she would rather be there with someone else, and pasted the best smile she could on her face as they walked through the ornate wood doors into the palace ball room. A smattering of applause sounded in the room. Her slightly-older twin brother and his new girlfriend were announced about the time Ana and Jonathan reached the bottom of the steps. When Jonathan stopped next to their seats, the crier called again.

"Our guests of honor, Her Royal Highness, Crown Princess Adeline of Montevaro and her husband, Prince Charlemagne Brewer."

"I bet he hates that," she muttered to herself.

"What?"

She looked up to see Jonathan staring down at her, an

amused look on his face. "I bet Charlie hates being introduced as Charlemagne all the time."

Jonathan chuckled. "I can imagine." He held her seat out for her as she sat down. Once he sat down next her, he leaned over to whisper in her ear. "You know, we both know you would rather be here with someone else, and we both know your mother would never allow you to attend with the escort of you would have chosen, so can we just make the best of this?"

Ana scanned the ballroom until her eyes landed on the dark wavy locks and laughing blue eyes of Montevaro's most renowned pediatrician. When he looked her way, she broke eye contact and stared at the family crest on her plate.

"I'd guess he'd probably rather be here with you, too."

"It does not matter. You were correct when you said my mother would never permit it. Perhaps once Adeline is queen..."

"That's only two days away. Once all this pomp and circumstance is over, your mother will relax."

Ana watched Dr. Fontaine as he smiled at the woman sitting next to him and her heart twisted, just a bit. She struggled through dinner, knowing her sister would point it out if she didn't eat well. Jonathan respected her space and did not try to draw her out in conversation.

When the dancing started, Addie and Charlie took the floor first. Partway through the dance, Rick - as the second in line for the throne - and Ellie joined them. The protocol secretary nodded at Ana, who allowed Jonathan to help her to her feet and join her brother and sister for the last third of the song.

Once the first dance was over, anyone could join in. She and Jonathan traded partners and she found herself dancing with her brother.

"Why so glum, chum?" Rick's eyes twinkled at her.

"Don't get all psychological on me." If she wasn't careful, he'd dig and dig, until he figured it out. "How are things going with Ellie?"

"Ah. You're changing the subject, little sister. Are you not completely enamored with your date?"

"You know I'm not. Jonathan is a nice man, but when it didn't work out between him and Addie, Mother decided she wanted him in the family anyway. That means me."

"And you would rather be here with the good doctor?"

Ana glared up at her brother but didn't reply.

"He was on the shortlist for Addie, so why not for you?" Rick twirled her out and back in. "That is your real question, is it not?"

How well he knew her. They had shared a womb. "Maybe."

Rick leaned down until there was no chance any of the other couple nearby would hear him. "I have it on good authority he's interested in my sister."

"Don't be silly, Rick. The man doesn't even know I'm alive except as the spare of the spare for the throne of Montevaro."

He held her hand to his chest and let his head fall back dramatically. "The spare? You wound me, sister."

If they hadn't been dancing at one of the most important balls of her lifetime, she would have smacked him right in the arm. The music began to wind down for this song and she knew tradition dictated the third dance be with whoever was on the lady's right. She just hoped her brother wouldn't her land next to one of the stuffed shirts from Parliament. Instead, as he took a step back and bowed, she noted the glint in his eye.

She turned to her right and her heart stopped. The man bowed while she gave a slight curtsy. One hand rested on his shoulder while the other fit snugly inside his. "Dr. Fontaine, it is a pleasure."

Could she make it through this dance without embarrassing herself?

He smiled down at her. "Oh no, Princess Ana. The pleasure is all mine."

Dr. Jonah Fontaine could hardly believe his luck. He'd expected the princess to end up with her escort for this dance as well, but when he'd looked to his left and saw her standing there, his heart leapt in his chest. As Princess Anastasia tucked her hand in his, he reached for her waist, settling his other hand on her hip, the smooth satin of her gown cool beneath his fingertips. He lead her through the first bars of the next song, found his sister's eyes on him and her wink said she was more than happy to relinquish her hold on him for the evening.

But he needed to take this chance before it slipped away.

"Are you enjoying yourself, Princess Anastasia?"

"Ana, please."

She wouldn't look directly at him. "Princess Ana, then." He noted the Ah-na sound she used to pronounce it and did his best to replicate, though he wasn't sure he succeeded, not with his Texas twang. "Are you enjoying yourself?"

"So far it has been a lovely evening."

"The meal was delicious. I will have to mention to your sister what an excellent job they did with the choices."

Was it just his imagination or did Princess Ana stiffen at the mention of her sister?

"I am afraid it would be a waste of time to mention it to Adeline, sir. My brother organized this ball. The charity auction later this evening will benefit my sister's charities as a celebration of her coronation."

"Of course. I will have to mention it to Prince Richard then, if I have the chance." He had only met the prince once or twice, though he and Adeline were on a first name basis. It made him uncomfortable, given her position, but he knew she didn't let friends into her inner circle lightly and he was grateful to be counted among them. He'd treated her new stepdaughter several months earlier when Charlie and Lindsey had flown to Montevaro less than two weeks after Lindsey's appendix burst.

The dance was passing much too quickly. He needed to find a way to spend more time with her. "We would love to have you tour the children's wing, Your Highness."

"I will see if I can work a visit into my schedule before the fall term begins."

Jonah felt his brow furrow. "I thought for certain I had heard you graduated this spring."

"I did. I am considering a Master's degree."

They continued to move around the floor and Jonah tried his best to come up with something to say. Adeline got most of the attention because of her position, but Jonah had always thought Ana was the more beautiful of the two.

"May I call on you, Princess Ana?" The words were out of his mouth before he could think about it.

She finally looked up at him, long, dark lashes covering bright blue eyes as she blinked rapidly. "Pardon?"

He sucked in a deep breath. "May I call you? Take you to dinner sometime after all the hoopla has settled down a bit?"

Ana just looked into his eyes, searching for something. He didn't know what, but if she didn't answer soon the dance would be over. As the last notes soared through the room, she gave a single nod. "I will see that you have details on how to contact me before you leave this evening." She took a single step backward. "I do hope you have a lovely time."

Jonah bowed slightly from the waist. "Perhaps I can have another dance before the night ends?"

"I doubt I will have many openings, sir, but if the occasion presents itself..." She bit her lip then released it.

"Perhaps at the auction." Jonah could have kicked himself. If he didn't bid on her last dance, he'd look like a cad. If he did bid - and was outbid by a large amount as he suspected would be the case - she'd see the paltry sum he could afford and never agree to dinner.

Ana gave him a small smile and a man stepped between them, cutting off his view of her. He turned to find Adeline standing there, smiling at him.

She smirked as the dance began and Ana was twirled away. "You could ask me to dance, you know."

Jonah bowed at the waist, more deeply than he'd bowed to her sister. "May I have the pleasure of this dance, Your Highness?"

"Of course." As he led her through the steps, she looked straight at him. "Do not give up, Jonah."

The truth of the matter burned in his core. "You know, Princess Adeline, I have only met your sister twice before this evening. Very briefly both times. An introduction during a receiving line. I doubt she has any idea who I am."

Adeline gave him a big smile. "Oh, she knows, Jonah."

He didn't contradict the woman who would be his queen in just a couple of days, but instead continued the dance with her.

"Bid for her last dance," Adeline told him. "Go as high as you need to and I will see that you're reimbursed."

He shook his head. "Thank you, ma'am, but I couldn't win her dance that way." Jonah turned when he felt a tap on his shoulder.

"May I cut in?" Charlie stood next to them, a smile on his face. "I need to speak with my wife a moment."

Adeline's face colored at the sound of her husband's voice.

Jonah had no choice but to step away. "Of course, Your Highness."

This was going to be a long night.

The one thing Ana hated most about balls were her aching feet. She'd never liked heels much, but she had little choice in the matter. With a ball gown, you wear heels. Period.

She'd danced every dance and never with the same man twice, not even Jonathan. As her escort, he'd have the last dance before the auction.

"You look like you're about ready to get out of here." She turned to she Charlie standing there holding out his hand. "I haven't had the chance to dance with my favorite sister-in-law yet."

Ana shook her head slightly. "I'm your only sister-in-law."

"Beside the point."

She noticed how much he'd improved over the last few months. Her last dance with him had been after he'd been knighted and his parents awarded the titles of Marquis and Marchioness of Montago for service to the crown. And she told him so.

He grinned. "It's not much of a chore to practice with Addie. I'll dance with her any chance I get."

Ana smiled back. "I would imagine so." She giggled. "And you don't have to say good night anymore."

Charlie chuckled. "I can't say I'm disappointed we spend, ah, more time together."

"I know you had a hard time finding time for each other the last few months."

"And I know after the coronation things will still be busy but hopefully the extreme busyness will calm down some."

"How is Lindsey adapting to all of it?"

"She loves Addie. That's all that really matters to her. She gets to live at the palace now, instead of with my parents, and we should get to have family dinners soon. Addie has missed her, too." He spun her in a circle. "Now, how enamored are you with Jonathan? Is it a love match?"

Ana looked over to see Jonathan dancing with Christiana, queen of Ravenzario - one of Montevaro's two sister countries. "I don't believe so. He's a nice man and I enjoy spending time with him, but I don't believe we will be a great love story like you and Adeline are." An ache had been building in her heart and the conversation with Charlie caused it to spread. She wanted to rub her chest with the heel of her hand in the hopes it would dissipate.

"There's someone out there for you, Ana. I know there is."

"I'm certain you're right, Charlie. I hope, for Papa's sake, I find him soon. He was exceptionally glad to walk Addie down the aisle before..." She looked around. No one was too close, but the news of her father's Parkinson's Disease had not yet been made public.

"I know." Charlie squeezed her hand.

Tears pooled in her eyes as she thought of her father's deteriorating health. "If I don't find someone soon, Charlie, would you do me the honor of walking me down the aisle? If Papa can't?"

He let go of her and grasped her hand, headed for the balcony. Before they could escape, the music changed. Charlie groaned. "I'm sorry, Ana."

She nodded. "I know. Go find Addie." He squeezed her hand and walked off. Ana continued her walk to the balcony, breathing deeply of the cool night air.

"Are you okay?" Jonathan's voice reached her seconds before he did. Without asking he pulled her into his arms and she rested her head on his chest, tears slowly seeping out of her eyes and into the shirt of his tuxedo. "What is it? Did Charlie upset you?"

"No. Not really. I just started wondering if my father would actually be well enough to walk me down the aisle when the time comes." She sniffled. "It could be years before I get married."

She sniffed again. Very unladylike, much less princess-y. But Jonathan tipped her head up to look at him.

"Then marry me."

Along Came a Prince

AVAILABLE NOW!

Princess Anastasia has grown up in the shadow of her older siblings and foster sister, Queen Christiana of Ravenzario. Ana longs for an identity beyond that of a princess. More than anything she wants someone to see her as more than just a tiara and a pretty face. Two men vie for her attentions but only one believes in her, believes she can make a difference by using her royal status to draw attention to the plight of those less fortunate.

American Jonathan William Langley-Cranston IV has dated both her sister and her soon-to-be sister-in-law, but he and Ana seem to have something extra special. When his brother disappears without a trace, she returns to the States to become the public face of his family.

In Montevaro, Dr. Jonah Fontaine wants to help. And unlike most people, he's willing to roll up his sleeves and get his hands dirty. He spends his vacations going places most people couldn't be paid enough to visit. As much as he wants to, he doesn't understand why Ana and others like her won't put their time and effort where their money is.

When Ana takes Jonah up on his challenge to join him at an orphanage in Ravenzario, they find themselves facing a crisis. A little girl, recently diagnosed with juvenile diabetes, is threatened by rising flood waters after a rare Mediterranean hurricane makes landfall. Jonathan, with the help of Queen Christiana, desperately searches for them, praying rescue won't come too late.

Her head knows which man, Jonah or Jonathan, is the wise choice. Too bad her heart has different ideas. Which one will win? Will Ana be able to convince either one of them of her worth as *More than a Princess*?

Previews may not be in their final form and are subject to change.

Finding

Mr.

Write

<u>Available NOW!</u>

Local Woman Arrested For Stalking Favorite Author

Dorrie Miller could see the headline now. She held the phone between her ear and shoulder as she shoved a pair of jeans in the drawer. "Did you really buy night vision goggles?"

"What do you think?" Sarcasm deepened the Appalachian accent until Dorrie could barely understand Anise.

Of course she had.

Anise had bought the night vision goggles and the ear wig thingies, the ones that looked like hearing aids, and heaven only knew what else.

Within two days of being at their first major national conference for writers, they'd be cooling their heels in a jail cell, hoping no one would use their escapades for story fodder. CANDID stood for Christian Author's Network, Dedicated to Inspirational Distinction, not detention.

"We're really going to stalk this woman? I know you want to meet her. I do, too. But stalking? That's a felony." Or a serious misdemeanor. Whichever. It wouldn't be good. "We'll have restraining orders and never be able to show our face at CANDID again." Dorrie checked her appearance in the mirror once more. Passable. "And how do you know MEL is going to be at conference, anyway?"

As administrator of the Mya Elizabeth Linscott Facebook page, Dorrie should know when the author had appearances scheduled. Dorrie had read all of MEL's books so many times she could quote large sections of them. Her collection would be complete with autographs, but the only way to get signed copies was to get them off MEL's website for twice the cover price. Sure, the extra money went to charity but Dorrie still didn't have that kind of cash. Instead, she had a standing order with the local Christian bookstore to get the latest book as soon as it released.

She'd even emailed with MEL a few times. Okay. MEL's assistant, but still.

How did she not know MEL would be making her first public appearance ever?

Anise hemmed and hawed for a second or two. "Well, I don't know for sure MEL's coming. But the bookstore coordinator sent me a list of authors who are going to have books and she's on it."

"One of her books is up for a CANDID Award," Dorrie pointed out. "Those are automatically stocked. She's up for an award every year. Those books are always there." Not that Dorrie had been at the other conferences, but she knew people and heard all about it.

"I know that. But she has 'five books' in parentheses next to her name. She'd only have one if it was just the book up for a CANDID Award."

Anise had a point. "Okay. She might be there."

"Let's plan how we're going to make sure we get to meet her. And bring your copies because they have a place where you can put them to be signed."

"You really think she'll sign them for free? Everyone else does, but she never has. She gives away ten free signed copies of each book when it comes out, but that's it." Dorrie had never won, no matter how hard she tried.

"You never know."

A glance at the clock showed Dorrie she had ten minutes before it was time to leave for her fourth ever local CANDID meeting. The one she was in charge of. What had she been thinking when she volunteered to be the coordinator? Dorrie half-listened to Anise prattle on as doubts assailed her once again.

Visions of George Costanza danced in her head to a Brad Paisley soundtrack as a dull ache began to seep into the edges of her brain. So much cooler in the online world. She should stay home where no one would discover she didn't belong with the cool kids.

Online, Dorrie knew she was a blast. Always fun. Always up for something. Or pretend something anyway. There weren't any real consequences to plotting with other readers to cyber-steal a flash drive with a manuscript on it from a favorite author when nothing actually changed hands. Or to resort to bribery with her peanut butter cookies. Dorrie had been known to send a box or two. Not that it had gotten her anywhere.

Another look toward the bookcase where her first edition Mya Elizabeth Linscott novels sat, unsigned, spurred her onward. She had to go. She had to follow her dream of becoming an author. No matter what anyone, especially her dad, said about it. In two and a half months, Dorrie could finally have a chance to meet her writing hero. If she was really lucky, have two, maybe even three, minutes to pick MEL's brain about the publishing world.

"Dorrie!" Anise's voice jolted her back to the present. "Can you get the walkie talkies?"

With a sigh, Dorrie turned to the conversation at hand. "Yes, I have walkies. I fail to see why we need them if we're using earwigs."

"Back-up. You know that. Back-up your back-ups. It holds true for manuscripts and trying to meet your favorite authors."

Anise was even more obsessed with back-ups than Dorrie had ever been. The advent of "the cloud" and "cloud storage" helped, but one could never be sure it was enough. The loss of a Publisher file with hours worth of tweaks to a floor plan for her character's house proved that.

Dorrie heard something in the background. A dog barking. Dishes crashing. Followed by, "I gotta run, darlin', and I know you've got your meeting. I'll talk to you soon. Knock 'em dead."

"Ha! Love you, Licorice."

"I'm not licorice. I'm Anise."

"Pa-tay-to, pa-tah-to. Same thing." The spice, anise, had a licorice flavor to it. Dorrie rarely let an opportunity to mention it pass her by. Of course, the spice was pronounced an-iss, but her friend hailed from Appalachia and said her name uh-nese.

"Love you, too. I think. See you in a few weeks!"

They hung up. Dorrie headed from her hometown of Serenity Landing, Missouri to Springfield and her first CANDID meeting with a for-real published author as the guest.

She just prayed she wouldn't make a fool of herself.

Dorrie sat at a table in Panera Bread wiping her hands on her dress slacks. The nice ones. The ones that made her feel a little more professional than jeans or her usual scrubs. It was only the fourth meeting but who was she to think she should be the one running a group like this? At twenty-three, Dorrie felt woefully unprepared to run the local meeting of the country's premiere group for Christian writers. Unpublished. Unagented. Uneverything. And inadequate.

And with a line-up of such prestigious guest speakers coming? Why her? Right. No one else volunteered to do it.

And just one guest speaker for now, .but Dorrie had to introduce her to everyone.

So what if "everyone" meant seven people?

Kathleen Watson really was very nice. Dorrie knew because they'd been talking on Facebook for months.

Dorrie took a deep breath and jumped in. "Okay, everyone!" Her voice echoed in the almost empty room as her nerves took a beating. "I think everybody's got their food, so it's time for the Springfield Area Christian Authors' Network, Dedicated to Inspiration Distinction group to welcome best-selling, award winning author, Kathleen Watson." What a mouthful! It made her even more grateful everyone just called the organization CANDID.

The half dozen or so writers gave a polite smattering of applause as Kathleen moved to sit on the table at the front of the meeting room. "Thanks so much for having me today. I was thinking I'd tell you a bit about me, my journey to publication, and life since then. Afterwards, we'll open it up for questions."

The door opened and in walked Prince Caspian – fresh off his voyage through the Seven Seas on the Dawn Treader. Dorrie's logical side knew it couldn't be the Narnian king, but had to be his doppelganger. Her romantic side didn't care. He was, after all, about six feet tall with longish chestnut colored hair that looked silky enough for every girl in the room to be jealous, and eyes the color of Hershey's chocolate.

"Is this the CANDID meeting?" His voice, smooth as velvet, melted Dorrie's insides.

"Um, yes," she managed to stammer. "Have a seat. We're just getting started."

He smiled, though Dorrie had the impression his full grin was much more drool-worthy.

Before she realized what he was doing, he slid into the chair next to her. If he got any closer Dorrie would be wearing his cologne. Very nice smelling cologne, too. Not at all like she expected from someone who spent most of his time on a boat with a giant talking mouse.

How was she supposed to concentrate? Ask insightful questions? Keep everyone on task during the Q and A if she spent the next two hours wondering if he'd take her back to Narnia with him?

Somehow, Dorrie managed to focus on Kathleen. She talked about what the industry had been like twenty years earlier when she first broke into publishing and how it differed now.

After about thirty minutes, Kathleen looked at Dorrie. "You know what? Why don't we skip straight to questions? You guys ask me what you want to know about life as an author. I don't know all of you so why don't we do introductions, then questions?" The look she gave left it up to Dorrie.

Dorrie moved to the front of the room to direct the conversation and told them a bit about herself when one of the other gals interrupted.

"Did I see your name on the New Beginnings list?"

Heat rose in Dorrie's cheeks. "I had two manuscripts final in different categories."

"New Beginnings is the CANDID contest for unpublished authors, right?" The question came from the other new member. Dorrie didn't think she'd heard the lady's name yet.

With a nod, Dorrie confirmed the statement but turned to the next person. All but two of the other seven people she'd met several times and halfway tuned them out. The newbie who'd asked about the contest introduced herself as Julie Harders. And then they got to Prince Caspian.

"I'm Jeremiah Jacobs. I've been writing for years, but decided to switch genres to political thrillers."

"What did you write before?" Kathleen asked.

He shrugged and looked uncomfortable. "A bit of everything

trying to find the elusive voice. I think I've found it writing political thrillers."

"Good." Kathleen turned to Dorrie. "Do you want to handle the Q and A?"

Dorrie gave a half-shrug. "Up to you."

They spent the next hour asking Kathleen questions about how she came up with new ideas year after year, about what life was like on deadline, how to avoid the deadline crunch, and on and on. Two hours after the meeting began, they wrapped up, chatting a bit in little groups until an employee stuck her head in and said another group was coming in a few minutes.

Grabbing her laptop bag, Dorrie thanked Julie for coming and asked her to come again. She needed to do the same with Jeremiah. If only she'd out-grown the high school "stammer-when-I-talk-to-cute-boys" phase.

"Jeremiah?" Here went nothing.

He looked up from where he was gathering his trash. Don't look him in the eyes. You'll drown in pools of chocolate that would make Willy Wonka jealous. The glimpse or two she'd gotten had been more than enough to realize drowning would be a marvelous way to go.

His voice jolted her back to Panera. And there were those eyes. Could he be smiling at her? "Thank you for letting me join you today."

"Of course. Are you new to CANDID?" She'd been told someone would send her an email telling her when a new member from the area joined, but she hadn't gotten one yet.

He shook his head. "No. I'm here for a few months trying to decide if this is where I want to move." At her puzzled look, he went on. "I work from home so it doesn't matter where I am and I'm tired of Chicago. I thought I'd try out a few other places before making a decision."

"That's smart. How do you like the Ozarks so far?"

"I've only been here ten days, but one of the things I looked at when deciding where to go was a CANDID group. It's not a requirement for wherever I settle, but it would be nice."

"Well, we're glad to have you for as long as you're here." Dorrie told him when the next meeting would be and got his email address so she could put him on the mailing list.

Dorrie went to take a sip of her soda, but the condensation on the plastic made it more slippery than she realized.

Like one of those slow motion scenes from the Matrix movies, every drop became individually visible from every other as the dark liquid first flew upward then plummeted down to Jeremiah's laptop bag. Dorrie could see his eyes widen as they both followed the trajectory of the cup downward. He grabbed for his bag, but it was too late. The sloshing brought everything back to real speed. At least it seemed to be in the non-laptop portion of the bag.

"I'm so sorry." Dorrie reached for the napkins sitting on the table next to her, frantically blotting at the papers inside.

Jeremiah pulled them out, spreading them on the table as he muttered something that sounded a lot like, "No, no, no, no, no."

Dorrie continued to blot at the papers. When she moved one of the file folders, papers and photos fell out – a sticky, wet mess.

Dropping to the floor to pick them up, tears filled her eyes. Just what she needed to make a good first impression on this guy. Not that she really thought he'd be interested in her of all people, but this ensured he would not. Especially if she ruined his photos.

She flipped one over and gaped.

He reached for it, but Dorrie sat back on her heels and stared. "Why do you have this?" The words escaped before she could stop them.

"Give it to me."

"This is the cover for the new Mya Elizabeth Linscott Cambridge Family Saga book. Not the one coming out in a couple months but the one that comes out in January. The title hasn't even been announced yet." Of course, after seeing the picture Dorrie knew, but the official announcement wouldn't come until the day before MEL's August book released. MEL would send out a newsletter with information on upcoming promotions, like when her eBooks would be discounted, and at the end, she'd announce the title and preview the cover of her next book.

Dorrie looked up at him. His face was an unreadable mask. She had to know. "How'd you get this?"

AVAILABLE NOW!

Jeremiah Jacobs moved to the Ozarks for a fresh start. He knows no one and has no plans to get romantically involved with anyone. Ever. He's already had his heart ripped out once and once is enough. Besides he has contractual obligations that prevent him from talking about work - and what woman would want to be involved with a man who has to keep his job a secret? When he attends his first local writers' group meeting, he finds the leader so intriguing, his instant attraction to her threatens to complicate his currently uncomplicated life.

Dorrie Miller has never been good enough. Not for her father or any of the guys she's dated in the past. She's pushed beyond her father's disapproval to have a good career while pursuing her dream of becoming a published novelist. The Christian Authors Network – Dedicated to Inspirational Distinction, or CANDID, is hosting their annual conference in Indianapolis and who's rumored to be in attendance? The super reclusive, super-star author, Mya Elizabeth Linscott.

The hunky new member of her local CANDID group, Jeremiah, wants to carpool to Indy. Dorrie can handle not making a fool of herself for eight hours each way. Right? But she never imagined doing a favor for someone during the conference would leave her accidentally married to the gorgeous guy she barely knows. How will she get out of this mess, married to a near stranger? Does she want to? Will her insecurities and Jeremiah's secrets tear them apart? Or can she trust that, all along, God's been helping her with Finding Mr. Write?

Finding Mr. Write is a mega-romantic story with amazing chemistry between the two characters, and Jeremiah is one of the most memorable and loveable heroes I've read in a long time. Carol Moncado's writing reeled me in and hooked me, and I was eager to see how Dorrie and Jeremiah would overcome their secrets and unusual circumstances to find true love. I loved this story! **~ Melanie Dickerson, award winning author of The Healer's Apprentice**

Previews may not be in their final form and are subject to change.

When she's not writing about her imaginary friends, Carol Moncado is hanging out with her husband, four kids, and a dog who weighs less than most hard cover books. She prefers watching *NCIS* to just about anything, except maybe watching *Castle*, or possibly *Girl Meets World* with her kids. She believes peanut butter M&Ms are the perfect food and Dr. Pepper should come in an IV. When not watching her kids - and the dog - race around her big backyard in Southwest Missouri, she's teaching American Government at a local community college. She's a founding member and President of MozArks ACFW, category coordinator for First Impressions, blogger at InspyRomance, and represented by Tamela Hancock Murray of The Steve Laube Agency.

CANDID
Romance

Finding Mr. Write

Available NOW!

Finally Mr. Write

Available NOW!

Falling for Mr. Write

Available NOW!

The Montevaro Monarchy

Good Enough for a Princess
Preorder now!
Available NOW!

Along Came a Prince

Available NOW!

More Than a Princess

Available NOW!

The Brides of Bellas Montagnes

Coming Summer 2015

The royal families of Mevendia and Ravenzario are no different than the rest of us. They just want to find someone to love, and now that their Montevaran cousins are settling down, the pressure is on.

Hand-me-down Princess

Prince Malachi of Mevendia has no intention of getting married. His father has a different plan.

Queen of His Heart

Ravenzario's Queen Christiana's life has been turned upside down. The wedding to the man of her dreams will fix that, won't it?

Prince from her Past

Princess Yvette of Mevendia has been betrothed since before her first birthday. Her intended groom disappeared not long after. The wedding is supposed to be next week. Now what?

44038051R00184

Made in the USA
Charleston, SC
15 July 2015